INDIAN COUNTRY NOIR

Indian Country Noir

EDITED BY SARAH CORTEZ & LIZ MARTÍNEZ

Published by Akashic Books
©2010 Akashic Books

Series concept by Tim McLoughlin and Johnny Temple
Map by Aaron Petrovich

ISBN-13: 978-1-936070-05-3
Library of Congress Control Number: 2009939086
All rights reserved
Printed in Canada
First printing

Akashic Books
PO Box 1456
New York, NY 10009
info@akashicbooks.com
www.akashicbooks.com

ALSO IN THE AKASHIC NOIR SERIES:

Baltimore Noir, edited by Laura Lippman
Boston Noir, edited by Dennis Lehane
Bronx Noir, edited by S.J. Rozan
Brooklyn Noir, edited by Tim McLoughlin
Brooklyn Noir 2: The Classics, edited by Tim McLoughlin
Brooklyn Noir 3: Nothing but the Truth
edited by Tim McLoughlin & Thomas Adcock
Chicago Noir, edited by Neal Pollack
D.C. Noir, edited by George Pelecanos
D.C. Noir 2: The Classics, edited by George Pelecanos
Delhi Noir (India), edited by Hirsh Sawhney
Detroit Noir, edited by E.J. Olsen & John C. Hocking
Dublin Noir (Ireland), edited by Ken Bruen
Havana Noir (Cuba), edited by Achy Obejas
Istanbul Noir (Turkey), edited by Mustafa Ziyalan & Amy Spangler
Las Vegas Noir, edited by Jarret Keene & Todd James Pierce
London Noir (England), edited by Cathi Unsworth
Los Angeles Noir, edited by Denise Hamilton
Los Angeles Noir 2: The Classics, edited by Denise Hamilton
Manhattan Noir, edited by Lawrence Block
Manhattan Noir 2: The Classics, edited by Lawrence Block
Mexico City Noir (Mexico), edited by Paco I. Taibo II
Miami Noir, edited by Les Standiford
Moscow Noir (Russia), edited by Natalia Smirnova & Julia Goumen
New Orleans Noir, edited by Julie Smith
Orange County Noir, edited by Gary Phillips
Paris Noir (France), edited by Aurélien Masson
Phoenix Noir, edited by Patrick Millikin
Portland Noir, edited by Kevin Sampsell
Queens Noir, edited by Robert Knightly
Richmond Noir, edited by edited by Andrew Blossom,
Brian Castleberry & Tom De Haven
Rome Noir (Italy), edited by Chiara Stangalino & Maxim Jakubowski
San Francisco Noir, edited by Peter Maravelis
San Francisco Noir 2: The Classics, edited by Peter Maravelis
Seattle Noir, edited by Curt Colbert
Toronto Noir (Canada), edited by Janine Armin & Nathaniel G. Moore
Trinidad Noir, Lisa Allen-Agostini & Jeanne Mason
Twin Cities Noir, edited by Julie Schaper & Steven Horwitz
Wall Street Noir, edited by Peter Spiegelman

FORTHCOMING:

Barcelona Noir (Spain), edited by Adriana Lopez & Carmen Ospina
Cape Cod Noir, edited by David L. Ulin
Copenhagen Noir (Denmark), edited by Bo Tao Michaelis
Haiti Noir, edited by Edwidge Danticat
Lagos Noir (Nigeria), edited by Chris Abani
Lone Star Noir, edited by Bobby Byrd & John Byrd
Mumbai Noir (India), edited by Altaf Tyrewala
Philadelphia Noir, edited by Carlin Romano

Alberta
CANADA
Ashland, Montana
UNITED STATES OF AMERICA
Los Angeles, California
Tucson, Arizona
MEXICO

Ontario

Eastern Woodlands

Upper Peninsula, Michigan

Adirondacks, New York

New York, New York

Chicago, Illinois

Charlotte, North Carolina

Memphis, Tennessee

New Orleans, Louisiana

San Juan, Puerto Rico

TABLE OF CONTENTS

11   *Foreword by Richard B. Williams*

13   *Introduction*

PART I: EAST

17   **JOSEPH BRUCHAC**   Adirondacks, New York
        Helper

37   **JEAN RAE BAXTER**   Eastern Woodlands, Canada
        Osprey Lake

59   **GERARD HOUARNER**   New York, New York
        Dead Medicine Snake Woman

85   **MELISSA YI**   Ontario, Canada
        Indian Time

PART II: SOUTH

103   **A.A. HEDGECOKE**   Charlotte, North Carolina
        On Drowning Pond

109   **MISTINA BATES**   Memphis, Tennessee
        Daddy's Girl

129   **O'NEIL DE NOUX**   New Orleans, Louisiana
        The Raven and the Wolf

150   **R. NARVAEZ**   San Juan, Puerto Rico
        Juracán

PART III: WEST

177   **DAVID COLE**   Tucson, Arizona
JaneJohnDoe.com

201   **LEONARD SCHONBERG**   Ashland, Montana
Lame Elk

214   **REED FARREL COLEMAN**   Los Angeles, California
Another Role

PART IV: NORTH

241   **LAWRENCE BLOCK**   Upper Peninsula, Michigan
Getting Lucky

252   **LIZ MARTÍNEZ**   Chicago, Illinois
Prowling Wolves

273   **KIMBERLY ROPPOLO**   Alberta, Canada
Quilt like a Night Sky

280   **About the Contributors**

FOREWORD

BY RICHARD B. WILLIAMS

Stories have been central to communication among Indian people for thousands of years. And the stories you are about to read are truly incredible. They will make your blood boil with fear, anger, passion, and, ultimately, remorse.

These stories are so real that you believe without questioning, so loving that you accept without strings attached, and yet so challenging that your soul is tugged by hundreds of lost spirits. Each tale leaves the reader feeling vulnerable to inner voices calling for you to do something, yet wondering what it is that you are supposed to do.

How can you tell if dreams are real? What do you do when there is such deep sadness because there is no hope? Why is there no real word for goodbye? Does Ashland, Montana really exist? Does being Indian mean that life will be filled with death, pain, shootings, drugs, alcohol, and abuse? I can't answer these questions for you. You have to read and experience this book yourself to understand.

For centuries, Indian people faced extinction, brutality, and racism. Ours was a harsh existence, where success meant survival. In our world, boarding schools were killing children, war heroes were dying without hope or dignity, and gifted and talented writers were lost in their own intellectualism with no place to tell their stories.

That horrible existence finally began to change in the

1960s. Since then we have seen a resurgence of Native pride. People are returning to their Indian culture for a sense of who they are. This renaissance is captured powerfully in the work of these authors. Each story evokes deep emotions for the reader. Yet introspection is always a challenge. In these stories, by both Native and non-Native writers, cultures are being exposed; lies, and truths as well, are being told; and all you can do is shake your head and try to determine what is real.

The beauty of Natives writing their own stories means that the experience comes without boundaries, literally and figuratively. These stories from all across North America do not carry the burden of Western political, philosophical, and literary expectations. The results are spectacular and will cause you to raise your eyebrows repeatedly.

We are pleased and honored to share these stories as examples of the passion, violence, and beauty that our people have to share, underscoring the centuries of acquired knowledge that we carry. I can hear the Indian haters saying, *What are those damn Indians thinking?* The beauty is, of course, that Indian people *are* thinking, using their natural intellect. Gone is the time when the sole focus was on survival. Now the focus is on thriving.

As you read this volume, remember: it's fiction . . . or is it?

Richard B. Williams is the president and CEO of the American Indian College Fund.

INTRODUCTION
SPIRITUAL TRANSGRESSION

Welcome to Indian Country . . . It lies within the physical and emotional antipodes of North–South–East–West, and encompasses territory both familiar and unknown. Many who inhabit Indian Country love it, and they often stay after their time on Earth is done. Others have died trying to claim it. They continue to wander there in the endless circle of time. This book has stories by both Native and non-Native authors reflecting them all.

The circle defined by the cardinal directions of the Medicine Wheel is your reminder that a harmonious relationship with nature and all living beings is how creation was ordained, with all of us equal and connected. Thus, all directions lead to each other, just as all these stories, in turn, point toward one another through a shared ethos.

As you step back into the troubled history of Joseph Bruchac's "Helper" and Liz Martínez's "Prowling Wolves," you will find yourself swept up by a fresh and powerful look into personal revisionist histories. It is, perhaps, not unpredicable that some of these tales show the narrator partaking in what appears to be an eminently satisfying dose of revenge: Jean Rae Baxter's "Osprey Lake," Mistina Bates's "Daddy's Girl," and David Cole's "JaneJohnDoe.com" among them. And while eliminating the person perceived as evil may have its own brand of dark glee, Melissa Yi's "Indian Time" gives us a truly haunting tale of twisted intention and vengeance.

Two of the stories are breathtakingly lyrical in their approach and articulation of the hard price paid by some Indians for spiritual homelessness and transgression: Kimberly Roppolo's "Quilt like a Night Sky" and A.A. HedgeCoke's "On Drowning Pond." Leonard Schonberg's "Lame Elk" takes us to the bitter cold of January in Montana for another tale of a crushed life.

For a glimpse at how a contemporary character with Indian blood functions in an urban environment, enjoy the fast-paced lives created by O'Neil De Noux in "The Raven and the Wolf" and R. Narvaez in "Juracán." Gerard Houarner keeps us in a contemporary setting in Manhattan's underground, yet masterfully weaves the mythological and historical through several different planes of reality. And speaking of myths, are there any stronger, especially in our media-driven society, than that of the "American Indian"? See how non-Native authors Lawrence Block in "Getting Lucky" and Reed Farrel Coleman in "Another Role" use the Hollywood-engendered mythos to bring us to yet other unexpected places.

Before you journey with these talented authors through the north, south, east, and west of Indian Country, you might wish to reflect upon the words of the famous Oglala Lakota teacher Black Elk: "Birds make their nests in circles; we dance in circles; the circle stands for the Sun and Moon and all round things in the natural world. The circle is an endless creation, with endless connections to the present, all that went before and all that will come in the future."

Sarah Cortez
Houston, Texas
March 2010

PART I

EAST

HELPER

BY JOSEPH BRUCHAC
Adirondacks, New York

The one with the missing front teeth. He's the one who shot me. Before his teeth were missing.

Getting shot was, in a way, my fault. I heard them coming when they were still a mile away. I could've run. But running never suited me, even before I got this piece of German steel in my hip. My Helper. Plus I'd been heating the stones for my sweat lodge since the sun was a hand high above the hill. I run off, the fire would burn down and they'd cool off. Wouldn't be respectful to those stones.

See what they want, I figured. Probably just deer hunters who'd heard about my reputation. You want to get a trophy, hire Indian Charley.

Yup, that was what it had to be. A couple of flatlanders out to hire me to guide them for the weekend. Boys who'd seen the piece about me in the paper, posing with two good old boys from Brooklyn and the twelve pointer they bagged. Good picture of me, actually. Too good, I realized later. But that wasn't what I was thinking then. Just about potential customers. Not that I needed the money. But a man has to keep busy. And it was better in general if folks just saw me as a typical Indian. Scraping by, not too well educated, a threat to no one. Good old Indian Charley.

Make me a sawbuck or two, get them a buck or two. Good trade.

I was ready to say that to them. Rehearsing it in my head. For a sawbuck or two, I'll get you boys a buck or two. Good trade. Indian humor. Funny enough to get me killed.

I really should have made myself scarce when I heard their voices clear enough to make out what the fat one was saying. It was also when I felt the first twinge in my hip. They were struggling up the last two hundred yards of the trail. That's when I should have done it. Not ran, maybe. But faded back into the hemlocks.

Son of a bidgin' Indin, the heavy-footed one said. And kept on saying it in between labored breaths and the sound of his heavy feet, slipping and dislodging stones. The other one, who wasn't so clumsy but was still making more noise than a lame moose, didn't say anything.

I imagined Heavy Foot was just ticked off at me for making my camp two miles from the road and the last of it straight up. It may have discouraged some who might've hired me. But it weeded out the weaker clientele. And the view was worth it, hills rolling away down to the river that glistened with the rising sun like a silver bracelet, the town on the other side that turned into a constellation of lights mirroring the stars in the sky above it at night.

The arrowhead-shaped piece of metal in my flesh sent another little shiver down the outside of my thigh. I ignored it again. Not a smart thing to do, but I was curious about my visitors.

Curiosity killed the Chippewa, as my grampa, who had also been to Carlisle, used to joke.

For some reason the picture of the superintendent's long face the last day I saw him came to mind. Twenty years ago. He was sitting behind his desk, his pale face getting red as one of those beets I'd spent two summers digging on the farm where they sent me to work for slave labor wages—like every other Indian kid at the school. The superintendent got his cut, of course. How many farm hands and house maids do you need? We got hundreds of them here at Carlisle. Nice, civilized, docile little Indian boys and girls. Do whatever you want with them.

That was before I got my growth and Pop Warner saw me and made me one of his athletic boys. Special quarters, good food and lots of it, an expense account at Blumenthal's department store, a share of the gate. Plus a chance to get as many concussions as any young warrior could ever dream of, butting heads against the linemen of Harvard and Syracuse and Army. I also found some of the best friends I ever had on that football squad.

It was because of one of them that I'd been able to end up here on this hilltop—which, according to my name on a piece of paper filed in the county seat belonged to me. As well as the other two hundred acres all the way down to the river. I'd worked hard for the money that made it possible for me to get my name on that deed. But that's another story to tell another time.

As Heavy Foot and his quieter companion labored up the last narrow stretch of trail, where it passed through a hemlock thicket and then came out on an open face of bedrock, I was still replaying that scene in the superintendent's office.

You can't come in here like this.

I just did.

I'll have you expelled.

I almost laughed at that one. Throw an Indian out of Carlisle? Where some children were brought in chains? Where they cut our hair, stole the fine jewelry that our parents arrayed us in, took our clothes, changed our names, dressed us in military uniforms, and turned us into little soldiers? Where more kids ran away than ever graduated?

You won't get the chance. I held up my hand and made a fist.

The super cringed back when I did that. I suppose when you have bear paw hands like mine, they could be a little scary to someone with a guilty conscience.

I lifted my little finger. First, I said, I'm not here alone. I looked back over my shoulder where the boys of the Carlisle football team were waiting in the hall.

I held up my ring finger. Second, I talk; you listen.

Middle finger. Third, he goes. Out of here. Today.

The super knew who I meant. The head disciplinarian of the school. Mr. Morissey. Who was already packing his bags with the help of our two tackles. Help Morissey needed because of his dislocated right shoulder and broken jaw.

The super started to say something. But the sound of my other hand coming down hard on his desk stopped his words as effectively as a cork in a bottle. His nervous eyes focused for a second on the skinned knuckles of my hand.

Fourth, I said, extending my index finger. No one will ever be sent to that farm again. No, don't talk. You know the one I mean. Just nod if you understand. Good.

Last, my thumb extended, leaning forward so that it touched his nose. You never mention my name again. You do not contact the agent on my reservation or anyone else. You just take me out of the records. I am a violent Indian. Maybe I have killed people. You do not ever want to see me again. Just nod.

The super nodded.

Good, I said. Now, my hand patting the air as if I was giving a command to a dog, stay!

He stayed. I walked out into the hall where every man on the football squad except for our two tackles was waiting, including our Indian coach. The super stayed in his office as they all shook my hand, patted me on the back. No one said goodbye. There's no word for goodbye. Travel good. Maybe we see you further down the road.

The super didn't even come out as they moved with me to the school gate, past the mansion built with the big bucks from football ticket sales where Pop Warner had lived. As I walked away, down to the train station, never looking back, the super remained in his seat. His legs too weak with fear for him to stand. According to what I heard later in France—from Gus Welch, who was my company commander and had been our quarterback at Carlisle—the superintendent sat there for the rest of the day without moving. The football boys finally took pity on him and sent one of the girls from the sewing class in to tell him that Charles, the big dangerous Indian, was gone and he could come out now.

Gus laughed. You know what he said when she told him that? Don't mention his name. That's what he said.

I might have been smiling at the memory when the two men came into view, but that wasn't where my recollections had stopped. They'd kept walking me past the Carlisle gate, down the road to the trolley tracks. They'd taken me on the journey I made back then, by rail, by wagon, and on foot, until I reached the dark hills that surrounded that farm. The one more Carlisle kids had run away from than any other. Or at least it was reported that they had run away—too many of them were never seen again

That had been the first time I acted on the voice that spoke within me. An old voice with clear purpose. I'd sat down on the slope under an old apple tree and watched, feeling the wrongness of the place. I waited until it was late, the face of the Night Traveler looking sadly down from the sky. Then I made my way downhill to the place that Thomas Goodwaters, age eleven, had come to me about because he knew I'd help after he told me what happened there. Told me after he'd been beaten by the school disciplinarian for running away from his Outing assignment at the Bullweather Farm. But the older, half-healed marks on his back had not come from the disciplinarian's cane.

Just the start, he'd told me, his voice calm despite it all, speaking Chippewa. They were going to do worse. I heard what they said they'd done before.

I knew his people back home. Cousins of mine. Good people, canoe makers. A family peaceful at heart, that shared with everyone and that hoped their son who'd been forced away to that school would at least be taught things he could use to help the people. Like how to scrub someone else's kitchen floor.

He'd broken out the small window of the building where they kept him locked up every night. It was a tiny window, but he was so skinny by then from malnourishment that he'd been able to worm his way free. Plus his family were Eel People and known to be able to slip through almost any narrow place.

Two dogs, he said. Bad ones. Don't bark. Just come at you.

But he'd planned his escape well. The bag he'd filled with black pepper from the kitchen and hidden in his pants was out and in his hand as soon as he hit the ground. He'd left the two bad dogs coughing and sneezing as he ran and kept running.

As his closest relative, I was the one he had been running to before Morissey caught him.

You'll do something, Tommy Goodwaters said. It was not a question. You will help.

I was halfway down the hill and had just climbed over the barbed-wire fence when the dogs got to me. I'd heard them coming, their feet thudding the ground, their eager panting. Nowhere near as quiet as wolves—not that wolves will ever attack a man. So I was ready when the first one leaped and latched its long jaws around my right forearm. Its long canines didn't get through the football pads and tape I'd wrapped around both arms. The second one, snarling like a wolverine, was having just as hard a time with my equally well-protected left leg that it attacked from the back. They were big dogs, probably about eighty pounds each. But I was two hundred pounds bigger. I lifted up the first one as it held on to my arm like grim death and brought my other forearm down hard across the back of its neck. That broke its neck. The second one let go when I kicked it in the belly hard enough to make a fifty-yard field goal. Its heart stopped when I brought my knee and the full weight of my body down on its chest.

Yeah, they were just dogs. But I showed no mercy. If they'd been eating what Tommy told me—and I had no reason to doubt him—there was no place for such animals to be walking this Earth with humans.

Then I went to the place out behind the cow barn. I found a shovel leaned against the building. Convenient. Looked well used. It didn't take much searching. It wasn't just the softer ground, but what I felt in my mind. The call of a person's murdered spirit when their body has been hidden in such a place as this. A place they don't belong.

It was more than one spirit calling for help. By the time the night was half over I'd found all of them. All that was left of five Carlisle boys and girls who'd never be seen alive again by grieving relatives. Mostly just bones. Clean enough to have had the flesh boiled off them. Some gnawed. Would have been no way to tell them apart if it hadn't been for what I found in each of those unmarked graves with them. I don't know why, but there was a large thick canvass bag for each of them. Each bag had a wooden tag tied to it with the name and, God love me, even the tribe of the child. Those people—if I can call them that—knew who they were dealing with. Five bags of clothing, meager possessions and bones. None of them were Chippewas, but they were all my little brothers and sisters. If I still drew breath after that night was over, their bones and possessions, at least, would go home. When I looked up at the moon, her face seemed red. I felt as if I was in an old, painful story.

I won't say what I did after that. Just that when the dawn rose I was long gone and all that remained of the house and the buildings were charred timbers. I didn't think anyone saw me as I left that valley, carrying those five bags. But I was wrong. If I'd seen the newspapers from the nearby town the next day—and not been on my way west, to the Sac & Fox and Osage Agencies in Oklahoma, the Wind River Reservation in Wyoming, the lands of the Crows and the Cheyennes in Montana, the Cahuilla of California—I would have read about the tragic death by fire of almost an entire family. Almost.

I blinked away that memory and focused on the two men who paused only briefly at the top of the trail and then headed straight toward me where I was squatting down by the fire pit. As soon as I saw them clearly I didn't have to question the signal my Helper was giving me. I knew they were trouble.

Funny how much you can think of in the space of an eyeblink. Back in the hospital after getting hit by the shrapnel. The tall, skinny masked doctor bending over me with a scalpel in one hand and some kind of shiny bent metal instrument in the other.

My left hand grabbing the surgeon's wrist before the scapel touched my skin.

It stays.

The ether. A French accent. You are supposed to be out.

I'm not.

Oui. I see this. My wrist, you are hurting it.

Pardon. But I didn't let go.

Why?

It says it's going to be my Helper. It's talking to me.

They might have just given me more ether, but by then Gus Welch had pushed his way in the tent. He'd heard it all.

He began talking French to the doctor, faster than I could follow. Whatever it was he said, it worked.

The doctor turned back to me, no scalpel this time.

You are Red Indian.

Mais oui.

A smile visible even under the mask. Head nodding. *Bien.* We just sew you up then.

Another blink of an eye and I was back watching the two armed men come closer. The tall, lanky one was built a little like that doctor I'd last seen in 1918. No mask, though. I could see that he had one of those Abraham Lincoln faces, all angles and jutting jaw—but with none of that long-gone president's compassion. He was carrying a Remington .303. The fat one with the thick lips and small eyes, Heavy Foot for sure, had a lever-action Winchester 30-06. I'd heard him jack a shell into the chamber just before they came into view.

Good guns, but not in the hands of good guys.

Both of them were in full uniform. High-crowned hats,

black boots, and all. Not the brown doughboy togs in which I had once looked so dapper. Their khaki duds had the words *Game Warden* sewed over their breast pockets.

They stopped thirty feet away from me.

Charley Bear, the Lincoln impersonator, said in a flat voice, We have a warrant for your arrest for trespassing. Stand up.

I stayed crouching. It was clear to me they didn't know I owned the land I was on. Not that most people in the area knew. After all, it was registered under my official white name of Charles B. Island. If they were really serving a warrant from a judge, they'd know that. Plus there was one other thing wrong.

Game wardens don't serve warrants, I said.

They said he was a smart one, Luth, Heavy Foot growled. Too smart for his own good.

My Helper sent a wave of fire through my whole leg and I rolled sideways just as Luth raised his gun and pulled the trigger. It was pretty good for a snap shot. The hot lead whizzed past most of my face with the exception of the flesh it tore off along my left cheekbone, leaving a two-inch wound like a claw mark from an eagle's talon.

As I rolled, I hurled sidearm the first of the baseball-sized rocks I'd palmed from the outside of the firepit. Not as fast as when I struck out Jim Thorpe twice back at Indian school. But high and hard enough to hit the strike zone in the center of Luth's face. Bye-bye front teeth.

Heavy Foot had hesitated before bringing his gun up to his shoulder. By then I'd shifted the second stone to my throwing hand. I came up to one knee and let it fly. It struck square in the soft spot just above the fat man's belly.

Ooof!

His gun went flying off to the side and he fell back clutching his gut.

Luth had lost his .303 when the first rock struck him. He was curled up, his hands clasped over his face.

I picked up both guns before I did anything else. Shucked out the shells and then, despite the fact that I hated to do it seeing as how guns themselves are innocent of evil intent, I tossed both weapons spinning over the edge of the cliff. By the time they hit the rocks below I had already rolled Heavy Foot over and yanked his belt out of his pants. I wrapped it around his elbows, which I'd pulled behind his back, cinched it tight enough for him to groan in protest.

I pried Luth's hands from his bloody face, levered them behind his back, and did the same for him that I'd done for his fat buddy. Then I grabbed the two restraining belts, one in each hand, and dragged them over to the place where the cliff dropped off.

By then Luth had recovered enough, despite the blood and the broken teeth, to glare at me. But Heavy Foot began weeping like a baby when I propped them both upright at the edge where it wouldn't take more than a push to send them over.

Shut up, Braddie, Luth said through his bleeding lips, his voice still flat as stone. Then he stared at me. I've killed people worse than you.

But not better, I replied.

A sense of humor is wasted on some people. Luth merely intensified his stare.

A hard case. But not Braddie.

Miss your gun? I asked. You can join it.

I lifted my foot.

No, Braddie blubbered. Whaddaya want? Anything.

A name.

Braddie gave it to me.

I left them on the cliff edge, each one fastened to his own big rock that I'd rolled over to them. The additional rope I'd gotten from my shack insured they wouldn't be freeing themselves.

Stay still, boys. Wish me luck.

Go to hell, Luth snarled. Tough as ever.

But he looked a little less tough after I explained that he'd better hope I had good luck. Otherwise I wouldn't be likely to come back and set them loose. I also pointed out that if they struggled too much there was a good chance those delicately balanced big stones I'd lashed them to would roll over the edge. Them too.

I took my time going down the mountain—and I didn't use the main trail. There was always the chance that Luth and Braddie had not been alone. But their truck, a new '34 Ford, was empty. An hour's quiet watch of it from the shelter of the pines made me fairly certain no one else was around. They'd thoughtfully left the keys in the ignition. It made me feel better about them that they were so trusting and willing to share.

As I drove into town I had even more time to think. Not about what to do. But how to do it. And whether or not my hunch was right.

I parked the car in a grove of maples half a mile this side of the edge of town. Indian Charley behind the wheel of a new truck would not have fit my image in the eyes of the good citizens of Corinth. Matter of fact, aside from Will, most of them would have been surprised to see I knew how to drive. Then I walked in to Will's office.

Wyllis Dunham, Attorney at Law, read the sign on the modest door, which opened off the main street. I walked in without knocking and nodded to the petite stylishly dressed young woman who sat behind the desk with a magazine in her nicely manicured fingers.

Maud, I said, touching my knuckles to my forehead in salute.

Charles, she drawled, somehow making my name into a sardonic remark the way she said it. What kind of trouble you plan on getting us into today?

Nothing we can't handle.

Why does that not make me feel reassured?

Then we both laughed and I thought again how if she wasn't Will's wife I'd probably be thinking of asking her to marry me.

What happened to your cheek? Maud stood up, took a cloth from her purse, wetted it with her lips, and brushed at the place where the bullet had grazed me and the blood had dried. I stood patiently until she was done.

Thanks, nurse.

You'll get my bill.

He in?

For you. She gestured me past her and went back to reading *Ladies' Home Journal*.

I walked into the back room where Will sat with his extremely long legs propped up on his desk, his head back against a couch pillow, his eyes closed.

Before you ask, I am not asleep on the job. I am thinking. Being the town lawyer of a bustling metropolis such as this tends to wear a man out.

Don't let Maud see you with your feet up on that desk.

His eyes opened at that and as he quickly lowered his feet to the floor he looked toward the door, a little furtively, before recovering his composure. Though Will had the degree and was twice her size, it was Maud who laid down the law in their household.

He placed his elbows on the desk and made a pyramid with his fingers. The univeral lawyer's sign of superior intellect and position, but done with a little conscious irony in Will's case. Ever since I had helped him and Maud with a little problem two years back, we'd had a special relationship that included Thursday night card games of cutthroat canasta.

Wellll? he asked.

Two questions.

Do I plead the Fifth Amendment now?

I held up my little finger. First question. Did George Good retire as game warden, has the Department of Conservation started using new brown uniforms that look like they came from a costume shop, and were two new men from downstate sent up here as his replacement?

Technically, Charles, that's three questions. But they all have one answer.

No?

Bingo. He snapped his fingers.

Which was what I had suspected. My two well-trussed friends on the mountaintop with their city accents were as phony as their warrant.

Two. I held up my ring finger. Anybody been in town asking about me since that article in the Albany paper with my picture came out?

Will couldn't keep the smile off his face. If there was such a thing as an information magnet for this town, Will Dunham was it. He prided himself on quietly knowing everything that was going on—public and private—before anyone else even knew he knew it. With another loud snap of his long fingers he plucked a business card from his breast pocket and handed it to me with a magician's flourish.

Voilà!

The address was in the State Office Building. The name was not exactly the one I expected, but it still sent a shiver down my spine and the metal spearpoint in my hip muscle twinged. Unfinished business.

I noticed that Will had been talking. I picked up his words in mid-sentence.

. . . so Avery figured that he should give the card to me, seeing as how he knew you were our regular helper what with you taking on odd jobs for us now and then. Repair work, cutting wood . . . and so on. Of course, by the time he thought to pass it on to me Avery'd been holding onto it since two weeks ago which was when the man came into his filling station asking about you and wanting you to give him a call. So, did he get tired of waiting and decide to look you up himself?

In a manner of speaking.

Say again?

See you later, Will.

The beauty of America's trolley system is that a man could go all the way from New York City to Boston just by changing cars once you got to the end of town and one line ended where another picked up. So the time it took me to run the ten miles to where the line started in Middle Grove was longer than it took to travel the remaining forty miles to Albany and cost me no more than half the coins in my pocket.

I hadn't bothered to go back home to change into the slightly better clothes I had. My nondescript well-worn apparel was just fine for what I had in mind. No one ever notices laborers. The white painter's cap, the brush, and the can of Putnam's bone-white that I borrowed from the hand truck in front of the building were all I needed to amble in unimpeded and take the elevator to the sixteenth floor.

The name on the door matched the moniker on the card—just as fancy and in big gold letters, even bigger than the word INVESTMENTS below it. I turned the knob and pushed the door open with my shoulder, backed in diffidently, holding my paint can and brush as proof of identity and motive. Nobody said anything, and when I turned to look I saw that the receptionist's desk was empty as I'd hoped. Five o'clock. Quitting time. But the door was unlocked, the light still on in the boss's office.

I took off the cap, put down the paint can and brush, and stepped through the door.

He was standing by the window, looking down toward the street below.

Put it on my desk, he said.

Whatever it is, I don't have it, I replied.

He turned around faster than I had expected. But whatever he had in mind left him when I pulled my right hand out of my shirt and showed him the bone-handled skinning knife I'd just pulled from the sheath under my left arm. He froze.

You? he said.

Only one word, but it was as good as an entire book. No doubt about it now. My Helper felt like a burning coal.

Me, I agreed.

Where? he asked. I had to hand it to him. He was really good at one-word questions that spoke volumes.

You mean Mutt and Jeff? They're not coming. They got tied up elsewhere.

You should be dead.

Disappointing. Now that he was speaking in longer sentences he was telling me things I already knew, though he was still talking about himself when I gave his words a second thought.

You'd think with the current state of the market, I observed, that you would have left the Bull at the start of your name, Mr. Weathers. Then you might have given your investors some confidence.

My second attempt at humorous banter fell as flat as the first. No response other than opening his mouth a little wider. Time to get serious

I'm not going to kill you here, I said. Even though you deserve it for what you and your family did back then. How old were you? Eighteen, right? But you took part just as much as they did. A coward too. You just watched without trying to save them from me? Where were you?

Up on the hill, he said. His lips tight. There was sweat on his forehead now.

So, aside from investments, what have you been doing since then? Keeping up the family hobbies?

I looked over at the safe against the wall. You have a souvenir or two in there? No, don't open it to show me. People keep guns in safes. Sit. Not at the desk. Right there on the windowsill.

What are you going to do?

Deliver you to the police. I took a pad and a pen off the desk. Along with a confession. Write it now, starting with what you and your family did at your farm and including anyone else you've hurt since then.

There was an almost eager look on his weaselly face as he took the paper and pen from my hands. That look grew calmer and more superior as he wrote. Clearly, he knew he was a being of a different order than common humans. As far above us as those self-centered scientists say modern men are above the chimpanzees. Like the politicians who sent in the federal troops against the army of veterans who'd camped in

Washington, D.C. this past summer asking that the bonuses they'd been promised for their service be paid to them. Men I knew who'd survived the trenches of Belgium and France dying on American soil at the hands of General MacArthur's troops.

The light outside faded as the sun went down while he wrote. By the time he was done he'd filled twenty pages, each one numbered at the bottom, several of them with intricate explicatory drawings.

I took his confession and the pen. I placed the pad on the desk, kept one eye on him as I flipped the pages with the tip of the pen. He'd been busy. Though he'd moved on beyond Indian kids, his tastes were still for the young, the weak, those powerless enough to not be missed or mourned by the powers that be. Not like the Lindbergh baby whose abduction and death had made world news this past spring. No children of the famous or even the moderately well off. Just those no one writes about. Indians, migrant workers, Negro children, immigrants . . .

He tried not to smirk as I looked up from the words that made me sick to my stomach.

Ready to take me in now?

I knew what he was thinking. A confession like this, forced at the point of a knife by a . . . person . . . who was nothing more than an insane, ignorant Indian. Him a man of money and standing, afraid for his life, ready to write anything no matter how ridiculous. When we went to any police station, all he had to do was shout for help and I'd be the one who'd end up in custody.

One more thing, I said.

You have the knife. His voice rational, agreeable.

I handed him back the pad and pen.

On the last page, print *I'm sorry* in big letters and then sign it.

Of course he wasn't and of course he did.

Thank you, I said, taking the pad. I glanced over his shoulder out the window at the empty sidewalk far below.

There, I said, pointing into the darkness.

He turned his head to look. Then I pushed him.

I didn't lie, I said, even though I doubt he could hear me with the wind whistling past his face as he hurtled down past floor after floor. I didn't kill you. The ground did.

And I'd delivered him to the police, who would be scraping him up off the sidewalk.

Cap back on my head, brush and paint can in hand, I descended all the way to the basement, then walked up the back stairs to leave the building from the side away from where the first police cars would soon arrive.

I slept that night in the park and caught the first trolley north in the morning. It was mid-afternoon by the time I reached the top of the trail.

Only one rock and its human companion stood at the edge of the cliff. Luth had stayed hard, I guessed. Too hard to have the common sense to sit still. But not as hard as those rocks he'd gotten acquainted with two hundred feet below. I'd decide in the morning whether to climb down there, so far off any trail, and bury him. Or just leave the remains for the crows.

I rested my hand on the rock to which the fat man's inert body was still fastened. I let my gaze wander out over the forested slope below, the open fields, the meandering S of the river, the town where the few streetlights would soon be coming on. There was a cloud floating in the western sky, almost the shape of an arrowhead. The setting sun was turning its lower edge crimson. I took a deep breath.

Then I untied Braddie. Even though he was limp and smelled bad, he was still breathing. Spilled some water on his cracked lips. Then let him drink a little.

Don't kill me, he croaked. Please. I didn't want to. I never hurt no one. Never. Luth made me help him. I hated him.

I saw how young he was then.

Okay, I said. We're going back downhill. Your truck is there. You get in it. Far as I know it's yours to keep. You just drive south and don't look back.

I will. I won't never look back. I swear to God.

I took him at his word. There's a time for that, just as there's a time when words end.

OSPREY LAKE

BY JEAN RAE BAXTER

Eastern Woodlands, Canada

A frosty halo circled the moon. It was going to snow. Eight inches by morning, the 6 o'clock forecast had predicted. Heather hoped it would hold off until they got wherever they were going. So far, the roads were bare.

"Turn right at the crossroads," Don said.

She touched the brake. Signs nailed to a tall post pointed to cottages east, west, and straight ahead. Some signs were too faded to read, but on others Heather could make out the lettering: *Brad & Judy Smith, The MacTeers, Bide-a-wee, The Pitts.*

"Are we going to one of those?"

"No. Our sign fell off years ago. I know the way."

The ruts were four inches deep. Frozen mud as hard as granite. Wilderness crowded the road. The bare twig ends of birch and maple trees and the swishing boughs of spruce, fir, and balsam brushed the Mustang's sides.

The track was getting worse. Heather leaned forward, high beams on, studying the ruts. "Are we nearly there?"

Don's lighter flared. "Ten minutes."

"There hasn't been a turnoff for half a mile."

"That's right. We've passed Mud Fish Lake. That's as far as they've brought the hydro. Osprey Lake is next."

"Does anybody live there?"

"There used to be Ojibwas, but we cleared them out years ago. Now it's just cottagers in summer."

"What about winter?"

"There's a permanent village at the far end of Osprey Lake. Maybe fifty people. What's left of the Ojibwas."

The car jolted in and out of the ruts. She pulled the wheel to the right to miss a rock outcrop twenty feet high. Just in time, she saw a tree with a two-foot-diameter trunk lying across the track. Heather braked hard.

"Shit!" Don said.

"What now?"

"We walk." He picked up the gym bag and opened the car door.

She wasn't dressed for this. Pant boots with three-inch heels, jeans, and a leather bomber jacket. Walking bent over, hugging herself for warmth, Heather couldn't see any path. Don walked purposefully. She stumbled after him.

Heather tripped. Don didn't notice; he kept on moving. She struggled to her feet, tripped again. The heel of one boot had snapped off. On her knees, she fumbled amidst the pine needles lying on the frozen ground. When she found the heel, she shoved it into her jacket pocket and lurched after Don.

The cottage's tall windows were what she saw first, a dull gleam of glass facing the lake. Trees and shadow obscured the rest of the structure. Behind it rose a wooded hill.

"Here we are," Don said.

"How do we get in?"

"There's a key."

He disappeared into a grove of evergreens and emerged with a key in his hand. He unlocked the door and stepped inside, motioning her to follow.

"It's colder in here than it was outside," she said.

"That's because you expected it to be warmer."

Don set down the gym bag and pulled out his lighter.

Its brief flare revealed a massive stone fireplace. He stepped across the room, lit a candle that stood on the mantel.

The room came more clearly into view. Open rafters. Walls paneled with wide boards. Pictures on the walls. A plank table and half a dozen wooden chairs. A cluster of tubular furniture with loose cushions.

"Hasn't changed," he said.

"Since when?"

"Eight years ago. The last time I was here."

"Who owns it?"

"My grandfather's estate."

So that was the connection. A loser like Don had summered here as a child. It didn't fit.

"This way," he said. She hobbled after him into a room at the back. He closed the door. "If we stay here in the bedroom, nobody out on the ice can see a light."

"Who's out there to see anything?"

"You never can tell."

"At 4 in the morning when it's ten below?"

A squall of wind rattled the windows.

She looked around. There was a double bed with an iron bedstead, a chest of drawers, and an open closet with wire hangers on a rod.

He set down the candle. Pulling two sleeping bags from the closet shelf, he thrust one at her. The fabric was riddled with tiny holes.

"You take the inside," he said.

"Okay." Why the inside? Because it would be harder for her to escape? But she wasn't going anywhere. Not tonight.

Heather spread out her sleeping bag but made no move to get into it.

"What are you waiting for?"

"I need to go to the bathroom."

"Bathroom!" he snorted. "There's a privy outside, if it hasn't fallen down."

"Where?"

"Up the hill. I'll show you."

She limped after him back to the main room.

"Did you twist your ankle?" he asked.

"Thanks for finally noticing. The heel broke off my boot."

"Huh!" He started to laugh, and then seemed to change his mind.

The back door was to the right of the fireplace. Don pulled the bolt. "Straight up the path."

Through the darkness Heather could see a shed. That must be it. She scrambled up the path on hands and knees. When she reached the privy and pulled on the latch, the door fell off, knocking her backwards.

She pushed the door aside and hauled herself to her feet.

No time to be squeamish. Heather pulled down her jeans and panties and lowered her bottom over the hole in the board seat. Gasping at the blast of frigid air, she imagined monsters with icy fingers reaching up from the dark lagoon.

When she returned, Don was sitting on the side of the bed, smoking.

"How do you like our privy?"

"The door fell off and knocked me over."

"Is that right? When I was a kid, I thought the privy was haunted. I never went there at night."

"First time I ever heard of a haunted privy."

"Family secret. When my grandfather dug the pit, he uncovered a skull and a bunch of bones. Old Indian grave. There were arrowheads and shell beads and a clay pipe."

She shuddered. "Under the privy?"

"It wasn't a privy then."

"All the same, he should have put it someplace else."

"Anywhere on that hillside would have been the same." He tossed his cigarette on the floor and ground it out.

Heather kicked off her boots, crawled into the sleeping bag, and pulled up the zipper. She didn't stop shivering until her body heat had finally warmed the narrow space. That was when the smell took over. Mouse dirt and mold. Her throat tickled and her breath wheezed.

Don went outside, but not for long enough to go up to the privy. When he returned, he pinched out the candle and lay down.

The mattress sagged. Heather had to hold on to the edge to keep from rolling into the hollow in the middle. Sometime during the night, gravity won. Her grip on the mattress loosened, and she woke up to feel Don's body against hers. Then she went to sleep again.

The mattress creaked. Heather half opened her eyes. It was morning. Don was sitting on the edge of the bed, smoking a cigarette.

"Are you awake?"

"Uh-huh."

"Look out the window."

Rising on one elbow, she peered through the dirty glass.

Snow filled the air with feathery clumps. It would already be over the tops of her pant boots, and it was still falling.

"Do you know how to light a Coleman?" Don asked.

"A what?"

"Jeez! Don't you know anything? It's a stove. It's for cooking."

"You mean there's food?"

"Look in the kitchen."

"Where's the kitchen?"

"In a three-room cottage, you should be able to find it."

She unzipped her sleeping bag and crawled past him. Christ, it was cold! With the sleeping bag draped over her shoulders, she tottered into the main room. The gym bag was no longer there.

Daylight brought to life the pictures hanging on the board walls. Some were the usual Canadiana: water, rocks, and trees. Others were blown-up snapshots of people having fun. A laughing girl in a canoe. A raccoon accepting food from a woman's outstretched hand. A boy holding up a string of fish. She took a second to observe the boy. A skinny kid with narrow shoulders and fair hair. He might have been Don at twelve or thirteen.

He came up behind her as she studied the picture.

"Is that you?" she asked.

"My kid brother."

"I never heard you mention him."

"He's dead."

"Oh. Sorry."

The kitchen was a narrow room with a door at the far end and a window that overlooked the lake. On the counter was a chipped enamel sink with a rusty hand pump mounted beside it. Also on the counter stood a metal object that looked like a hotplate crossed with a barbecue.

"That's the Coleman," Don said. He fiddled with a knob and flicked his lighter. A ring of blue flames spurted.

"Cool. But what's there to cook?"

He pointed to a row of large, dusty jars labeled with masking tape, all empty except for *Sugar*, *Rice*, *Flour*, and *Macaroni*.

"That's it." He picked up a pail. "I'm going outside to get snow we can melt for water."

"Doesn't the pump work?"

"Jeez, at ten below?"

Heather boiled rice for breakfast. Don smoked right through the meal. After eating, he brought in logs from the woodpile outside the back door and lit a fire in the big stone hearth. Heather stretched out her hands to the warmth.

"Enjoy it while you can," he said. "When the snow stops, I'll have to put out the fire. Smoke from the chimney is a dead giveaway somebody's here." He dragged a chair to the hearth and settled himself.

Heather looked at her surroundings. The dark blue seat cushions were stained. Dirty white stuffing bulged from their burst seams. Dust covered everything.

"Doesn't anybody ever come here?" she asked.

"A guy from the village checks every so often."

"I mean come for a vacation."

"Not anymore."

"Why not?"

"There was an accident." He paused, shook his head. "Sooner or later the place will be sold. My dad and uncle are suing each other over the estate. Both their lawyers told them to stay away." His lank hair fell across his eyes, and he pushed it back irritably. He hated questions, but if she didn't ask, how would she find out anything?

"What are you going to do about the car?"

"Nothing, right now."

"You can't just leave it there. It's covered with DNA."

"I'll figure out something."

She suspected that Don hadn't a clue what to do next. They were both in a bad spot. But Don's was worse. What would he face if he got caught? Life? Twenty-five years? That was his problem. She wasn't the one who had killed the Paki. Her smart idea was to turn herself in.

All this trouble to steal a few lousy bucks from the till of a corner store. Why had she let him talk her into it? Why was she such a fool?

Heather sat in front of the fire on a love seat with dirty cushions and stared at the flames. Don was dozing in his chair with his skinny legs stretched toward the fire.

This might be a good time to do something about her boots. She pulled the broken heel from her pocket. To make the two heels match, all she needed was a knife. This would be simple. She stood up, wincing when her feet met the cold floor, and carried her boots into the kitchen.

Don sighed, shifted in his chair.

In the drawer that held the cutlery, she found a knife with a saw-toothed blade. That should do. Holding the unbroken boot firmly against the countertop, she started to saw. The knife squeaked as it chewed.

Don must have heard. He bounded across the floor.

"What are you doing?" His fingers squeezed her wrist so tightly she dropped the knife.

"Fixing my boots."

"Leave them."

"I want to walk like a normal person."

"You aren't going anywhere." Wrenching one arm behind her back, he propelled her to the love seat and dumped her onto it. "If you're thinking of running away, forget it." He stalked back to the kitchen, picked up her boots, strode across the room, and hurled them into the fire.

"No!" she yelled. Jumping up, she made a dash for the fireplace tongs. Before she could fork her boots from the fire, Don grabbed her shoulders. He held her fast while tongues of blue and green flames licked the leather of her boots. The soles peeled away from the vamps, and the heels sweated beads of glue. He didn't let her go until two charred lumps were all that remained.

Morning sunshine sparkled on the lake. Around the cottage, evergreen boughs bent under their burden of snow. Don put out the fire.

"We're going to freeze," Heather whimpered.

"The fireplace will hold heat for a couple of days."

"And then we'll freeze." The food wouldn't last more than a few days anyway. Freeze or starve. What difference did it make?

She padded across the cold floor to the windows. Now that the air was clear, she could see the village at the end of the lake, smoke rising from snow-covered roofs. There was a tiny island in the middle of the lake. The only tree on the island was a dead pine. A rough platform of sticks balanced on the top, capped with snow.

"What's that thing on the dead tree?"

"Osprey nest."

"You're kidding."

"Why should I be kidding? This is Osprey Lake. Ospreys live here."

"It doesn't look like they live here now."

"They fly south for the winter."

"They're not so dumb. At least they're smarter than the people in those houses, stuck up here in the snow. What do they do all winter long?"

"They tend their trap lines. Except for Rosemary Bear

Paw. She's a bootlegger. When we were kids, she supplied us with smokes and liquor. She never asked questions. Never told secrets. Her house was painted blue."

"Why blue?"

"So people would know which house was hers. There are no street addresses up here, you know."

This was interesting. Rosemary Bear Paw must own a snowmobile. What would she charge for a lift to . . . where? Huntsville? Anywhere with a bus station. Heather had ninety dollars in her wallet. Would that be enough?

But first she would have to walk to the village—one mile across the frozen lake.

There was a junk room on the far side of the kitchen door. Heather had looked in several times, but never entered. Maybe the next time Don dozed off, she could search there for something to wear on her feet. She might even find the gym bag. Don must have hidden it somewhere.

She would like to know how much money was in that bag. She was entitled to half, wasn't she? She had driven the car.

"Tell me about your brother," she said as they sat at the wooden table eating their supper of boiled rice. "The boy in the photograph."

"Why do you want to know?"

"Just wondered. Was he a lot younger than you?"

"Five years younger. He was twelve when he died.

"You told me there was an accident. Was that it?"

"Yeah. Charlie drowned." Don set down his spoon.

"Poor kid."

"He bugged me to bring him up here fishing. I used to come up with some other guys. We didn't want Charlie along, but Dad said we had to take him. We paddled over to the village and bought a couple of forty-ouncers from Rosemary Bear Paw. Charlie never had a drink before. The guys thought he went outside to throw up. Drowned in six inches of water right by the shore." Don banged his fist on the table. "It wasn't my fault. What kind of parents would throw out a seventeen-year-old kid because of an accident? When I phoned my grandfather, he hung up on me. It's their fault I ended up on the street."

"You weren't exactly on the street when I met you," she said. "You had a job pumping gas. As I remember, you had big plans."

"I was waiting for a break."

It had been a warm July day when Don first came into the drugstore where Heather worked. He had bought toothpaste. She remembered that because of his smile—the kind of smile that sells toothpaste on TV. Their fingers brushed when she handed him his change.

Next day he was back buying condoms. When she saw what they were, blood rushed to her face and she couldn't meet his eyes.

"When are you done working?" he had asked.

She didn't answer. But at 4 o'clock, the end of her shift, her heart beat fast to see him leaning against a black Mustang in the drugstore parking lot. He wore tight jeans and a dark green shirt open at the neck.

"Can I give you a lift?"

"No thanks. I don't have far to walk."

He had smiled. "We can go for a drive." Something shivered in the air between them.

"All right." I shouldn't be doing this, she told herself as she climbed into the car. From the beginning, she couldn't say no to Don.

"Name's Don," he had said.

"I'm Heather."

"I know."

"How?"

"Your badge."

"Oh. Of course." She had felt her cheeks redden.

He drove fast, with the window open and one arm along the back of the passenger seat. They had stopped for a hamburger at a crossroads restaurant, and then kept on going. He'd parked his car down by a river just past a little town. It was very quiet, almost as if the town were miles away, not barely out of sight behind a hill.

He removed a green plaid blanket from the trunk. Heather, pretending she didn't know what was coming, wished that she were wearing sexy underwear instead of cotton briefs. As he pulled her down onto the blanket, she remembered the condoms. Don was prepared. But he took a lot for granted, didn't he?

With her next paycheck, Heather had purchased five pairs of lace panties at La Senza. For the rest of the summer, she and Don had made love a couple of times a week, either on the plaid blanket or in the backseat—depending on the weather. In November they rented an apartment together.

To help out with expenses, Heather stole things from the drugstore: condoms, toothpaste, aftershave, deodorant. It was easy.

While they were sharing a joint one afternoon, Don said, "I've figured out a way to make some real money."

"How?"

"There's stuff with street value in that drugstore. Uppers. Downs. Dexedrine. Cold remedies. We can make crystal meth out of cold remedies right here in the kitchen." His eyes locked on hers. "What about it?"

She had felt scared. "I can't. I don't have access to the dispensary."

"I don't see any bars keeping you out."

"Only the pharmacists ever go behind that counter."

"Come on, Heather. Don't tell me you can't." A deep sigh. "This is the first thing I've ever asked you to do."

Don had pushed her for a couple of weeks before giving up. A cloud settled over their relationship. She had let him down.

A few weeks later, Mr. Stonefield, the drugstore owner, caught her sneaking a bottle of aftershave into her handbag. Peering at her through his trifocals, he said she was lucky he didn't press charges. This was true. But now she had no job, no income, and no chance to pick up little extras for Don. Again, she had let him down.

While Don napped—all he ever did was smoke and sleep— Heather grabbed her chance to rummage in the junk room. There she found a man's rubber boot mixed up with rusted buckets, fishing poles, kerosene cans, and coils of rope. Embossed in the boot's red sole was the number 13. Further searching produced the boot's mate. When she turned the second boot upside down, mouse dirt and popcorn kernels rained onto the floor.

Gingerly she pulled on the boots and took a few steps. It was like trying to walk with her feet in a pair of cardboard cartons.

Don opened his eyes as she stomped into the main room. "You look like a circus clown," he said.

She didn't care what she looked like, as long as he didn't

take away the rubber boots. For the rest of the day she tramped around the cottage, bumping into furniture and tripping over her own feet—sometimes on purpose, to demonstrate that she couldn't run fast enough to escape with them on her feet. He let her keep the boots.

An airplane droned in the distance, louder and louder, coming from the south. Heather, wrapped in her sleeping bag on the love seat, looked up. Through the tall windows she saw the plane's black shape against the gray sky.

"Cessna," Don said. "Single engine."

"Is it coming here?"

"How would I know?"

"It *is* coming here!" As it descended, she saw that the plane was yellow, not black, and that it had skis instead of wheels. Heather's heart pounded. She wanted to run out onto the snow-covered lake, wave her arms, and shout: This way! Save me!

But before reaching Osprey Lake, the plane dipped behind the trees and disappeared.

Don walked over to the window. "Not coming here. It's landing on Mud Fish. Could be the air ambulance." He lit a cigarette, smoked it to the butt, and then lit another from it. The engine's drone continued.

"He's not sticking around or he'd have killed the engine," Don said. "He's picking up somebody or letting somebody off."

The air rumbled as the plane took off. It reappeared above the trees, circled, and headed south. An ache of loneliness came over her. She felt abandoned, like a castaway on a desert island who watches a ship draw near and then sail away. She squeezed her eyes shut to stop her tears as she listened to the receding drone.

Don flopped into a chair. "How about something to eat?"

"There's nothing left but sugar and flour."

"Can't you make something out of them?"

"Such as?"

"Bread, maybe?"

"Christ! And you think I'm dumb!"

Heather pulled on the rubber boots, clomped into the kitchen, and lit the Coleman. A skin of ice had formed on the water that she had melted from snow two hours earlier. She broke the ice, poured water into a saucepan, and stirred in half a cup of flour and a spoonful of sugar.

While she was bringing it to a boil, she heard Don go out the back door. It sounded like he was straightening the wood-pile, which was pointless since he wouldn't let them have a fire anyway. By the time he returned, the liquid in the pan had thickened enough to coat a spoon. She sipped a few drops, added a dash of sugar, then sipped again. Slightly better. After filling a couple of mugs, she carried them into the main room.

Don stood by the windows, staring south at a pillar of black smoke that funneled into the sky. Something was burning, back there along the track.

She handed him a mug. Don cradled it in his hands.

"Looks like a big fire," she said.

"Yeah. Somebody's torched the car." He raised the mug to his lips, grimaced as he swallowed. "What do you call this stuff?"

"Gruel, I guess."

"It's disgusting." He put his mug on the table. "We have to clear out."

"When?"

"First thing in the morning."

* * *

It was pitch dark outside when she heard the creak of the mattress. She knew that sound—how the mattress squeaked when you sat up, squeaked again when you rose from bed. Why was Don getting up?

The floor now creaked. He had left the bedroom. He had reached the back door. Maybe he just needed to pee. She turned her head, looked out the window, and there was Don, the gym bag in his hand. For an instant she could not believe it. Don was taking off with the money, and he was leaving her here alone.

She pulled herself out of the sleeping bag and, draping it over her shoulders, stumbled into the front room. She could see him from the window, heading toward the road.

"You greedy bastard," she said, right out loud. What kind of boyfriend would leave his girl to starve or freeze? Should she go after him? For the past six months she had been trotting after him like a love-sick puppy.

The thought filled her with sudden disgust. Let him go. He was welcome to the money in the gym bag. Providing she got out of here alive, she would be happy to never see him again.

I can walk to that village, she told herself. Find the blue house. Ask Rosemary Bear Paw to help me. She might know when the bus goes through Huntsville. Or maybe there's a closer stop, a depot in some country store along the way. Heather glanced at her wristwatch. Nearly 7 o'clock. It would soon be light.

Between the cottage and the hill there was shelter from the wind. But the moment she turned the corner, the wind slammed into her face. It howled across the lake, lashing her cheeks with icy grains that stung like tiny needles. The osprey nest at the top of the dead pine rocked in the wind.

Heather plodded on, her head bent to the wind. When she got back to Toronto, she'd find a job. Any kind of job. She didn't need much—a small apartment with a bathroom. Tub and shower. Lots of fluffy, warm towels. She wanted a kitchenette too, with a microwave and cupboards to store the delicious food she would buy. Kraft dinners. Chocolate chip cookies. Tim Hortons coffee. Would she tell the police about the hold-up? Definitely not. She never wanted to see Don again. Not in court. Not in prison. Not anywhere. If love was a sickness, she was cured. How could she ever have cared for such a loser?

Nearing the village, she saw that each snow-topped shanty had a snowmobile parked near its door. Except for one, the houses looked as if no paintbrush had ever touched them. That one house was blue.

Heather stumbled onto the shore and reached into her pocket for a tissue to wipe her dripping nose. She hadn't a clue what to say to Rosemary Bear Paw, beyond asking for a lift.

There was no sign of life in any of the houses. Outside the blue house, a scruffy brown dog lifted its leg against a yellow and black snowmobile. When the dog finished, it trotted to the house, acknowledging her with a glance over its shoulder. At the door it gave a sharp bark. The door opened just enough to admit the dog, then closed.

At her knock, the door opened again with a blast of warm air that smelled of tobacco and smoked fish. In front of Heather stood an enormous woman wearing a lumberjack shirt. She had a neck like a bull, and her shoulders sloped. Her face was coppery brown with wide cheekbones. Not an ancient face, but a face out of an ancient time. Beady eyes embedded in fat pouches regarded Heather with more suspicion than surprise. At her feet, the dog growled.

"Where'd *you* come from?" The woman had a tiny Cupid's bow mouth that scarcely opened when she spoke.

"Across the lake. I . . . uh . . . need a ride to the bus."

The woman eyed Heather from head to foot. She saw it all: the bomber jacket, the tight jeans, the rubber boots.

"I'll take you over for fifty bucks."

"Fine."

She opened the door wider. "Come inside before all the warm air gets out."

Heather stepped into a small room that was almost filled by the woman's bulk. In one corner stood a cast iron stove. On top of it a copper kettle steamed. A bed covered by a red blanket pressed against one wall. Near the opposite wall stood a wooden table and three chairs that did not match.

"Are you Rosemary Bear Paw?"

"You know my name? You come from Lawfords' place, I think." She took a green mug and a bottle of rye whiskey from a shelf, poured a shot, and handed it to Heather. "This will warm you up. You drink, then we go."

Heather did not want it. She had tried whiskey before— nasty stuff that tasted like nail polish remover. But as the warmth slid down her throat, she changed her mind.

Rosemary Bear Paw's dark eyes studied Heather's face. "I knew somebody was staying at the Lawford place. It don't take much to show me that. I don't ask questions. Been plenty trouble there already."

She lowered her bulk onto the bed and pulled on her boots, huffing as she leaned forward to lace them. "That hillside—in the old days, we buried our people there. Sacred land. My father told old man Lawford not to build there, but he don't listen. There's a curse on that place." With a grunt, she stood up and pulled her parka from a hook. "That Lawford boy and his friends used to come up here to get drunk. They said they come to fish, but I don't see nobody put their line in the water. Then the little kid drowned. That killed the old man." She wrestled her arms into the parka's sleeves. "For eight years, I don't see no family there." She finished with a pucker of her lips and a popping sound, like a kiss. "Huh! I tell you, the ancestors never leave this land."

I'm glad I'm leaving, Heather thought. The ancestors can keep it. I never want to see Osprey Lake again.

The woman held out her hand, which was dimpled and remarkably small, considering the size of her body. "Fifty dollars."

Heather handed over two twenties and a ten. The money went straight into a coffee tin on the table. Rosemary Bear Paw pulled on a pair of leather gauntlets decorated with bright beadwork—red, green, black, and white.

"We go before anybody else wake up."

Heather looked around but saw no sign of another person in the house.

"I mean neighbors. They're still sleeping. Nobody needs to know you been here." The dog followed them to the door. "Not this time," the woman added. The dog trotted over to the stove, turned around three times, and flopped onto the floor.

The snowmobile looked like a monster insect. No, not exactly an insect. More like that contraption the Space Centre sent up to Mars. It was a new machine, and probably worth more than all the houses of the village put together.

"You like it, eh? Ski-Doo Skandic SUV. Electric starter. Never stalls in the cold."

"Very nice."

"Hop on," the woman grunted. "We don't have all day."

For a moment, as she climbed onto the seat, Heather

thought of asking if she could first use the bathroom. But the thought of another hole in a board over a stinking pit was too gross.

"Is it far to the bus station?" she asked, conjuring in her mind a modern facility. Shiny ceramic tiles. Flush toilets. Sinks with hot and cold running water.

"Not far." Rosemary Bear Paw started the engine.

The hills that rose up on either side seemed to channel the Ski-doo from lake to lake. The wind screamed in Heather's ears. This won't take long, she thought. But one lake led into another, and then another. No sign of a highway, a road, or a town. Where was this woman taking her? Heather saw nothing but rocks, trees, and the occasional boarded-up summer cottage.

If she had known it would take this long, she definitely would have asked to use the washroom. Her bladder pressed sorely. The vibration of the machine made it worse. She panicked. What if she wet herself? She would rather die than go into a bus depot with pee leaked all over her pants.

By the time she let go of the right-hand grip to thump Rosemary Bear Paw on the back, it was nearly too late.

The snowmobile stopped, its motor still turning over. The woman shouted over her shoulder, "What's your problem?"

"I need to pee."

"Help yourself." Her tiny mouth spat out the words.

Heather dismounted and waded off through the snow. When she was a few yards behind the snowmobile, she unzipped her jeans. Rosemary Bear Paw swiveled on her seat to watch. Did she expect Heather to pee while being stared at? Why was she looking at her like that, taunting with those beady eyes? Heather felt like screaming: Turn your goddamn back! Not until Heather's panties and jeans were around her ankles did the woman avert her eyes.

Such a relief to release the flow, to feel the pressure ease! Heather relaxed as much as anyone could relax while squatting bare-bottomed in the snow.

The revving of the motor took her by surprise. She was still peeing when the engine roared and the Ski-doo sped away.

"Hey! Wait a minute!" she shouted, as if the snowmobile's departure were mere carelessness—a failure to notice that the passenger was not on board.

It took Heather ten seconds to realize that the snowmobile was not going to stop, another ten to claw her clothing into place. She stumbled through the snow, hollering, "Don't leave me here!" She chased after the Ski-doo, the diminishing roar of its motor humming in her ears even when it had disappeared behind a hill.

After disbelief, shock set in. The truth swept over her, buried her like an avalanche. She was alone in the middle of a frozen lake. The Ski-doo's track, a long scar in the white snow, was the only sign that it had ever been here. Everything else seemed like a bad dream. Only the track was real, and only it could save her. She had to follow that track, and quickly, before drifting snow erased it.

Which way should she go? Forward or back? It must be twenty miles back to Osprey Lake.

Forward, she decided. There would be a town beyond the next hill. She would come upon it soon. Snow swirled in every direction. Soon it covered the snowmobile's track.

Heather walked and walked until she lost all sense of time and place. There was a buzzing in her head. Images swam vaguely in her mind. For a while, someone seemed to walk beside her, a presence felt rather than seen. When she turned her head, nothing was there but swirling snow.

Then a heavy drowsiness came upon her. She felt her knees

give way and her body sink into the softness. Rest and sleep, she thought. Rest and sleep. Memories passed like strands of mist, like fragments of a dream. It was summer, and Don lay beside her on the plaid blanket, down by a river, just past a little town that was out of sight behind a hill. She made an effort to touch his face. But she was too tired.

There were voices in the wind. They came from above her and from every side, chanting in a language she did not know. She heard drums too, but that might have been her blood beating in her ears, fainter now and far away.

DEAD MEDICINE SNAKE WOMAN

BY GERARD HOUARNER

New York, New York

S he was a different kind of incoming, bursting like a hungry T-Rex through the City Hall subway platform crowd thick from track pit to tile wall with suits and stiffs. Her eyes zeroed in on half a dozen guys, me included, for a split second before dismissing us all. We weren't on the menu. I wouldn't have minded, even after she near knocked me over chasing a train that hadn't come in yet.

Funny how little of my life sticks with me. But, of course, things sticking to me isn't the problem at all.

She put a good lick into me with her shoulder. Played some games, that one. Curtain of black hair had my heart racing before I remembered her lips, thin because they were pursed, and her small nose, nostrils flaring like a horse in full gallop. I liked the way her hips shoved the sides of a loose cotton top out as she bulled her way through a New York crowd that really didn't give a shit about being pushed around by her.

Almost like they forgot she'd been there as soon as she passed. But I didn't.

Wake up, white man, and see what's coming.

That's what Grandpa said, inside my head. Normally, I'm sleeping when I hear him. Usually, I'm dreaming when I see the world so sharp it hurts, in a quick-cut slide, down a looping water ride that doesn't ever want to stop. Like a house-to-house fire fight. Or an RPG blazing a smoke trail for a Humvee parked at a market.

Grandpa says I should take up the pipe if I want to understand where I'm going and what I'm seeing in these dreams. Then he laughs when I think about it, and tells me I don't have enough First in me to handle a pipe. Yeah, and you weren't there when I needed you, ghost warrior.

I couldn't remember the last time he warned about something in real time.

I turned, a little slow because I didn't want to let go of her, and looked. Got two looks in, really. First take was of a big, goofy, golden-haired boy with porcelain skin and muscles on top of muscles packed under a shiny custom suit, slipping and sliding his way through the crowd like a king snake with a thousand *excuse-me*'s slithering from his mouth in a few different languages. Pretty. Officer candidate material. The type that goes down hard and doesn't bounce. People didn't look twice at him either.

Second take went toward the same place as Grandpa's voice.

I never saw nothing in any dream like what was coming on my second take. Sure, I've spent time with ravens, cougars, coyotes, rabbits, squirrels, even talking water bugs. Trees and leaves turning into freaky faces, speaking words I can't understand, and even when I do, I still don't get what's up—yeah, plenty of that.

But this check-off got me a vision full of toothy, mangy, wild-eyed wilderness surging like a market crowd running from a bomb blast. Where the eyes were supposed to be in the lump that might have been a head, there were holes, red-rimmed fire pockets like sniper muzzles loaded with bullets with names on them.

Two faces. Walking in the waking world.

Something inside me felt cold, but it wasn't really me. Grandpa was upset.

The station already smelled like meat turned bad from the mass of sweaty bodies perfumed for the day at the office, but what I saw pushed out a shockwave stench like a body cooked in burning wreckage. Or a fresh, dug-up grave stacked with the dead.

Two-face didn't single me out. It was stalking the woman.

I moved. Didn't think twice. Not scared. Hell, Grandpa'd been talking to me since I was a kid, saying he's in my blood and telling me I should do this or that crazy thing. Scared always bounced off of me, even in that shit-and-rock country they sent me to after I enlisted. This was just one more dream I was walking through.

I left a wake of curses. Guess I was the only one running who wasn't invisible. Put out a hand, caught a flap of cloth that felt slippery. Kept the other tight for a punch to what I hoped were ribs.

Two-face raised an elbow and I barely cleared a broken jaw. The thing shrugged and I heard the buzzing of a nest full of hornets barreling into my ear drums.

I went down, sparks flying. No concussion or ringing eardrums, no smoke curling from singed cloth. No flashbacks either. Got up quick. People muttering didn't bother me. I'm used to folks thinking I'm crazy. Best four years of my life were in the service. I was normal there. Bugfuck as I wanted to be. Grandpa didn't visit me. Not even in dreams. No signs or warnings. Reality was the dream. I'd been sent all alone to the mountaintop in a shit storm to find my way, my tribe, my vision.

You had to make it on your own, is what Grandpa told me

when I came back and he started speaking to me again.

Where's my way, my tribe, my guide?

You on the path for it now.

Thanks for nothing.

I followed in the big man's wake, catching up, thinking about what I was going to do—jump up and grab the choke or go low and take out the knees. He stayed mostly man, which made it easier to think. Of course, when you have to think about these things before you do them, they don't turn out well.

I wasn't fast enough. Good thing, or else I wouldn't be talking about it now. And the woman, she'd be dead.

He caught up to her and shoved. She screamed as she went flying into naked air, and when she stopped flying she vanished into the track pit.

A gust of warm, humid air blew in, then surged out of the tunnel.

The man kept moving on through the crowd as I came to the platform edge. A few suits shouted, stirred from their iPod cocoons by a sense of having just missed something. I knew the feeling. A young girl in a school uniform pointed down at the tracks. A knot of teenage boys whooped and laughed. Maybe there was something down there, maybe there wasn't. A fat rat plodded away to the other side of the station. Fast food wrappings and newspaper pages danced in the air. A roar was building.

The big man wasn't so big anymore, like he was making his way down a different horizon line than everyone else. He looked back at something way behind me, maybe the distant crowd of us and his victim, and then he dipped below the range of shoulders and was gone. There was no two-faced man. No woman either.

Grandpa settled down inside me. I never knew he could get upset like that.

On the uptown side of the station, a twenty-something who looked like he'd stayed up from a night of clubbing broke into a free-form flow like he was the headliner and we'd all come to hear him and the sound of that train coming was our love and adulation taking him higher and higher. I have no idea what he was rapping about.

So I jumped.

The lights of the lead subway car were the eyes of that thing I'd seen on the second take of Mr. Muscle, only they were flashing with the fire from full clips being dumped on me.

My hand settled on something warm, soft. Moaning. There she was. I grabbed an arm, pulled. Got hold of her hip, slid my hand up under the other shoulder. There was space below the platform. I dragged her to cover.

Happened to me once. Small, smelly guy, spilling blood himself, pulled me from a burning wreckage over stone and dust and sheet metal, through a tangle of poles and beach umbrellas and plastic sheeting, to a quiet little spot underneath sides of meat quietly flaming. We listened to gunfire crackling and kids crying for a while. Don't know what happened to him after the evac.

I held the woman tight against my chest, legs around her hips to keep her from rolling. Her hair flew and crawled all around my face and head as the train blasted past us inches away. For a second I didn't know where I was anymore. Too many dreams, too much reality.

She was a warm, trembling bundle against my beating heart. I closed my eyes, and turned my head so her hair could get all of me, neck, ears, eyes, and lips—like she cared—and her fingers were memorizing the shape of me and I was something special to her.

But the train screeched to a stop and we choked and coughed on a burnt, electric stink and dust and she broke free but knocked her head against a car's undercarriage and stared at me like I was the one who'd thrown her down there.

Her face was rounder than I thought, now that I could see it with her hair flowing away, reaching for the light and the air and freedom.

"Sorry," I said, pulling my legs away from her because I was afraid that even with everything going on I'd get a hard-on and that would make the situation a complete cluster fuck.

People were shouting above me and I thought I was okay, though my knees and hips were singing like an out-of-tune choir. I thought we could crawl to one end of the station and get out, so I pointed and started moving. If there's one thing hearing voices, much less combat, taught me, it was recovery. If you just lay there, you're screwed. Keep moving.

I grabbed her arm. She brushed me off. "Don't touch me," she said, like it was the worst thing that had happened to her so far that day.

You can't touch the moon.

Great, Grandpa.

I said, "Hey, I just saved your life." Getting pissed now. Like when you take fire from people you're supposed to be saving and you want to lob a few shells back to say, *You're welcome.*

Somebody with training interrupted from above and got me to answer her questions: no blood, moving my limbs, breathing regular. "The woman's fine too," I added.

All I got back was "What woman?" and "Stay calm" and "Help is coming." After a few whispers, the voice asked, "What meds are you on?"

My heartbeat woman was still staring at me, hard, reading between my lips and holding on to steel-smoking motor mounts that looked hot to me. But her skin wasn't blistering and I figured, well, I don't know what. She had to be in shock. I was. So I told the voice from above, who identified herself as a nurse, what had happened: I saw a man chasing a woman through the crowd, tried to stop him, couldn't catch up, and he pushed her into the train tracks. I jumped down after her.

I didn't mention the vision I had of that man, or that I was in love with the girl in the tracks.

This is the stuff of heroes, I was thinking. I mean, I'm a Marine. A vet. Doing my warrior thing. That meant name in lights, spot on the *Late Show*, cash rewards. I'd have to play down the Java programmer angle, though. Nobody wants to know about a smart vet.

"You saw the monster," my heartbeat woman said.

"Yeah. If that's what you call it."

My father killed something on high steel when he was young.

Thanks, Grandpa, but I'm busy right now.

"I'm real to you." She looked into my eyes like she was trying to see through them.

"Shit, yeah."

He killed something like that. And afterwards, the bridge came down.

Yeah, Grandpa. Quebec Bridge. Mohawk disaster. I remember. Can we talk about it later?

"You're not afraid to die."

"Right." Easy to stay loose about the death end of life when the living part doesn't stick.

Its blood's a curse. Mixed with ours. The dealing with it is our duty. Even down to you.

Blood? What? Never told me that one, Grandpa.

"I can't save everyone," she said, and in that dark place tears shone in her eyes. "I can't do more for you. I have others to take care of."

In that small space she seemed to be crawling backwards away from me. I reached for her again, but this time I missed, like my hand went right through her.

I thought it had to be that thing's blood that drew me to you. Hard as it is to believe.

And here I thought I was special.

You are. Though I've been wondering if that thing was ever going to show up. You carry the responsibility.

What responsibility?

There aren't many descendents left. Seems like you're all that's left.

For what?

Did my best to show you the way. Wish your father'd lived long enough.

And then she was already halfway under the subway car, folded over but still facing me almost between her own feet like a circus contortionist, sliding back without making a sound or moving a muscle. Her eyes were darker than any space in the tunnel or under the train, darker than a night without stars and moon, or a dreamless sleep. But when I looked into them, I gave that darkness a touch of light and she nearly cracked a smile. That's when I knew I'd been talking to the wrong ghost. Family just never knows when to get out of the way.

"Wait, what's your name?" If this had been a Manhattan lounge maybe she would have said something like Cinderella and I'd never have seen her again.

"Medicine Snake Woman."

"What the hell kind of name is that?"

"You're welcome," she said, and flashed me a small, sad

smile like she'd already read everything she needed to know between my lips and she was moving on to bigger and better things.

Then she was gone, and it hit me. She was the one who should have said thanks, and "You're welcome" should have been my line.

I woke up dizzy back in the real world underneath a train with police and EMTs talking to me through the crevice between the platform and the train, rats piling up around the third rail wondering if the lunch buffet had arrived.

Sucks to be you, don't it.

At least I'm alive, Grandpa.

Alive. Yeah. That woman, she made me feel alive. I didn't care what was happening or if I was finally coming down with PTSD. Screw all that. I needed her.

I crawled out on my own while they warned me to stay put. The rest of the day was a fancy necklace of diamond reality moments strung on a flimsy line of breaking-heartbeat woman dream—emergency room, police report, psych eval, criminal and military record check, even a call to my old foster home to confirm I had no psychiatric history. There was also that golden call to the boss saying I wouldn't be working the Java today because I just jumped in front of a train.

Through it all, I couldn't get Medicine Snake Woman out of my mind. When we married, what would I call her—Medicine? Med? Snake? What would we name our kids? How would we be in bed—a dance, a firestorm, a tsunami? Would I be able to support her, or was I expected to stay home while she went on with whatever it was she did for a living?

Would my mixed heritage be a problem for her family, who obviously took pride in their lineage? What would it feel like to be scared of losing her?

Hell, I already knew that answer.

The dream came apart and was replaced by another when I fell asleep after a beer later that night.

Bet you think you're something special.

Grandpa likes to talk from out of trees most times, but this night he was a big-ass bear standing on two legs taking a dump in the woods. His paw was bigger than me. So was his dump.

I studied the acorns by my foot and said, No, just crazy, like everybody says I am.

You can't let her go, can you?

I didn't answer because I knew it was going to be one of *those* dreams, like the one that took me to Afghanistan for four years to make a warrior out of me. Or the time in junior high when I landed in the hospital for standing up to older bullies picking on a skinny black kid who was also in a foster home. Or, best yet, who can forget popping my nine-year-old dream cherry the first time Grandpa paid a visit and convinced me my real mother lived in the next town over and I needed to see her because blood called to blood. Maybe I'd seen her last when I was two or three. Couldn't remember her much, or my father.

Things didn't stick to me even back then.

Grandpa even showed me where my foster parents kept the real cash stash and what bus to take when and where and the best time to go over to catch Mom. Ran away on a Friday night with a forged note for the bus driver just in case, and sure enough I found my birth mother, who told me about how my daddy died in the service with honor even if it was an accident. How she fell apart and had to give me up and was too ashamed of letting me and her husband and their families down to ever stay clean long enough to take me back. So she left me with people who could love me the right way until she got herself together.

Said she'd been trying. Told me, "You know how it is."

By Monday I was back in my foster home, and we all knew that was the best place for me after that weekend. She gave me up for adoption. My foster parents made me theirs.

After the Marines, I never went back. Sent them a postcard every now and then. Guess they didn't stick either. Sweet folks. They were a comfort, making me feel like I was loved. And I thought Mom loved me still, so that made two places. But not everything that loved was true.

Not sure what exactly made me stop owning my life and maybe my death. Might have been seeing my mother in her drunken junkie glory. Could have been afterwards, when Grandpa sent me to my father's military cemetery and I saw Dad standing there on a Sunday morning, trees and grave marker visible right through him. Looked like he'd been waiting for me, seeing me coming from years away. Didn't say nothing. Not that kind of spirit, Grandpa said. Killed before his time came to pick up the fight.

I never asked what Grandpa meant by that. I mean, bad enough I was doing whatever a voice in my head told me to do. Dad looked at me like he knew what was coming and couldn't do anything to protect me. We couldn't talk no matter how hard we tried, and Grandpa didn't translate or act like a telephone between us. Dad did try touching my face. All I felt was cold. Wish it was him in my head instead of Grandpa. But apparently there wasn't enough First in him to carry on that part of the tradition either. Well, I guess that was Grandpa's fault.

Wish I'd cared enough to run away again and look for my daddy's family. Ran away for everything else that popped into my head. But Grandpa told me they had enough problems without me, and I still believe him.

Wish a lot of things I can never have.

So here I was again in dream time, feeling Grandpa trying to steer me away again, but this time I wasn't having it. I wasn't letting life go through me again. And I wasn't going to wait for that blood-cursed monster to hunt me down somewhere down the road. It was here, and so was I. I was going after it.

You're going after it, aren't you.

I still didn't say anything. Didn't ask about responsibility either. I knew I'd get a load of tradition and spirit talk. Grandpa came down on all fours with a thump that almost woke me up and stared at me through one eye, up close, so that it seemed I was peering through a furry porthole at a wooded landscape of rolling hills and bright streams under a golden full moon. I wanted to hump the moon.

What's wrong with that?

You can't have her.

Why? Because I'm not Indian enough?

Nobody gets her. She's from the other world.

Same place as the monster?

Yes.

So the ones from the other world get us but we can't get them?

That getting is a transgression. That's why the ones who get us are monsters. If one of us caught her, that one would become a monster.

I held her.

That's sweet. But it wasn't getting. Do you need a talk about the difference?

I didn't bother answering. Instead, I climbed up on to Grandpa's back and rode while he walked through the woods, grabbing a beehive full of honey and gurgling up fish by dipping his jaws into a stream and snapping them closed when they swam over his tongue. Didn't mind the fishing, but the pissed-off bees were a pain.

She likes me.

She likes everyone who's brave and strong and full of medicine.

She ever like you?

Never saw her in my life.

Then you're just jealous.

She's going to be the death of you. Or the life. Either way, it'll be the hardest thing you've done with your life yet.

Why?

This time it was Grandpa who didn't answer. He shrugged me off on a hilltop and left me sitting on a rock. Waiting for a vision.

You ever fight the monster? I asked Grandpa.

But he didn't answer that question either.

I woke up too late to get to work on time and thought I deserved a sick day to recover and said so when I called in. Showered, dressed in the nice jeans and shirt, the clean boots, just in case I found her. Put the 1911 .45 under my shirt, just in case I found the monster too. I call it a memento from the service, but of course they don't issue .45s anymore.

I went out into the busy city day looking for my heartbeat woman.

I started at the train station where I'd made my jump. Scene of the crime. Works in old movies.

The train was pulling out just as I went through the turnstile. After rush hour and a train, the platform was empty, except for the requisite homeless guy on a seat with a bag between his legs, head down, asleep.

I walked yesterday's walk. Saw her running through again, and the thing. Felt her bump. Smelled her smell. Retraced the path I'd taken to the edge. Went back down, slow and easy this time. Looked for clues. A scarf. A shoe. A tiny stone from a piece of jewelry. A purse with ID. The kinds of things left behind in old movies to get the hero to the woman who was going to be the death of him.

No train was coming, but the minute I spent down there was sad and crazy and made me feel as vulnerable as a blasted bleeding body in a combat zone. I struggled to get back up on the deck, searching for the Homeland Security camera and thinking I'd better use the other exit, when the homeless man hooked me under the armpit and helped me up.

A sign of life. Maybe this station was home. He could've seen something. The clue.

I brushed myself off. "Thanks, guy. I know this looks weird, but I was here yesterday, the guy who jumped down there, maybe you saw me? I'm trying to find the girl," I explained, reaching into my pocket to pull out a fiver, whether he knew anything or not. "She fell down first, but nobody believed me—"

"So am I."

Yeah. It was that kind of movie.

The homeless man looked like a braided rope of sinewy, dried meat nearly lost inside a soiled overcoat, face hidden under a massive beard, smelling like an open sewer. He picked a crisp, fresh shirt and pants out of the shopping bag next to him, slipped out of the coat, started changing.

I headed back the way I'd come, figuring the token booth clerk had already called the cops about the terrorist on the tracks who he'd spotted in his monitors. But the booth was closed. Could have sworn it was open when I came down. I went for the exit, but the gate was locked into place. Darkness flooded the stairs leading to the street. The lights went out on the MetroCard machines, then in the overhead fixtures. Something pushed my chest and I fell back into the monster, fully dressed and itself again: overlapping out-of-synch images of a blond slab of muscle and a thatch of shadows grinning teeth and blazing laser-painting eyes.

What was I thinking? These are the moments I need Grandpa, I said to myself. What good is not being afraid if you can't figure out what needs to be done.

I pulled the gun out—what I should have done in the first place—and stuck the muzzle in the vague borderland between the monster's neck and head. "Where is she?" I demanded, keeping the question as simple as the threat of a released safety.

"I don't know."

I lowered the gun and put a round in its kneecap. The explosion was muffled, the kick subdued. The monster didn't fall, but its blond mask hair ruffled. I put one in the hip. Nothing. Elbow. Shoulder. Sternum. I finished the clip into its head out of sheer defiance. When I was done, I dropped the gun. It felt like I'd been firing a .38.

"You didn't die, so she didn't," the monster said.

"Is that important?"

"Yes."

The strong arm ending in a big bruiser hand grabbed me by the material at the back of my neck like a kitten, lifted, and carried me off. Except the fingers felt like claws scratching the bones of my spine.

We went off into the subway tunnel gloom, monster feet splashing through puddles and kicking refuse. My head got knocked into a few caged lights along the way.

As a warning gust of air blew at our backs, a side tunnel opened up. The tracks ended, the lighting dimmed. The monster's footsteps were drowned by the screech and grind of a train turning out of the station.

Someone cried out from a niche and scuttled away as we passed.

We entered another station, the mix of raw rock face, rusted wrought-iron gates, and bare sculptured sconces and pendants telling the sad story of abandoned visions of grandeur. Faded graffiti peppered tiled walls curving into the arched ceiling decorated with an incomplete mosaic. Something mythological. Modern banks of lamps set high on the wall at each tunnel mouth defined the boundaries of the excavated cave. The monster threw me onto the steel and rotten wood platform and hopped up after me, making the floor tremble.

It was the laser-pointer eyes pricking the back of my eyeballs with burning needles that made me blink and flinch. Not fear.

Looking back on the situation, the smart move would have been picking up right away on the monster not knowing where Medicine Snake Woman was and blowing its eyes out to buy time to get away. But I wanted her. And this thing was my only connection to her. The way to my Medicine Woman was through it. Plus, it tried to kill her. And I never got an actual clean shot at the monster.

And here was my true warrior moment. The one that came after the last ass kicking. And the best I could do was say, "What do you want?"

"Her."

"Can't help you there, big fella."

"Yes."

"How?"

"Because she'll come for you."

See, in the movies and books, this works the other way around—she's supposed to be the bad guy's prisoner and I'm the one who's supposed to do the rescuing. Of course, that's when I stumble into the setup and maybe I die but for sure I lose the woman and the bad guy puts a hurt on everybody.

I remembered that look she gave the bunch of us in the station when she was running, and wondered if she'd been searching for a chump. I like to think it was a warrior she'd been after.

But right then I felt like my long-lost cousins and distant great-uncles walking high iron without nets or cables. Only on this job, I'd run out of bolts and there was no way off the beams, and that iron was shaking and it was 1907 and the Quebec Bridge was falling into the St. Lawrence River all over again. Grandpa told me everything he could about living through that terrible day, losing his father, mourning with the rest of the Kahnawake Mohawks, but this was the first time I'd connected with the words he'd whispered in my head.

This time, the past was sticking to me, and it weighed more than all the steel that fell into the river that day. That past, it was as heavy as the spirits of the men who died under the steel, and the sorrow of their families, and the strength it took for those left to keep living another day.

The monster, it watched me like it couldn't decide if it was time for me to die yet. So I did the only thing there was left to do.

Sat down. Not so hard, carrying that weight. Waved a hand at the space in front of me. All I needed was a pipe to share a smoke with a monster.

"Why her?" I asked, like I had something to trade of equal value.

The monster grumbled and clicked. Tree trunks snapped somewhere inside it. I think it was laughing. "Medicine."

"Yeah, everybody wants medicine."

"Yes."

"She doesn't know me, doesn't even like me. You've got a long wait coming."

"No."

The thing became its stubborn resolve, standing by the rusting iron gate to a shadowy set of stairs, arms by its sides, blond hair and coal-fire eyes fading, until it was just a part of the background—another ruined, incomplete part of the city's foundation. Trains rumbled in the distance. Traffic sounds from the street above filtered through air vents. I watched a water bug dart in spurts around me.

Then she was there. Standing next to me. Out of nowhere.

"Get out of here!" I yelled, and then I cursed, because if the monster had been sleeping, he was awake now.

Of course, it had always been awake.

It rolled great shoulders and shifted forward like a landslide, its porcelain mask of skin breaking, shattering the illusion of humanity. The brooding muscle man became a mountain of broken stone, an avalanche of pebbles that might have been the calcified souls of the dead, on which floated a thatch of pale wood that, if alive, would have been a badge of life in a cold and forbidding world, but since the wood was bare and brittle, could only be a sign of death.

And I waited for her to fold us out of there, or produce a magic gun, or call on some other kind of moving monstrosity to do her dirty work, but no, she just stood by my side and the monster took her in both its great paws and lifted her high overhead until she screamed.

Her voice cut into me, clean and fast, a saber slice through the heart, and my blood ran ghost cold and my muscles stiffened hard as roadside dead and my brain sizzled like a ball of dough in burning oil.

And I saw, as clearly as the city spread out under me from

the high steel, that Medicine Spirit Woman wasn't there to save me. No. She'd come to see if I could save her.

And I wanted to. With that need, I was alive, more than I'd ever been. Everyone I'd ever known and left behind—from my quiet and steady foster parents to my scarred, bony mom to that asshole whose ass I kicked in junior high and even that Taliban bastard whose head I opened up real wide with four from the 9mm when he came at me through a window—was alive, inside, welcoming me back to my own life with arms spread.

Where are you, Grandpa?

No answer. No words of wisdom. Again. But I thought I understood. Fighting was for the living, and that's what I had to do for her. No gun, but I was a warrior. Maybe I should have brought a knife.

Jump in. Just do it. That's what warriors do.

I tackled the thing low and from the side, wrapping arms around hips in a solid tackle. Figured Medicine could take the fall. But I grabbed a crumbling pile of debris and landed flat on my face. It stomped on my back once before I rolled and kicked, ducked a sweeping arm that managed to clip my knee.

The good news when I got myself standing was that Medicine was free. But she wasn't running away. No, she was standing there, watching. Waiting for me to be all I could be.

The monster's first punch sent my flying into solid rock wall. The second broke a couple of ribs. The third spun me into a heap that fell through rotten boards and left me hanging ass high halfway down a pit, a horn screaming in my ears and an earthquake rocking my head. That one brought me back to the war.

The thing dragged me out and whipped me into tile work hard enough to chip teeth and ceramic.

This was when I found out it wasn't only the past that could stick to me. Fear could too.

Things weren't going right. Not such a big deal. Didn't know what to do. No news there. Pain. I'd had plenty of that before.

Too much white man, not enough Indian, Grandpa might have said if he'd been talking. If you say so. None of that was what was making dread creep out my gut to squeeze my heart.

I was scared because I was losing her. My Medicine Snake Woman. She was the future, a hope, the breath of life. I didn't care what she really was or where she came from, I just needed her.

Suddenly, I felt bad for my real mom. She'd come to need what was the death of her, just like me. Medicine was all inside my head, sticking hard, making me think, holding me back. I lost that space of doing something when you're ahead of fear, when it just can't catch you. Couldn't walk the heights no more.

The monster wasn't done with me, but its priorities were clear. Medicine Snake Woman came first. Blood curse–carrying duty-bound man later. It went back after her.

And Medicine didn't move. Didn't look to the monster for mercy or to me for help. She stood her ground, full of her life, her strength, standing or falling to whatever came, whether it was musket fire, cavalry charge, flood, or fire. Or a monster. Leaving it all to me to do what had to be done. But I had nothing.

Maybe she loved so much she was setting me free by dying.

No.

How much do you love her?

His voice shocked me. I hoped I was in a dream, but my body told me otherwise.

Grandpa, help me.

Do you love her more than anything?

Do something.

More than yourself?

Yes.

The monster picked her up. Twisted an arm. She cried out. It liked the sound, shuddering and rattling as if laughing. If there'd been a fire, it might have stuck Medicine on a spit and watched her roast. It slapped her with a finger. Poked her. She sagged, shuddered, a doll in a fighting pit. She was already dead, but her death hadn't caught up to her yet.

And even on the precipice, half-broken but still breathing and peering out at the world through eyes that didn't seem able to close, she was larger than anything I'd ever known, full of promise and beauty, a treasure fallen from the sky, a thing no man, not even all living men put together, could wrap their arms around and hold.

Then the questions hit. Not as hard as the monster, but they hit. They'd both warned me. Loving the moon was one thing, but wanting to possess something that wasn't mine, that was bigger than me and the monster and the whole damn city, country, world—that was a problem. A transgression. It wasn't her, and it wasn't my own life sticking to me, slowing me down to a stop. It was my need for her, for all that love I thought was missing, that was keeping me down.

Well, that and a royal ass kicking.

I had to get back to having no fear. I had to put all of that crap about wanting and losing out of my mind. Be strong. Be alive. Now. Not in the past or in the future. Just alive walking on high steel like I was on solid ground getting the job done. A part of everything, holding on to nothing.

I would have to kill her, in my heart.

I slipped past the smiling faces of the welcoming committee

to my life, headed for the back room where the mother who gave me up hides out, along with the father who couldn't keep himself alive for me. There was a blackboard back there full of rules. Along the walls stood a police lineup of white, black, brown people, Indians, Asians, a motley mess of mutts like me, all proud and pissed. There was that hard-ass DI who smelled Indian on me and didn't like it. Shadows in the mountains lobbing mortar shells and setting off IEDs. And there was her.

I dove into my life. Went deep. Drowned in all the pain and hurt I'd been through, the bugfuck craziness of talking to a ghost in my head and being blown up and falling in love with the moon.

Went quiet. Silent. Dark. Closed the door to that back room, and when I did another opened with stairs moving up to a light.

Went up high, walking on girders across the sky, not afraid. Doing what I had to do. Walking in the steps of my ancestors.

I had to kill Medicine Snake Woman in my human heart to keep her in my spirit's heart. To walk without fear in the sky. To perform my duty to all my people.

I stood. Rattled, creaked, and bled. Walked the broken bits of my body step by step to the monster, staring hard at its back, not listening to Medicine's panting, her small cries, the rustle of her blouse, the sounds her bones made.

She didn't belong to me. She was everybody's.

Easy as stepping through clouds, I reached the monster while it played with its catch and slid my hand through the gravel pit of its back, sank my arm deep, to the shoulder, until I touched what I knew I'd find. Everything alive has one. Even the ones who've transgressed, just like the ones who stay pure and true.

It was small and wet, but it beat hard and fast, like mine

had when I'd held Medicine in my arms. The monster stiffened, squeezing Medicine to screaming and locking my elbow to the breaking point. Another moment and my arm would have been dead, and so would I.

But I'd already closed my hand, crushing the monster's heart until it was mud dripping through my fingers. The avalanche of calcified souls collapsed, sending me flying back to keep from being buried and crushed. I landed bad and took another knock on the head. Decided to lay for a while and dream.

If Grandpa was there, he wasn't talking first.

You warned me, I said.

Nothing.

You helped me.

He was playing hard to get.

Why this time? I asked, spinning in my little lonely world. Not that I don't appreciate the effort, but there're about a hundred times I could name where I could've used the help. Like that RPG in the market.

This time, you were working with something from my world. You needed more than dreams.

You sorry I didn't listen?

You do what you're going to do.

Well, I got myself a monster. Does that make me a monster too?

Grandpa didn't answer right away, so I did it for him: I guess that's why they call it a curse. Or responsibility.

Maybe you got some First in you after all.

I gave her up. Killed her inside me.

She's still with you. With everybody. She's carrying the medicine of our return from where the First came from. All the First, and not just for one man, but for everybody. For everyone you're keeping inside you, and the ones you let go.

That's some powerful shit.

Best there is.

Something caressed my face, and I thought it was Medicine Snake Woman saying her farewell. But her touch was cold and then I thought she was dead. I opened my eyes, resolving not to let my heart break again when I looked up at her face. Instead of her, I saw the head of a giant white snake over me, tongue tasting the air, one cold eye fixed on me.

Your great-grandfather died because he killed his monster.

Snake. Talking. I wasn't having it.

That bridge collapse wasn't his fault.

No, but battle has its cost.

The design was flawed. The builders didn't correct it. I looked it up.

If your grandfather hadn't fought as long and hard as he did to win, the weight would have held long enough for the men to leave at day's end. But if he'd lost, far more terrible things would have come to the Kahnawake. And to more. Your grandfather, he was killed by the one that came for him.

My heart jumped. Grandpa? You never told me.

And terrible things followed. Fire. And blood. For the world.

And Dad—my dad . . .

Your father was killed before his time came. You carried his burden, as well as your own.

So, what's the cost of *my* winning? Am I going to die? Is my apartment building going to collapse—

You paid your price, in your heart.

I didn't like the way that sounded. Already, I was feeling like I needed a way to let everything slide off of me. Maybe even lose Grandpa in my head. So I said, Am I done? Is the blood and the duty part of my life over?

You're not that special.

Ideas burst out of the little boxes I'd tried keeping them locked up in. They chased each other around in my head like mice running from a cat, and the circle of my little life suddenly grew bigger. Medicine Snake Woman. Monsters. Dead people in my head. A burden of duty. I got a little cold thinking about how lucky I'd been, with Grandpa in my head and Medicine Snake Woman being there to give me a way to come out on top. And then I was cold as the far side of the moon, thinking of Great-Grandpa all alone on high steel against something like that. And Grandpa, going down, then Dad, never getting the chance to even fight, having to watch me come to his grave searching for answers and not being able to give me any.

Then I remembered it wasn't Grandpa talking. It was the damned snake.

"What the hell are you?" My question echoed in the big empty train station, and I looked to the tunnel entrances for someone new to come into my life.

That's your animal spirit, boy. Snake. Must be the white man part of you.

Grandpa.

I gave a look back into that snake's eye. Why?

Gift from Medicine Snake Woman. Consider it your love child.

I pushed myself up and saw her standing on the platform edge smiling at me, though her face was bruised. She favored one leg and kept her hands behind her back.

"Thanks—" I started to say, but she was already gone.

And then I remembered, she'd already said, "You're welcome."

The snake curled around me, gave me a squeeze. I saw stars. Python, boa constrictor, I couldn't decide. But after the thing finished hugging and sliding over me, I felt a lot better, though by the end the snake was down to the size of a string I could tie around my finger.

I picked up the little snake, which wriggled in my palm, and asked it, "How did you know that stuff about my father and grandpa?"

Of course, there was no answer. Still, I was grateful. For a little while.

Medicine Snake Woman was already fading from my heart. She was dead, at least to my flesh-and-blood heart. I'd done a good job killing and burying her. Pretty soon, the surprise and sorrow and pride I'd felt knowing what happened to my ancestors would slide off of me too. Because nothing sticks with me, not for long.

But the circle I was running in was still bigger. My life was taking a turn. I figured maybe I'd finally found that path Grandpa liked to talk about, yet the crossroads I was bound to run into looked like it was going to be serious trouble, if this monster was just the start. But I was sure the snake was going to come in handy.

Just shows you can't always be right.

I talked to the pale string of wriggling meat in my palm. "So you're supposed to be my guide, my medicine, my healer? White snake for the white man in me. Very funny. So what do you have to say, Snake? You and Grandpa. Who am I? What am I here for? What's next?"

It wasn't one voice that answered, but two, both in my head. Yeah, I was on the path, all right, walking through high places and sure to see more and bigger monsters in days to come. And for a long time to come, I knew I'd be hearing Snake and Grandpa saying just what they said when I asked them all those stupid questions: *You ain't that special.*

INDIAN TIME

BY MELISSA YI

Ontario, Canada

I'm impressed you showed up," says Mrs. Saunders.

"Thanks." I look behind her for my boys. I'm not here to fight. I'm here to take my boys out.

"I kept them in their rooms. I didn't want them to be disappointed." She lets her voice drift off, and I'm sixteen again, and Noelle and me are shooting up till nothing else matters. I shake that off. Noelle's dead, her mother's standing in the doorway, blocking me from seeing my sons, and as their dad, I'm not going to let her.

Mrs. Saunders shades her eyes. It's October in Cornwall, Ontario, so the sun's not blinding her. She's making a point. Noelle used to say you could tell a lot about someone from the hands. Mrs. Saunders's hands look pretty young for a woman who's almost seventy. Plus, she still wears her wedding ring even though Mr. Saunders has been dead for at least twenty years. She asks, "Who's that in the car?"

"My girlfriend Shana." I told her to stay outside. I knew it would get too messy. I raise my voice. "We're here to see Jake and Tommy."

The Buick door slams. I whip around, but Shana's already striding up to the porch with her best waitress grin. "It's nice to meet you, Mrs. Saunders. My name is Shana—"

"I'm sure," says Mrs. Saunders, letting Shana's hand hang in the breeze. "So nice of Fred to bring his latest girlfriend to meet the boys." I see her taking in Shana's brown skin, big nose, and bigger tits.

Shana doesn't get rattled. Like I said, she's a waitress. "I feel honored." She doesn't sound funny when she uses big words. She's saving up to go to college.

"Well, these courts think it's quite fashionable to give visitation rights, no matter what kind of parent it is. Jake! Thomas!" Her voice is like a rawhide whip and I'm not surprised when my boys' feet thunder up behind her. "My goodness. You sound like a herd of elephants! Let's try that again."

While she pushes them back, I squat down on the step with my arms out. I don't care what I look like. I haven't seen my guys in two years and I'm not about to let a stupid thing like pride trip me up. I've always been a big target for the world, but I'm not going to hide from my only two fans.

I call out, "They're just happy to see me, aren't you? Thing One and Thing Two?" That's what Noelle and I used to call them. It was a joke. But a bad one. I can see Mrs. Saunders filing it away to tell the lawyer. "It's from *The Cat in the Hat*," I tell her. Just then, I finally catch a glimpse of my boys' faces. They're both staring at me like they have no idea who I am.

Jake, my older guy, is five now. Way taller than I remember, and so serious, so skinny. Where'd his baby fat go? No smile either. Just arms dangling in a white dress shirt. Khaki dress pants and shiny shoes. They're wearing shoes inside? No wonder they sound like elephants. Kids should be playing, skidding around in bare feet or socks. They should be hugging their dads. They should be something.

Tommy. Tom Thumb. Two and a half, always our little smiley baby—at least that's how I remember him. But same as his brother, hair combed back like a '50s throwback, same white shirt and khaki pants and black leather lace-up shoes.

He starts to put his thumb in his mouth and I smile cause at least that's the same, it's even his left thumb, I remember—

"Thomas!" Whip voice again. "What did I tell you?"

Tom's face crumples up. Jake stands a bit in front of him. Tom drops his eyes and says, "Sowwy."

Still can't say his Rs. At least I haven't missed that.

"Pardon me?" from the Ice Queen.

"Pa-don me," Tom parrots, and it just breaks my heart.

I'm not a big fighter. Hell, most addicts would rather hurt themselves than anyone else. But I'm willing to beat up this old lady who's been sucking the life out of my boys. I take a step forward and something must show in my face, because Mrs. Saunders squares her shoulders, plants both feet, and smiles a little. A knowing smile. An I-knew-this-was-coming smile.

"*She:kon skennen kowa ken?*" Shana's cool voice drifts in between us.

I stop right there.

"Shay-cone?" repeats Mrs. Saunders, as if Shana has just sworn in Martian. Of course she doesn't know this most basic Mohawk greeting, but I'm too busy checking Jake's face to see if he remembers. I was no hell at Mohawk, but I did say a few nursery rhymes to him and stuff. Even for Tom, I sang lullabies before I got locked up.

Jake looks blank. Tom's staring at the ground. My throat chokes up, but Shana's already explaining. She squats right down on the porch too. She doesn't care if the white woman doesn't ever let us into her house. She gets down on their level so she can look them in the eye and she says to them, "It's our language. We say that instead of 'Hello, how are you doing?' A lot of people just say '*She:kon*,' like your grandma just did, but that's like saying 'Hey' instead of the whole greeting. And

I wanted to say the whole thing the first time I met you two very important people."

Jake stares at her like he can make some sense of it through the steadiness in her eyes. Tom hovers closer to her, like he doesn't get it but he likes her open face and lightly balanced feet.

With Shana by my side, I feel my anger start to drain and I can talk to my boys again. "*Skennen* means peace. And *she:kon* means still. So it means 'Do you still have the Great Peace?' Are you all right? Are we still friends?" It means more than that. It's asking if they're still part of the tribe, if they're okay not just in their bodies, but in their minds and spirits, but I'm trying to keep it simple. Shana's right. It's the perfect way to greet my boys, instead of calling them Thing One and Thing Two and beating up their grandmother. Thank God Shana's here.

Something flickers in Jake's eyes before he says, "We don't do any of that Indian stuff." He looks to his grandmother for approval.

Somehow, it hurts even more that I thought I was getting through to him. It's like a meat hook in my chest.

Tom stares from me to his brother to his grandmother. He doesn't know what to do.

Mrs. Saunders does. "That's right, Jake. You know that if your mother hadn't gotten mixed up with any of that stuff, she'd be alive and taking care of you today."

That stuff. That *Indian* stuff is *me*. Their father.

So that's what she's been doing. Poisoning them against me and making them hate themselves and their weak, dead mother.

I know this. I know this like I know which way is east even when I wake up after a bender. I'm a sorry excuse for an

Indian and maybe even for a human being, but I know people.
I know evil.

"*Tohsa sasa'nikon:hren,*" says Shana. *Don't forget*, she is saying. And I know what she means. Don't forget yourself. Don't
forget you are on probation. Don't let the woman rile you up
even as she's stealing your children away.

But I am riled. I've spent most of my twenty-five years
hating myself and I don't want my boys sucked into the same
rigged game. I stand up straight. I keep my gaze on Jake and
Tom. "I'm Indian. You guys are Indian too." Mrs. Saunders
makes a noise, but I talk over her. "You may not think that's a
good thing, and maybe it's not. People either think you want
a handout or they want you to teach them some great big
secret New Age woo-woo bull—" I catch myself just in time
"—pucky, and they think you get everything for free. But we
founded this place and we're not going anywhere. We're Mohawks." This time Shana makes a noise. She calls us Kanien-
kehaka, which means People of the Flint, cause Mohawk
means "man-eater," but I don't have time to explain that to
the boys. "We're tough. Some people say we're the most stubborn tribe around."

Tom's got his forehead puckered like he can't figure out
what I'm saying, but he wants to. And I feel a flicker of interest, or at least not hostility, from Jake, my big boy. I smile at
him until he says, "Is that why you've got hair like Anne of
Green Gables?"

Mrs. Saunders smothers a laugh, but this time I'm ready
for it. I may not be the sharpest tool in the box, but you can't
hit me the same way twice. Not even if you're my son. "Yeah,
pretty much, only mine's nicer. I use better conditioner."

The corners of Jake's mouth twitch. "Do you really use
conditioner?"

"Only the best." I toss my braids and make a serious face, my Indian chief statue pose. Shana giggles and Jake starts laughing. Even Mrs. Saunders defrosts a bit. She can let me have this role, the Indian clown part. That's the part I used to play with Noelle too.

Tom titters. He's checking his brother and grandmother, but he wants to join in the fun. I ache to scoop him up and kiss his chubby little cheeks. But I keep smiling through my pain. "Now. Why don't you all come out with me and Shana? Tell me what you want to do. You want burgers?"

"Yeah!" Jake slaps his hands together before he remembers to look at the killjoy.

"I don't allow the boys processed meat. We have organic beef or chicken once in a while, but we try to eat legumes and tofu instead."

Is she for real? My eyes bug out a bit, and I see the spark in Jake's eyes before he hides it again.

Shana says, "Well, they have salads now at McDonald's. Would you like to come along?"

I steel myself, but after a long moment Mrs. Saunders gives us the fish-eye and says, "Oh no. This is supposed to be your time." She smiles a little. "Indian time."

Jake grinds his toes in the floor. He knows it's an insult, but he doesn't know why. Just that he's ashamed.

"Right on," I say, too loud. "Indian time." And I usher the boys into my black Buick, trying not to think about the rust around the wheels or the cracked taillight and the bumper held on with a rigged-up coat hook. I was proud of that coat hook when I thought it up. Auto mechanics will hose you when all you need are elbow grease and quick thinking. But seeing my car through Mrs. Saunders's eyes, I feel the same thing as Jake. Shame.

"Can we do the drive-through?" Jake asks after I pull up to the McDonald's parking lot.

Shana and I exchange a look. I thought for sure they'd want to play inside. "Don't you want to jump on the balls and stuff?"

"Well, yeah, but—" He glances at my braids, and my heart just about stops. He doesn't want to be seen with the Indian.

Shana puts her hand on mine. "We can do whatever you want," she says. Jake relaxes in his booster seat and my throat closes against the pain.

"Your hair is almost as long as hers."

I turn to see Jake trudging behind me. His foot slips, but he catches himself on one knee and glares at me like it's my fault he's wearing sneakers on a hike in October. Shana thought fresh air would be better than McD's this time around.

Jake and I've got such a love-hate thing going on. I just stop and say, "Yeah, it's probably longer than Shana's."

"*Why?*"

Tommy's easier. I can chase him around and he shows me his big baby belly and I make giant raspberry kisses on it. Shana's carrying him on her hip right now and he's looking at the leaves, trying to touch one.

I drag my eyes away from Tommy. "Why not? What's the big deal about my hair?"

"It looks dumb! You look like a cartoon! You should at least, like, have a Mohawk!"

I sigh. I don't want to fight with him right now.

Shana catches up to us and sets Tommy on the ground. He toddles over to a puddle and tries to stamp in it.

"Hey, Jake. Did you know your dad does have a Mohawk?"

He scrunches up his face. "He does not!"

"What do you think a Mohawk haircut looks like?"

He rolls his eyes. "Are you gonna tell me it's a Mohawk because *he's* a Mohawk? That's lame."

She shakes her head. "For Indians, long hair is sacred. Men and women have long hair because that's what our Creator gave to us."

"It looks okay on *you*." Always the poison saved for me. "But everyone knows a Mohawk is that punk thing, you know, where you shave the sides and the middle sticks up in spikes."

Tommy slips and lands in the puddle on his butt. Man. We're going to have to change him on the trail. I pick him up and spin him around to get him to stop crying before I tackle his change. I can still hear Shana explaining.

"That haircut was like the army haircut. Going to war and taking someone's life was against everything the Creator, Shonkwaiatison, taught us. So if the people had to take a life, they'd cut off their hair. When they returned from war, they'd let their hair grow back."

I don't look at them. I pull a clean diaper and a pair of pants out of the diaper bag, even though Shana is way better at changing Tommy. I don't want to break the spell.

Then Jake bursts out, "I don't care! I'd rather have the army haircut!"

Shana laughs, and I do too. Laughing over the hurt. Laughing while I try to pull off Tommy's play pants with him wiggling like a minnow.

Shana says, "At least you're thinking about getting an Indian haircut now. So you wanna figure out what a puffball mushroom is? I can see one from here!"

She's so good with him. Jake's bouncing around now. He finds this giant puffball. It's as big as a bear paw, if a bear had a white Ontario Place dome mushroom kind of foot. And she's explaining how it's good to eat, but you want to eat the smaller kind because the big ones get yellow and mushy inside.

"You should only get mushrooms with me or your dad, because you could get mixed up with other ones, like the Death Cap or Destroying Angel."

"Destroying Angel! I want that one! I'd bring it to school!"

"No, you wouldn't. It would make you throw up and then it would kill you."

Tommy's pants aren't so bad under his play pants. I pull the play pants back up and let him splash in the puddles again.

I touch my hair. I don't know why I grew my hair after I got out of jail. It just seemed like the most rebellious thing I could do when the rest of me was heading mainstream. I've lost jobs because of it. But I never thought it might make me lose my son. I don't know why things are so hard between us. I don't know how far I would go to keep him.

While I'm thinking this, Tom yelps. He's wandered away from me to the edge of the trail and he's skidding on a fallen branch.

I dive. Yank up on his arm. He screams like I've ripped it out of its socket and falls in another mud puddle anyway.

Shana sprints to our side with Jake behind her yelling, "What is it?"

Tom is bawling and trying to fight me off. I'm doing my best, but he is damn strong for a two-year-old and it's all I can do to hold onto him when he's muddy and slippery and screaming.

Finally, he calms down and lets me hold him, but he's not using his left arm. It's just hanging there.

We take him to the emergency room. Wait there for three

hours. Jake gets bored. He keeps asking for stuff, so Shana brings him magazines and candy bars and answers his non-stop questions, everything from "Why is your nose so big?" to "You think there are any of those destroyer mushrooms around here?"

Jake sure talks a lot for an Indian. I didn't say a word until I was two and neither did my brothers. Maybe that's his mother's side coming out. He always talks to Shana, though. It's like he doesn't know what to say to me, or maybe his grandma has his head turned too far against me.

I keep holding Tom. He drinks some 7-Up and wanders a bit, touching magazines and toys with his right arm, but he mostly just wants to sit in my lap. I'm okay with that.

When we finally get to see the doctor, a pretty Asian woman in glasses, she talks way too fast and I don't get most of it. She pulls on Tommy's arm and twists it at the elbow and he gasps, but then she's like, "Can you use it, Tommy? Wanna touch my stethoscope?" After a minute, he reaches for Jake's toy motorcycle with his left arm. She says something about how one of Tom's arm bones isn't grown and something about a ligament slipping, but I don't care what except Tommy's arm is okay.

He turns to me and says, "Burger?"

When the phone rings and it's my lawyer, I know it's a problem. He sighs down the line. "What happened to your son Thomas?"

I explain about the fall and the emergency room and how he was fine and ate two kid's burgers afterward. But my stomach has more knots than my old golden retriever's tail.

"You have to tell me about this kind of thing."

"Why? He was okay." My heart is pounding even as I say it.

"Because your ex's mother already has her lawyer organized on charges of physical abuse—"

"Abuse?" My parents were so screwed up after being beaten up at residential schools, I would let my boys run me over with a truck before I raised a hand to them.

He says more stuff, like the boys were dirty when they came home and we feed them junk.

I can hardly talk. Shana takes the phone away from me and scribbles notes. She's good at stuff like that.

Dumb old Fred. Dumb old Indian. Suckered by the system again.

Before we can figure it out, Mrs. Saunders has it rigged so we have to have "supervised visits" with my boys. We're even supposed to pay for some chaperone. We don't have the money.

"So I can't see my boys?" I ask my lawyer.

He sighs and says, "I know some supervision visitation providers who don't charge that much. Maybe your band council can help you out."

I press the phone against my jaw. The construction season's almost over and Shana's saving up her waitress tips for school. I wouldn't ask her to spend more on my boys anyway. We could hardly afford the Happy Meals, but we did it because the toys made them smile and maybe think of us a little before they broke. I can hardly get the words out. "I don't think so. Can't you fight this?"

"I've got a lot of cases on the go, Fred, but I'll try and make this a priority. At least get you down to nonprofessional supervision provider so you don't have to pay for it."

Great. I start squeezing the phone receiver so hard I imagine the plastic splintering in my fist. "How 'bout the fact that I didn't do nothin'!"

More sighing. "I know, Fred."

Sure you will, white man. It's a real "priority" for you. I got to do my own thing.

Shana puts up with me for the next week while I try to figure out what to do. I'm not eating, I can't sleep, I'm walking around in the middle of the night and getting up at 6 to work. I even try to split up a tree that fell down two years ago in Shana's backyard. It's a messy job. I break the chain saw. I'm pretty useless with an axe. But I'm not drinking. And I'm not using.

"Sorry," I tell Shana when, for the first time, she wants to have sex and I just want to crash.

"It's okay." She kisses my cheek. "Just do the dishes for the next week and I'll forgive you."

That makes my eyes pop open. But she simply laughs and drags the covers over me. The quilt is soft. I sleep. And Saturday morning, when I should be seeing my boys, I know what to do instead. Go see Phil.

White people love to talk about native elders, but they're hard to come by. My parents were so screwed up by the schools where nuns beat them for speaking Mohawk or priests raped them just because they felt like it. My grandparents are dead and I don't really know the elders. They probably wouldn't understand my baby Mohawk anyway.

But I know Phil. He's a smart old guy. He used to have a job at CN Rail before he worked his way up at the paper mill and then retired on good money when the mill closed. Now he writes for the local paper. So I drop by the diner. Shana brings us coffee on the house.

Phil pushes his paper aside and asks, "What can I do you for?"

In a low voice, under the grill's sizzle and plates clattering and chairs bumping, I tell him what's going on.

He pours two creams and two sugars in his coffee and stirs it around until he finally answers. "She's in a lot of pain."

"Who?" For a second I think he means Shana, whose long legs just walked by.

"The grandmother."

"The *grandmother*? Come on, Phil, you going to side with a white woman instead of me?"

He shakes his head. "Not taking sides. I think she just has a lot of hurt and she's taking it out on you. Probably ever since her daughter died. She had Noelle late, a change-of-life baby, if I remember right."

I stare at him. Who is he, Sigmund friggin' Freud? Who cares how old she was when she had Noelle? "So what do you think I should do?"

"Get rid of that hurt. Then she won't hate you so much."

What a wise guy. I feel like hurling my coffee cup at him. I only put it down gently because it's Shana's place. "Thanks a lot." I sling a ten on the table.

"You've got to solve this yourself," he calls to my back.

Yeah. I knew that already.

DEATH NOTICE

Saunders, Francine (née Ferguson). Passed away on November 10, 2009. Survived by her grandsons, Jake and Thomas Redish. Predeceased by her daughter, Noelle, and husband, Jacob.

It should be a good Christmas. The best ever, in fact. One of my buddies gave me a tree, said it was a cast-off because of the dead needles. Shana rigged it so you can't even see the brown bits. She and Jake are hanging the balls, and Tommy and I are throwing tinsel at it. Mel Tormé's roasting chestnuts over an open fire, and things would be just perfect except for a few things.

I was going to take care of Mrs. Saunders. I really was. I wanted to bash her head in, but in the end I decided Phil was right. I set up an appointment with one of our mediation counselors. Mrs. Saunders would never set foot in Akwasasne, let alone allow an Indian tell her what to do, but all I could do was try.

Until she upped and died. She seemed okay, or at least her normal mean self, sending the boys to bed without any veg stew supper after Jake gave her "too much lip." Then she made them go to church the next morning with a neighbor. Said she wasn't feeling good.

They came home to find her dead in her own puke. The neighbor called 911, but it was too late; they took her to the emergency room anyway. We asked for no autopsy. Because she was almost seventy and had a heart condition, the coroner dropped it.

Sometimes I wish he hadn't.

Maybe I'm too suspicious. But I looked up what mushrooms do to you. The real deadly kind. You feel okay for twelve hours and then you start puking. You end up going pretty quick.

"Daddy!" Jake hollers, holding up the box of my mom's old Christmas stuff. "This one stinks! I think it's the candle!"

"Throw it out, then," I suggest. I'm looking at how he and Shana have their heads close together. Their hair is growing back, but Shana shaved both their heads after Mrs. Saunders died.

"I'll just throw out the candle," Shana says, and I smile at her because I still love her and she's such a good mother to my boys, even though I get goose bumps every time I see her butch hair.

Tommy tugs my pants. He wants me to kneel down. I do. He clambers in my arms and I lift him up to hang tinsel on high. His prickly little hair stands straight up now. He asked Shana to cut it off when she did his brother's.

I'm the only one who kept a crew cut. I feel really guilty. I don't know why. But when Tommy hugs me and Shana asks me to help Jake with the star, I can't help humming along with old Mel Tormé. Shana looks cute with short hair, kind of '80s punk rock. And Jake trusts me enough to hold him high while he crowns the tree with a silver and gold star.

PART II

SOUTH

ON DROWNING POND

BY A.A. HedgeCoke

Charlotte, North Carolina

I saw Jimmy earlier this week. Just before the discovery of
yet another fallen victim to the drowning way. He was
still the same Jimmy, drunk—wasted. Crouched on the
curb across from the market with a half-dozen longtime cro-
nies and their women. Women who have been on the down
edge so long their bodies have masculinized and hunched with
the depression of life lost to drink, hard sex, smoke.

I saw him and I remembered Jolene, her beautiful smiling
face, shining hair. Thought of her unrelinquished love for a
man who'd only one wife in his heart. Thought of this bottle
he'd fully committed to, of his smell, his ways. How she must
have longed for him. Leaving her there the way he did, looking
down on her maybe, thinking he was quite the man for taking
the young passionate breath she'd had, in his making over of
her brown body. Thought of his sudden losses of memory, and
willingness to go on in life so soon and in such close proximity
to her passing, and I wondered if he ever as much as poured a
drink on the ground in her memory, or if he held that drink so
precious to himself even a gulp would be too much to spare.

I saw him and I watched the walkers, those who've taken
to carrying signs and speaking out against the assailants they
believe they'll recognize once they stay the vigil until another
passing. And I remembered how Jolene was always a private
woman and doubted she would show her smiling face in a

crowd this immense—especially among the sober living. The waters may look still today, but each time I glance across the creek, use my peripheral vision, for a moment her easy presence forms here, waiting. It's here I leave some hope for her, a few presents now and then, and ask her to go easy on us—the living. Here, too, I vow to follow him, take him down to the water one night, bring her Southern Comfort.

Jolene came to mind just this morning, how the light illuminated the walking bridge rail above her resplendent body. The shining of her deep black hair, under the water, on the morning they found her two dozen years ago. Right here in the thick of Brooklyn Alley. Just west/northwest from the Double Door Inn and over from the Broken Bank, Marshall Park. I remember how she always smiled when asking for "just a few quarters to get by."

It was spring. Jolene, though barely grown, had already been married and separated twice. She had a young child, but her parents had taken custody in the recognition of her spirit gone to drink. She had lived among the other ghosts, friends still walking the Earth along Independence, panhandling, selling themselves, huddling together for warmth and for desire of the strange flesh necessary to endure the jaundiced and rotting skin they themselves wore. Those who had lost lives here already, and yet still breathed, still continued this walk among the living. The ones whose blood no longer held hemoglobin, red, nor white leukocyte to speak of, yet flowed with a powerful wine-red fire-rush of alcohol-permeated heat. Those whose tears bore no salt, yet swelled each time a lost love was mentioned in conversation. Worse still if one actually passed by, nonchalant, unknowing, a member of the living world still. Those who fill the deep underworld here, though the white-collars cannot see them.

Jolene had found a lover. A great man, great in size and truly experienced among these parts. His residency here dated back a good decade or more, since his mom was chain gang in South Carolina. Heard she died there. I knew him holding his own guts in his hands. Knew him to be unstoppable. He walked with a certainty. A macho strut. He was certain—of himself, of the drink he made vows with. Everybody knew him. This familiarity, this personal community knowledge, allowed her protection from the perpetrators who infiltrated the Brooklyn-side Charlotte streets on weekends, summers, and holidays. Those who came to prey on the already forgotten but not quite gone. Those who justified rolling drunks as "teaching them a lesson." Or roughing lobs to "make them understand." Ethnic cleansers. I despise them.

It was in the month of the eclipsed moon, that time of reddened sky, after a fresh rain and hail pummeling along the curb. Jolene and her man. They were along the newly constructed revision bank when the storm broke. They had gone into the bar to avoid the wetness and to engage some draws from the deep tap-well, at least until the panhandled earnings were exhausted.

They say when the lovers went back down the construction path, Jolene was so taken by the deepening colors of the flora around them, she swelled with passion in the green and purpled midst and they lay together in the wet grasses along the bank, experiencing the fullness of newborn spring. They say she slept there. Fell asleep during, some say. When they found her she was naked from the waist down, as brown as a summer doe, lying half-in and half-out of water. The half-in was the upper part of Jolene. They dragged her out by the bare heels poking up through the wild violets blooming.

You know, she smiled even in death and her heavy hair

flowed far past her physical body, much as the water flowed behind her. Jimmy was questioned but never arrested in her passing. He suffered from blackouts and seizures, and couldn't recall the last he saw her the night before. He was so sure she had returned to the bar with him. So were a few other regulars. They were all certain they saw her at least two hours after the coroner determined her expiration. They recounted Jolene hanging onto Jimmy's arm and smelling his breath and neck as if it were something scintillating. No one remembered her speaking, though Willie Notches said she tried to steal a cigarette right from his brother Tyrone's pocket but was so intoxicated she couldn't grab hold of it. Said his cousin Punchy Blackknees walked by and put a cigarette into her hand and she thought he was handing her a grasshopper since the clumsy numbness made the end shake up and down. Willie still laughed at the recollection. Others said they had seen her swimming near the city center at dawn, where elders and children were allowed to fish before the conversion of the city into cosmopolis. Said they averted their eyes to avoid embarrassing her obvious bathing. The city more concerned with gentrification than the fallen, then and now. Nothing was done. No follow-up, just over and buried, they say. They still claim such. Amazing.

Years passed. Winos would sometimes claim they saw a beautiful woman, underwater, facing up and smiling in the now white-collar park enclave. Back then, they'd leaned over and fallen in trying to get a better look at her before the shock of cold water woke them from drunken stupor. Then there was Tyrone. The creek-bum who hadn't seen a sober day in so many years his skin had grayed beyond redemption. Tyrone drank with Jimmy, for years they say, drank with Jolene once or twice in the living time. It was Tyrone whose death bristled my attention. Tyrone had claimed it was Jolene in the waters. Claimed she reached right out of the water for the Marlboro in his shirt and held him a moment, puckering wet lips and beckoning him with her muddy eyes. He said he'd shaken her off twice before and was afraid she would come for him again. He told Jimmy he believed her jealous of the woman Tyrone had introduced to Jimmy while he should have still been mourning her. As if the ones who lived on this bordering world were capable of remaining celibate for a year's time to mourn anyone. He drowned four years after they found Jolene. He surfaced around Freedom Park, no explaining it, the pocket completely ripped from his shirt and his trousers torn through the crotch, one entire pant leg missing.

Then there was that one up from the Catawba River for the Frontier Days rodeo. They said he looked and walked a lot like Jimmy and that he had drunk in the Double Door three days straight before going to "get some sleep" by the pond path. They said his breath had the strong smell of Peppermint Schnapps or Hot Damn over bad beer and cheap wine. Said the peppermint was the only thing kept him from getting picked up P.I. by Officer Wall on his lot patrol at the market. He surfaced exactly four years after Tyrone. After him, they came up more often.

A few full-bloods floated facedown after being lost for two or three days. They were strong men, well built, with the exception of the distended gut from too much drinking. All were known to have frequented the park and the Indian bar nearby. All were going through hard times and break-ups. Then two half-bloods rose from the bottom. One with his woman just twenty yards away, still sleeping after having relations. For a week she told the story of his sweetest day, their closest time together—ever. This day he had drowned. Then she took up with a guy who stayed over nearer the park and they poured wine on the ground for her man every time they took to drink together.

Once they found a drowned stranger, a sort-of stranger, a guy from another tribe who was a known exhibitionist and molested the street women, often paying them in cigarettes after he was finished with them. One had to be hospitalized— he had been so brutal in his business. When they pulled him from the water, his man-thing had been sheared by what appeared to be a sharp branch. They said he'd tried to bribe Jimmy for a turn at Jolene years ago.

Once, or twice maybe, a white man came floating and I began to believe Jolene had given up on Indian guys altogether. I've considered it myself, but can't stand the never-ending explaining you have to do to date outside. One came up so fast they found him minutes after he'd swallowed waters, yet no effort was made to clear his lungs by the followers or the police. I figure she shamed herself in seducing the historical enemy and wanted no part of being affiliated with him after the fact.

I saw Jimmy earlier this week. Maybe I'll follow him, take him down to the water tonight, bring her comfort. Soothe the blue-black night waters welling with Jolene. Soothe them.

DADDY'S GIRL

BY MISTINA BATES

Memphis, Tennessee

Standing behind her husband's left shoulder, the woman emitted hiccupping sobs that set Daniel Carson's teeth on edge. His skin prickled with the same sensation as if he'd raked his nails against a chalkboard. Carson forced himself to focus on his client's face. Failure to catch any lies could have fatal results.

The man pursed his porcine lips and shook his head. As if commiserating, his ice-blue gaze locked with Carson's, and he shrugged. "You have to understand, my wife is so upset because this is our only daughter."

Carson nodded once, as the fleeting image of his own daughter—a pigtailed girl with a gap-toothed grin—brought a twitch to his face.

Seizing on this minute gesture, the man leaned forward onto the leather blotter built into the massive mahogany desk. He steepled his fat fingers. "So, you're a family man?"

"My domestic situation has no bearing on the matter at hand."

The man blinked, and irritation flashed across his face. He quickly regained his composure, no doubt deciding it unwise to piss off a man in Carson's line of work. "You come highly recommended," he began, then paused, as if waiting for a response. Carson inclined his head but said nothing. Sighing, the man continued, "You understand that discretion is of the utmost importance."

"Naturally. Has there been any communication since your daughter's disappearance?"

This time the scowl remained planted on his face. "Only the one call, demanding a million in cash." The woman's sobs grew louder, and her husband reached up to pat the hand she laid on his shoulder.

"And the police are not involved?"

A firm shake of the head. "No. Given my position in the community, I'd prefer to handle this matter privately."

"Of course." An avid outdoorsman, true to his Cherokee heritage, Carson had no interest in antiques or other furnishings, yet even his untrained eye knew that the library in which they sat was the work of a well-funded interior designer—as was the rest of the manor that had once overseen the whole Norfleet family estate.

Now the home lay in the midst of an exclusive subdivision, dwarfing the expensive houses crammed into modest-sized lots. Carson knew from research that his client had bought the old home for half a million and tripled his investment within three years, according to the latest property tax assessment. Both the bluebloods and the nouveau riche alike would raise eyebrows if they knew what kind of man had purchased this piece of Memphis history and joined their polite society.

"What can you tell me about your daughter and the missing money?" Carson asked.

The man's frown deepened, and he clenched his hands. Then he paused to collect himself. He turned to his wife. "Darling, why don't you see after some coffee?" He glanced over at Carson with thinly veiled disdain. "Or maybe you'd rather have whiskey?"

A tiny muscle twitched at the back of Carson's jaw, but his expression remained neutral. "Coffee, please," he said in a soft voice to the raven-haired woman with gentle brown eyes. She nodded and left the room. As she passed through the doorway, she used a fist to stifle her sobs. When Carson returned his attention to his client, an edge clipped his words: "I don't drink."

Carson's eyes bored into those of his newest employer. After several tense seconds, while the older man struggled with his ego, common sense prevailed and he offered an almost-contrite smile. "Sorry. That was poor manners."

"Agreed." Carson's hooded expression warned of the consequences that a subsequent lapse in manners would incur. "You were telling me about your daughter's disappearance."

Carson leaned back into the leather armchair as his client started speaking. He studied the man's face as he committed the information to memory—notes could leave a trail. Just as he had scanned the land and vegetation as a boy—and later as a member of the elite Shadow Wolves in search of drug smugglers—he watched and measured each nuance of every expression, searching for signs of deception or evasion.

For the next two hours, his attention never wavered from the man before him. He extracted the details leading up to his client's employment of James Hicks, a Navy SEAL with a dishonorable discharge—the man who was now demanding one million dollars. Carson mentally recorded key facts from the sailor's personnel file. He also gathered information about Buddy Martin, his client's accountant.

After receiving the phone call, the businessman had contacted Buddy, his friend and confidant of more than twenty years. Since then the accountant had failed to answer repeated calls to his home, office, and cell phones, and Carson's client feared the worst.

"Why go after Buddy?" Carson asked.

"It could be as simple as the fact that he kept a sizable petty cash fund for me at his office."

"How sizable?"

"A quarter-million, give or take."

Carson studied the man's face for several seconds. "But there's more than petty cash involved, isn't there?"

"I've noticed that funds have started disappearing from my various business interests."

"You think Buddy's in on this?"

"It pains me, but I can't trust anyone at this point."

Carson's client had been given forty-eight hours, now down to twenty-eight, to turn over the money, or he would lose everything: his daughter, his reputation, his social status. The life that he had carefully built would be destroyed.

Carson maneuvered the Dodge Charger through the maze of East Memphis streets, guided by the robotic female voice of the global positioning system mounted on the windshield. Tara had laughed when he bought the device two years ago, chiding him for relying on technology, rather than the innate skills cultivated by his people over generations.

It was a matter of efficiency. Even allowing for the occasional error—when the gadget directed him to make an illegal left, for instance—his GPS had saved him countless hours plotting and memorizing the lay of the land in every city he worked.

As it wasn't yet 3 o'clock, Carson easily found a spot near the SEAL's apartment. He removed the Glock 17 from the space between the seat and armrest. He tucked the gun into the waistband of his Wranglers, where it was hidden beneath the hip-length leather jacket, and exited his car. After scanning the area for residents or visitors, Carson removed the gun when he reached the shared foyer.

His other hand reached for a reverse peephole viewer, which revealed stairs directly behind the door, a dining area to the left, and a hallway leading to the living room.

He pocketed the viewer and stepped to the side, ringing the doorbell. When several seconds had elapsed, he rapped firmly on the wooden door.

Nothing. The odds of a dog were slim to none.

Seconds later, Carson entered Hicks's home. The still, silent air confirmed that he was alone in the sparsely furnished town home.

Clearly, the man continued to follow the military's strict code for tidiness, at least downstairs. Not a scrap of paper was lying about. All the dishes were neatly put away in the cabinets. The remote controls were arranged side by side next to the cable box.

Upstairs reinforced Hicks's fastidious nature. Carson could have bounced a quarter off the queen-sized bed, the only piece of furniture in the room. After searching the closets and the bathroom, he moved on to the second bedroom, which was an office.

Here Carson found the only personal item in the entire apartment: a framed photo of a red-haired woman. He studied the picture. She was posing on a bench in New Orleans' Jackson Square, the St. Louis Cathedral soaring in the background. He removed the photo from the frame and tucked it into his breast pocket.

Driving downtown on Main Street, past the gentrified Mid America Mall, Carson slowed as he approached the converted warehouse that housed Buddy Martin's office. Half a dozen city vehicles, including four police cruisers, crowded the street. Carson casually turned west onto Linden, but not before spotting the sedan marked *Forensic Medical*.

The meat wagon had already arrived, so police must have been on scene for at least an hour or two. Given the looming deadline, Carson hated the delay but adjusted his plans.

He drove north and then east, returning to the revitalized section of downtown Memphis. He deposited the car in a public garage across from the commercial playground of Peabody Place, where he blended in with the tourists who thronged the shopping oasis in the still-bleak inner-city zone.

Carson joined the small crowd of gawkers who had assembled at the crime scene perimeter. Snatches of conversation confirmed that Buddy Martin had been found dead of multiple gunshot wounds, most likely killed the previous day. The receptionist had been out all week, visiting her mother in New Jersey.

After twenty minutes, Carson concluded that he had learned all he could. He headed north toward Charlie Vergos's famed Rendezvous. He could think of no better temporary office, preferring a slab of ribs to overpriced coffee any day of the week.

Carson had visited the Memphis institution on several occasions, but the surly waiter who seated him didn't recognize him. Perhaps because he now had dark blond hair and green eyes—a dramatic departure from his natural coal-black hair and brown eyes so dark they, too, looked black.

A few keystrokes later, Carson discovered that Hicks's black 2007 Land Rover was registered to a Jennifer McLaren of 1375 Agnes Place. He also confirmed the twenty-four-year-old Miss McLaren as the redhead from the photo in New Orleans.

Carson's food arrived and he made short order of the tender, smoky meat. As he ate, he scanned the current edition of the *Memphis Flyer*, the local tabloid, which he had picked up in the lobby. Carson turned to page seven, to an article on an exhibit opening referenced on the cover. On the lower right-hand corner of the page, his client's frosty blue gaze stared back at him—this time from the face of a stunning brunette, hair upswept to showcase a swanlike neck. He checked the caption, tore out the photo, and placed it with the snapshot of Jennifer McLaren.

"She's not here." Standing no more than five-foot-two, the elderly woman in the doorway managed to look formidable with her scrawny arms folded on top of an ample, but sagging bosom. The short, wide body and skinny appendages made her look like a dwarf, but Carson suspected that Jennifer McLaren's grandmother had been a magnificent specimen some forty years earlier.

"Can you tell me where she is, ma'am?" said Carson, returning his credentials to his back pocket.

Piercing green eyes peered out from the wizened face. "Why would I do that?"

"Because it looks like one of Jennifer's friends might be dangerous," said Carson. "One woman is already missing. For all we know, Jennifer could be next."

One birdlike claw, sporting a fresh coat of pink nail polish that clashed violently with the auburn hair dye, flew to her throat. "Dear God," she whimpered. Her mouth tightened in a crimson slash. "It's that Hicks boy, isn't it?" She studied Carson's face and then nodded to herself. "I told Jenny that boy was bad news. The damn fool kept handing over her hard-earned money every time he smiled at her . . . Well, come on in," she said at last, returning her gimlet stare to Carson. "Can I offer you some coffee?"

"That would be mighty kind of you."

He returned to the Charger, checking his watch. This time tomorrow, his client's daughter would either be dead or alive, depending on whether Carson completed his mission.

Jenny's grandmother had given him an address in New Orleans, where the girl had moved the previous month. The woman wasn't sure about the circumstances, but she thought that Jenny and Hicks had been having troubles.

Driving away, Carson considered his options. Leaving now would put him in New Orleans around midnight. If he waited to check out Buddy's office, it would be morning before he reached the Big Easy.

Of course, the link to New Orleans was circumstantial. He didn't have time for a dead end that would eat up more than half his remaining time.

Carson resigned himself to several hours of cooling his heels. He headed west on Union and returned to the garage near Peabody Place.

He took out his cell phone and dialed. "Daddy!" squealed a voice almost instantly.

"Were you waiting by the phone?"

"Yep," came the smug reply.

"How'd you know I was getting ready to call?"

"We women have our ways." The grown-up words coming from her eight-year-old mouth reminded Carson of the fleeting nature of childhood.

After a few minutes of banter and a recap of her day, he asked to speak with her mother.

"Hey, handsome." Tara's sultry voice never failed to warm him. "And where in the world is my husband now?"

Carson let her know that he was in Memphis and quickly

turned the conversation to her and their life in central Texas, what he thought of as his "real life"—separate from the world of his job.

Reluctantly, he ended the conversation. Carson snapped his phone shut and sat for a few minutes, savoring the peace that these conversations always produced.

He finally stirred himself and headed to Beale Street, where he passed the evening hours listening to a performer who sang like Johnny Cash and looked like Jerry Springer. At a quarter to 11, he settled the tab for his nachos and club soda and went back to work.

As Carson left the lights and activity of Beale Street and Peabody Place, he tossed his car keys in the air and caught them. He whistled softly while he walked, casually scanning the now-deserted section of Main Street.

By the time he arrived at the redbrick warehouse, Carson had confirmed that he was alone. He quickly dispatched the lock on the street-level door and entered. He turned left at the second-story landing. To his immediate left, yellow crime scene tape sealed the glass door with black-and-gold lettering that announced: *Sherman "Buddy" Martin, Certified Public Accountant.*

He sliced through the tape with his horn-handled pocket-knife and spent only a few seconds longer on the lock.

When he opened the door, the coppery scent assailed his keen senses like a blow to the gut.

Carson walked through the empty reception area and stood in the doorway of the main office. He surveyed the scene before him, aided by the narrow but bright beam of his mini Maglite. From the spatter of blood, brain, and bone on the wall, window, and floor, he could see the killer had used hollow-point ammunition. The top of the desk was bare; the police had confiscated everything.

He then turned his attention to the open closet door in the far corner of the room, which revealed a large steel safe, also open. And empty.

Carson methodically scanned the area, starting with the ceiling and working his way down to the floor. The light glinted off an object in the corner. He studied the space between him and the safe. Convinced that his passage wouldn't disturb anything, Carson crossed the room and kneeled in front of the safe.

He played the beam over the floor next to the wall and spotted the item that had caught his attention. Part of the object had fallen into the crack between two of the pine floorboards, and part had slipped under the radiator. Carson used the tip of his pocketknife to slide the article onto his gloved hand. It was a sterling silver earring in the form of a delicate three-inch chain that ended in a flat, pointed ellipse, similar to a feather or leaf.

Carson smiled, thinking how the nature symbolism would appeal to Tara, who insisted upon educating their daughter on her Cherokee heritage.

A thin hook at the top threaded through the ear. Holding the item in his hand, he realized how easy it would be for the wearer not to notice its loss; it weighed less than half an ounce.

Click.

Damn. Someone was coming in through the street-level door. He had maybe ten seconds before the newcomer arrived.

He chanced a glance out the window and saw a Crown Vic, the stereotypical unmarked police car. Things were getting complicated. Not impossible, but definitely complicated.

Carson stepped to the shadows in the opposite corner, on the same wall as the door. He heard the footsteps ascend the stairs and stop outside the reception area. The hallway door opened a few seconds later, just long enough for someone to pull out a weapon in response to the door's broken seal.

Carson braced himself for the sudden glare of the overhead light. Instead, a flashlight beam sliced through the darkness.

"Police! Step outside with your hands up." The words came out thick and imprecise.

Carson stood in the darkness, waiting for the officer's next move.

"This is your last warning." There was no mistaking the slur. "Step out or I will shoot."

Several seconds elapsed, and Carson held his breath. Finally, heavy treads approached. Carson tensed, ready to spring. The officer shone his flashlight into the interior space.

In his mind's eye, Carson saw himself reach forward and grab the service pistol, snapping the man's finger before de-gloving the digit and wrenching away the weapon. He quickly dismissed this option and pursued patience. No sense in stirring up a hornet's nest by leaving one of Memphis' finest bound and injured at a crime scene.

The man made a sloppy sweep of the room that failed to reach the corner where Carson waited.

Carson had a clear view of the slim man in a dark blazer and rumpled khakis. The sweet stench of Jack Daniel's turned his stomach, instantly bringing to mind his Uncle Joe—a man who embodied every negative stereotype of his people.

Forcing himself to the present, Carson watched the lawman weave his way toward the bookshelves on the wall opposite the safe. The man holstered his weapon and flashlight, kneeled down, and grabbed two large ledgers from the bottom shelf. While the officer's back was turned, Carson crossed the room in silence. When the man stood and turned to leave, his eyes locked with Carson's. He recoiled in surprise, and the heavy ledgers crashed to the floor. Carson secured the lawman's hands behind his back in an iron grip, forcing his face into the wall.

"Relax," said Carson. "I don't want to hurt you. And I'm guessing you don't want to advertise your presence here."

"What do you want?"

"I just want to find the person responsible for this mess," said Carson. "A more interesting question seems to be, what are *you* doing here?"

"None of your business, that's what." The alcohol made him sound like a petulant child.

Carson shrugged and increased the pressure on the man's wrists. "Suit yourself. I can leave you tied up here and place an anonymous call to the precinct. Or . . ."

"Or what?"

"Or we can try to work this out. So we both get what we want. That sound reasonable?"

The man hesitated, but then he nodded. "Okay. Let's talk."

"Good choice." Carson removed the firearm from the man's hip holster. He searched for additional weapons and pocketed the compact gun he found in an ankle holster. Finally, Carson took the flashlight before releasing the lawman to turn around. He offered an apologetic look as he trained the service pistol on its owner. "I'm sure you'd do the same."

The officer narrowed his gaze at Carson as he rubbed his arms. Carson wasn't sure if he was trying to intimidate—or to focus.

"You working this case?" asked Carson, slowly sweeping the light over the cop. The man's hesitation gave him his answer. Carson took in the distinctive alligator pattern on the man's shoes. Well-styled. Probably Italian. He caught a flash of gold as he moved the beam upward. "Mind showing me your watch?" The man pushed back his cuff. Diamond baguettes winked at Carson from a Rolex President. "Nice. Tell me, Officer . . ."

"It's Detective. Detective Aaron Lawry."

"Pleasure to make your acquaintance, detective," he said, emphasizing the title. "You come from money? Or is the city of Memphis exceptionally generous with its hazardous duty pay?" When Lawry remained silent, he continued, "Or does this have something to do your being here after your buddies have gone home?" The man glanced down at the ledgers, and Carson nodded. "I figured it was something like that. Something big enough that you'd risk the complications of a broken crime scene seal. I don't care what your business was with Buddy Martin," Carson said at last. "But I'm a man on a deadline, and I always meet my deadlines."

He told Lawry the tale of an unnamed damsel in distress, in the clutches of an ex-military mercenary who had brought Buddy's life to an untimely end.

"I'm afraid I can't disclose my client's name," said Carson. "But I can assure you that he is a major player in this town. And very generous."

"How generous?"

"Generous enough that, once this is done, I can give you fifty large, in cash, for less than a day's work."

"Sounds reasonable to me," Lawry said after a moment's consideration. "Can I have my guns back?"

"Not yet," Carson replied, tucking the pistols beside his

Glock. He made a sweeping gesture toward the office. "What do you know about the investigation?"

Lawry gave Carson a look of resentment, quickly replaced by resignation. He sighed. "Buddy was tortured. Every bone in his right hand broken." No prints other than Buddy's and his receptionist's, which suggested the attacker had worn gloves. Lawry glanced over at the safe and back at Carson.

"Yes?"

"We assume he was tortured for the combination," Lawry said. "Once your guy made sure it worked, he finished Buddy off with a couple shots to the head."

"Any idea where he went?"

"Since your client didn't report any of this, it sounds like you know more than we do at this point. You care to share?"

Carson told him about his research and his conversation with Jenny's grandmother. "The connection is tenuous, but I don't have anything else at this point."

"That's okay," said Lawry. "I think we might. Let me make a call. You mind?"

"I'll be right here." Carson jerked his thumb toward the outer office. He stepped into the next room and heard Lawry make his call. Despite the detective's hushed tones, Carson's acute senses allowed him to hear most of the one-sided conversation.

"It's me . . . Yeah, I'm here . . . Yeah, I got them, but we have a situation . . . Some guy here seems to know what's going on. He promised me a fifty-grand payout if I help him out . . . Give me some credit. If he's offering me fifty, he's got to be holding back at least that much for himself . . . Yeah, yeah. It's perfect. You get the collar, we get the cash, and the business with Buddy gets buried with him. But we got to deliver too . . ."

Having heard enough, Carson crossed over to the far side of the room. So that's how it was. Not that he was surprised, but he'd need to plan ahead. At least Detective Lawry had simplified the situation for him. He heard Lawry end the conversation.

"Hey, chief." Carson bristled and then turned to face his temporary partner, who now wore a look of confusion. "What's your name?"

Carson slowly stretched his mouth into what he hoped was a relaxed grin. "Faubion. Charles Faubion."

"You got some proof?"

"Of course." Carson smiled for real. No honor among thieves, he thought as he handed over an Arizona driver's license and a card identifying Charles Faubion as a licensed investigator in that state.

Lawry nodded, satisfied. "Okay, Charlie. Our crime scene boys found a note pad on Buddy's desk with the name Jenny and a New Orleans telephone number. That enough of a connection for you?"

A shave under six hours later, Carson pulled the Charger into the lot for the apartment complex at the address Dorothy McLaren had provided. They located Jenny's apartment and saw that the place was dark.

"Looks like she's either still asleep or she's already left," noted Lawry.

"Or she's just now getting home," added Carson, hunkering down in his seat as he pushed Lawry down in his.

The young woman in question drove past them in a red Corolla from the early '90s. They watched her walk up the ornate wrought-iron stairs and disappear into her apartment.

"Let's go," said Carson.

When she answered the door, Jenny McLaren had

scrubbed her face clean of the heavy makeup that revealed why she was returning home at dawn. She looked like a young co-ed, dressed in a Tulane sweatshirt and baggy jersey pants.

"Hello, Jenny," Carson said in a soft voice. "Mind if we talk?"

Fear flickered across her face, replaced by sullen suspicion, as Jenny assessed her visitors.

"Who are you and why would I talk to you?"

"Because we've tied you to a dead guy and a suspected killer."

Jenny stared at the men and then sneered. "I don't think you've got shit."

Before she could react, Carson stepped forward and spun Jenny around, pinning her arms behind her back. "Listen up. A woman's life is on the line, and I don't have time to waste. We're going inside, and you're going to talk."

Carson ignored the muttered epithet and guided Jenny into the tiny living room, where he released her. "Spill it," he snapped. "We've got James Hicks driving your SUV around, while you're in a tin can. We've also got your name and number in the office of the late Buddy Martin, who was supposed to be protecting my client's money."

Jenny covered her mouth with both hands, and tears welled in her eyes.

"Buddy's dead?" she whispered.

"Stone cold," said Lawry. "What's your connection?"

She took a deep breath. "We were lovers."

Both men stared at her.

"Maybe that's too strong a word," she admitted. "A few months back, James talked me into getting friendly with Buddy. He was a lonely old man." Jenny paused, as if remembering the accountant. "It wasn't hard for me to seduce him."

"So you sweet-talked him into stealing the money," said Carson.

She nodded, eyes downcast.

"Were you and Hicks planning to live happily ever after? Or did you know he was picking up a new high-class girlfriend?"

Her head snapped up. Surprised outrage sparked in her eyes.

Lawry turned to Carson. "I guess not."

Carson reached into his breast pocket and retrieved the newspaper clipping. He showed the photo to Jenny, who flinched as if Carson had struck her.

"You know this woman?"

Jenny brushed tears away with an impatient swipe. "Of course I do," she snorted. "She never shied away from a camera in her life. That lying son of a bitch told me to head down here while he wrapped things up in Memphis."

"Have you seen him?" asked Carson.

She nodded. "Yeah, he came over here last night, just before my shift. He's staying at some cheap motel about twenty minutes out."

Before they left, Carson asked Jenny for a pad of paper and a pen. She frowned but retrieved the items.

He jotted down a number and a short note. Then he folded the paper and handed it back to her with the pen.

"Call this number," Carson said. "If you're interested in making a change, they can help you out. If not, that's your choice. Either way, you'd do well to forget we were here."

Her face remained expressionless as she closed the door.

When Carson and Lawry pulled into the parking lot of the Motel 6 in Slidell, northeast of the city, the Land Rover was parked in front of room 114, just as Jenny had indicated it would be.

"What's the plan?" asked Lawry after Carson killed the engine.

"We go in, get the girl, and leave."

"You don't think your man's going to have a problem with that?"

"We won't give him a choice." Movement in the window confirmed that Jenny had followed his instructions and made the call. "I'll stay here and keep an eye on the room. Go show the manager your badge, and get the master key. One of us will open the door; the other will provide cover."

Lawry arched his brow with skepticism. "I'll provide cover. You open the door."

"Get the key."

The officer opened the car door and strode toward the office, oblivious as the entrance to room 114 cracked open. Carson opened his own door and crouched behind the vehicle, his silenced Glock ready. The report of a 9mm pistol shattered the morning air, and Lawry dropped to the pavement, the left side of his head missing. Any twinge of guilt Carson might have felt was neutralized by the knowledge that the dirty cop wasn't planning to let him walk away alive.

Hicks turned to see Carson's muzzle aimed at him. It was the last thing he saw before the slug in his forehead propelled him backward into the motel room.

Carson launched himself across the parking lot and into the narrow room, entering low with his gun in front. He nudged the body inside with his legs as he scoped out the room's interior.

Just as his brain registered that the main room was empty,

a petite figure emerged from the bathroom. Cold blue eyes stared at him from a doll-like face.

"Your father sent me," he said.

She took a step backward.

"We have to go. The police will be here any minute. Grab your things."

The woman took a shuddering breath and nodded. She cast one more wary glance at Carson and then turned to disappear into the bathroom. "It's not about the money, is it?" she asked.

On the porcelain vanity, Carson saw the mate to the earring he had picked up at Buddy's office, the same one she had worn to the museum event. He considered the question. "No. I think it's a matter of security. Peace of mind." He envisioned this same diminutive woman raising a gun to kill a man who had watched her grow up. Lawry had known that the murder was a two-person job and probably suspected the second player.

"Does the same go for you?"

"No. For me, it's a matter of honor."

In the mirror, he saw her reflection shoot him a withering glance. "Honor," she spat. "That's an interesting term for it."

Carson shrugged. "I only pursue those who have proven themselves dishonorable."

His bullet penetrated the back of her skull, and she crumpled to the floor.

Twenty-five minutes later, he was heading north on I-90, crossing the huge expanse of Lake Pontchartrain. He dialed his client from a disposable cell phone.

"It's done."

Silence. Just before Carson hung up, believing the conversation over, the man spoke.

"Thank you. I trust you collected the stolen cash as the remainder of your fee?"

"I haven't counted it, but I'm sure it's fine."

"Excellent. Our business is concluded."

The line went dead.

Carson rolled down the passenger-side window and tossed the cell phone, along with the spent shell casings, into the water.

He calculated the distance between New Orleans and Gatesville. Then he activated the Bluetooth device linked to his personal phone and dialed home.

His angel answered on the third ring. Once more, Carson found himself wondering how a relationship between father and daughter could go so wrong as to justify his latest assignment.

"Daddy?"

"Yes, sweetheart. I'll be home to tuck you in tonight."

THE RAVEN AND THE WOLF

BY O'NEIL DE NOUX

New Orleans, Louisiana

I t's all over the Channel 4 Eyewitness News at 10 p.m.—
police officer killed in her home.

Images of cops standing outside an apartment building fill my TV screen, flashing blue and red lights illuminating the powder-blue N.O.P.D. uniform shirts. I spot my former partner's yellow-blond hair as Detective Jodie Kintyre moves through the crowd and into the building. Jodie wears another of her skirt-suits, this one tan.

The camera pans to several cops crying, turning their heads away from the camera as the television news anchor explains, "The body of Fifth District police officer Kimberly Champagne was found this evening in her Tchoupitoulas Street apartment after she failed to show up for roll call."

Jesus Christ! I let out a long breath and, "Motha fuck!"

"The tragic killing of the popular officer is particularly heart-wrenching to the rank and file. Officer Champagne, a recent graduate of the police academy, was a rookie with a promising career ahead of her." A police ID picture of a smiling brunette with wide eyes comes on the screen as the anchor goes on to explain how Kimberly Champagne went to Sacred Heart Academy before attending Tulane University where she majored in Sociology.

I lift the bottle of Abita beer to my lips and finish it off. It's taking all my strength to keep from jumping out of the chair, grabbing my weapon, badge, and radio, and racing to the scene. I'm off duty and maybe it's my Lakota heritage (Sioux, as the white man calls us) that knows better than to go looking for trouble. It'll find me on its own. Or maybe it's the Cajun half of me that knows not to volunteer. Volunteers are from Tennessee, not south Louisiana.

I get up slowly to grab another Abita and sit back in the easy chair and wait for the sports to come on. Waves lap against the side of my houseboat and I hear the guttural noise of a big outboard as some boat slips away from Bucktown into Lake Pontchartrain. *Sad Lisa* rises slightly then gently settles as the waves subside, and I close my eyes for a moment and hear it again, in my mind. "*. . . cop killed . . .*"

A summer breeze flows through an open porthole of my houseboat carrying in the familiar scent of salt water. I can't stop my heart from racing no matter how hard I try.

Trouble is waiting for me the following morning as I walk into the detective bureau in the visage of my lieutenant's dark brown, scowling face. Dennis Merten, all six feet, 250 pounds, stands with his arms folded across his chest. He wears his usual black suit, narrow black tie loosened. He hasn't even had time to take off his jacket.

"Detective John Raven Beau," Merten calls out. "Just the man I'm looking for."

He growls as I approach. "I need you on Tchoupitoulas. Assist the evening watch with a canvass. A cop was killed last night."

"I know. Mind if I look over the dailies?" I'd like to know more about the case than what was on the damn news.

Merten walks away, snapping back at me, "Just don't take

all fuckin' morning." Then he stops and says, "I'm surprised you didn't go barreling over there last night."

"I'm on the day shift, remember?"

"'Bout time you learned that." Always in a good mood, that man.

Climbing from my unmarked Chevy Caprice, I leave my suit coat hanging in the backseat and reach in for my portable radio, note pad, and pen. I wear my black suit today, with a light gray tie. My hair is freshly cut and shorter than usual. It's still as dark brown as when I was a kid. My 5 o'clock shadow is in check with a close shave this morning.

A better description of me would mention I'm six-two and lean. An ex-girlfriend says my eyes are the color of dark sand. She also says I have a hawk nose and look like a raptor at times, a bird of prey.

I stare at the apartment house that was on TV last night. It's a redbrick building, old, a warehouse converted into condos. This entire area has been reclaimed—hulking buildings turned into apartment houses or small delis, coffee shops, a Kinko's at the corner of Julia Street.

Two marked police cars are parked directly in front of the building. I spot two uniforms standing down the street and one outside the front door of the place with Jodie, in a light yellow blouse and black slacks this morning. Her blond hair, freshly blow-dried as always, is longer than usual, a page-boy cut.

I tug up my pants as I start across the street. Must be losing weight, my stainless steel 9mm Beretta 92F, in its nylon holster on my right hip, weighs down my belt more than usual. Jodie nods at me as I approach and I recognize another familiar face. The uniformed cop smiles weakly at me and pushes a wild strand of dark brown hair from her face.

I met Officer Juanita Cruz a couple months ago at Charity Hospital when I worked the murder case we call *Shoot Me I'm Late*—a case she helped me solve. Wasn't much to it. Guy had his buddy shoot him in the leg so he wouldn't get in trouble with his domineering girlfriend for being late *again* for a date, only the guy died.

I'm about to ask what a Fifth District officer is doing downtown, but when a cop's killed, we all come out like the cavalry (may not be a very good analogy from a man whose ancestors wiped out Custer at Little Big Horn).

"Hold this," I say to Juanita, handing her my radio as I unfasten my belt and tighten it up a loop. That's better. Juanita's chocolate-brown eyes are wide and I wink. She looks as if she's lost weight too. She still wears her hair back in a bun, like most women in uniform do. As I recall, she's twenty-five, a good five years younger than me.

Jodie's cat eyes are weary as she lets out a long sigh. "We're going to recanvass the building first. I'll start at the top with Juanita. You start at the bottom, okay?"

I slip my radio into my back pocket.

It takes me six minutes to solve the murder.

Mindy Cellers, with a "C," an inquisitive seven-year-old who lives in apartment 1A on the first floor, stares at my gold star-and-crescent badge clipped to my belt as she tells me, "I know who killed her."

I go down on my haunches, eye level now, and ask the obvious, "Who?"

Mindy tugs at the sides of her reddish hair. "I tried to tell the police last night, but nobody would talk to me."

"I'm talking to you." I keep my voice low and soft. "Who killed her?"

"The Wolf." Her green eyes narrow as she nods. "That's what he calls himself. He visits her a lot."

"What does he look like?" Hoping she's not about to describe a canine from some childhood fantasy world.

"He's as big as you and thicker. And scary looking."

"Scary?"

"He's got a sharp face and big eyebrows." Mindy leans forward. "I think he's her boyfriend."

A door opens behind me and I turn to see an old man peek out.

"He saw the Wolf when he left." Mindy leans past me, speaking to the old man. "The Wolf almost knocked *you* over when he left, didn't he?"

I stand and the old man's gaze moves from my gun to my badge and he shrugs. He's barely five feet tall, balding with a craggy, sallow face. He's in a faded red plaid housecoat. Barefoot.

"I'm Detective Beau. Homicide. You saw someone yesterday?"

The man glances around, hand still on the door as if he's about to slam it and escape back inside. I recognize the look of fear; I ease forward.

"There's nothing to be afraid of. We'll get him, you know. Nobody kills a cop and gets away with it." I drop my voice menacingly. "Not in *New Orleans*."

"You don't know Wolf."

I slip my radio from my back pocket and call Jodie.

Allan O'Grady lives in 1B, an apartment decorated with timeworn furniture and old-fashioned lamps and smelling like sweaty socks. Jodie and I both jot O'Grady's story on our note pads.

Last night, at about 7 p.m., the former boyfriend of Kimberly Champagne who lives in apartment 2B came hurrying down the stairs, bumping into O'Grady who was coming back into the building from putting his garbage out. The Wolf, in a black jacket and baggy black pants, kept his hands in his pockets as he jammed his shoulder against the door to swing it open and rush away. An hour earlier O'Grady had heard several loud pops, but thought it was a car backfiring. Later, when the police arrived, O'Grady heard voices and crying but wouldn't answer his door no matter how many times people knocked on it. He'd turned off the lights.

Jodie asks why everyone knows this man as the Wolf and I spot Juanita Cruz easing in the open doorway. Her eyes are red and she nods me over. We step back into the hall where Mindy still waits in her doorway.

Juanita's face is scrunched up as if in pain. "I know him."

She takes a step back and sits on the stairs. "Kim broke up with him months ago."

I pull out my note pad as I watch her breathing heavily now.

"What's his real name?"

"Ahern Smith." She sucks in a deep breath. "Calls himself the Wolf or just Wolf. Always refers to himself in the third person. Like, 'The Wolf is hungry,' or, 'The Wolf thinks this is nice.'" She blinks up at me and tears flow from her eyes. "He's an ex–Green Beret."

I sit next to her and ask how long she'd known Kimberly Champagne.

"I broke her in when she came out of the academy." Juanita buries her face in her hands. "We were partners for six months."

Before leaving with Juanita, Jodie explains to me how the Wolf made it look like a break-in, as if Kim had stumbled on a burglar. "We've been looking at every goddamn 62-man in the computer."

Jodie shakes her head and thanks me before she heads back to the detective bureau to get a line on this Wolf character and secure the necessary warrants.

I'm left to take the formal statements from O'Grady and Miss Mindy Cellers with a "C."

"What's a 62-man?" Mindy asks.

"Burglar."

"I'm not afraid of the Wolf." She tilts her head to the side and smiles. "I know you'll get him."

I give her a long stare before I say, "I usually do."

Ahern Keith Smith, alias the Wolf, has no arrest record but did spend eight years in the U.S. Army. In a photo we secured from Kim Champagne's apartment, a picture we've distributed to all law enforcement, he looks a little like the actor River Phoenix, the kid who OD'd, only the Wolf's face is leaner and meaner-looking with an almost rabid glint in his blue eyes.

His condo is on St. Charles Avenue, corner of Peniston Street, in the center of a row of new town houses built on ground that once housed a mansion. On either side of the condos are mansions with antebellum columns, verandas and all.

At 4 a.m., I follow three S.W.A.T. men, decked out in all black, army helmets, bulky flak vests. The first one carries a sledgehammer, the second a bullet-proof shield. It's Jodie's case and her warrants, so she makes me put on a flak vest or I have to stay out. I'm in all-black too, black T-shirt, jeans, and running shoes, my Beretta cupped in both hands as we move up to the Wolf's front door. Jodie's right behind me, her own 9mm Beretta in hand. She's blacked-out also, her hair in a ponytail.

The condo is quiet. A voice booms "Police!" as the sledge-hammer shatters the deadbolt and the door flies open. Everybody wants him to be there with a weapon in hand so we can send the Wolf straight to hell, as painfully as possible.

He isn't there, but there's blood around the kitchen sink. Pulling on rubber gloves, we start rooting. In the Wolf's desk, I find detailed notes of his surveillance of Kim Champagne—her work schedule, times entering and leaving home, times and places she went to after work, along with black-and-white telephoto pictures of her. Just as I find the Wolf's night-vision goggles and binoculars, Jodie discovers six semi-automatic pistols and a World War II Browning Automatic Rifle, the famous B.A.R.

I can see the strain in Jodie's eyes. Under the bright lights of the condo, her smooth face is still void of age lines, although she's pushing forty. I remind her of that, just to break the tension, and she gets up on the balls of her feet, extends her five-seven frame, and gives me a rabbit punch in the solar plexus.

As the crime lab tech enters to collect the blood, headquarters calls Jodie on the radio to notify her that Ahern Smith's black SUV was just found abandoned on the Claiborne Avenue bridge over the Industrial Canal. There's blood in the car.

"Jesus! I gotta go." Jodie yanks off her gloves. "You got this?"

"I'll finish up," I tell her as she pulls the band from her hair, shakes out her ponytail, and hurries away.

When I find the Wolf's journal, I read the last entry where he says he's going to kill Kimberly, then himself. He even gives us the reason, a broken heart he calls *my heart's death* since she left him. I flip back through the pages as he describes his life without Kimberly, back through their relationship to the time he first saw her as they each stood outside Galatoire's, each with friends, waiting for Sunday breakfast at one of the most exclusive restaurants in a city of great restaurants. Kimberly wore a short red dress that day.

He admits his clever lines didn't impress her at first, but he succeeded in discovering where she worked and kept at her until she let him take her out. I skim over the details of their sex life and feel a sickness in my stomach, knowing all this will be read in open court when we catch the bastard, all the detailed descriptions of Kim's body.

I shake my head, my heart racing again.

As if he really jumped off the fuckin' bridge. If he wanted to kill himself, why didn't he do it at Kim's? I close the journal, which goes back three years. There are other girlfriends listed too, with more explicit details. I add the journal to the box of materials we're taking.

We've answered the question *why*, although *why* isn't important to a homicide detective. *Why* is only important in Sherlock Holmes stories and to the news media, which struggles to determine why everything occurs. In homicide, the who, what, when, where, and how of a murder is what leads us to the killer. But sometimes it helps to know why, I guess.

I slip on my extra-dark Ray Ban Balorama sunglasses as I sit at my desk in the bureau, the early-morning sun burning through the withered tint on the wall of windows while Jodie explains the case to the assembled cops. It's 10 a.m. now and I'm worn out. That's what I get, being thirty.

Yes, there was blood inside the Wolf's SUV. No, no one saw him jump. No one saw him walk away either. The ever-alert bridge operator didn't even notice the abandoned SUV until a passing Harbor Police car almost ran into it. Yes, we checked cabs and buses, but no one picked up anyone close to the Wolf's description.

The ever-efficient Harbor Police are dragging the Industrial Canal, only they're not optimistic. The canal's deep enough for ocean-going ships and they can't keep the locks closed for long. I feel myself dozing off.

No one in the room believes he jumped, so we set up a routine. Lt. Merten takes over, handing out assignments, sending detectives to cover all the Wolf's known haunts, houses of his relatives, places he's worked, whatever they've come up with from the computer.

I'm slipping now, my regular breathing lulling me to sleep.

I feel someone shaking me and raise my sunglasses to Juanita Cruz's eager face. "I'm going with you tonight. You want me to meet you here, or what?"

I pull my feet off my desk. "Come again? What did I miss?"

"I'm assigned to work with you." She sounds apologetic.

"No problem there." I stand and stretch. "What are we supposed to do?"

Juanita points to Jodie standing next to the coffee pot, waving us over.

"You two go sit on his ex-girlfriend," says Jodie. "The one he went out with just before Kim." She takes a sip of coffee. "We've notified everyone from his journals to be careful."

On our way out, Juanita remarks, "Everyone wants you to be the one to catch him."

I don't have to ask why.

Shortly after sunset, following some needed sleep and a

thick burger and fries at my favorite haunt, Flamingos Café in Bucktown, I sit parked in my unmarked car with Juanita. We're outside the Wolf's old girlfriend's apartment house on Constance Street just down from Howard Avenue, only three blocks from Kim's apartment. The building is three stories tall with a security front door and a gated garage out back.

Juanita and I both wear dark, short-sleeved dress shirts, unbuttoned and open over black T-shirts, black running shoes, and black jeans, with our 9mm's in nylon holsters on our hips. She wears her hair down and looks different. Even with only a hint of makeup, a brush of red on her lips, she's very pretty, with those sultry Latina looks.

"So what's this girl's name again?" She has her note pad open.

"Bessie Cleary, white female, twenty-three, five-five, thin, light brown hair. Went out with the Wolf for over a year. Lived with him. Jodie talked with her and Bessie doesn't think the lovely Mr. Ahern Smith would ever hurt her."

Juanita looks up from her notes. "You sure he can't get in the back way to this place?"

"I'm not sure. But the security guard's retired N.O.P.D. and he's just chomping for a shot at the Wolf. Carries a Glock 35, .40 caliber, seventeen rounds. Itching to shoot."

I stretch out my legs as best I can. Even with the windows down it's still steamy, not even a breath of wind. The only smell is Juanita's light perfume, which is kind of nice actually.

"So, your girlfriend's mad at you?"

I'd mentioned it when I picked her up. "Yeah. Another night alone. She said it's getting old all these hours I put in."

I don't tell her how many girlfriends have given up on me. Don't want to sound pathetic. Heartache's part of the job, I keep telling myself. Suddenly, the Wolf's words, *heart's death*, come to mind, and I brush them away. Fuckin' bastard.

"Kim thought the Wolf was the one." Juanita's voice is husky with emotion. "Soul mate, you know." She takes in a deep breath. "I remember the first time I saw Kim, all bright-eyed and eager, right out of the academy. She smiled all through that first shift." Her voice cracks.

"You were her training officer?"

She nods, catches her breath, and continues in a staccato voice filled with emotion. "Her family's rich. She was an ath-lete. Played tennis in high school. Had *two* college degrees. Was going to go to law school, but went to the academy instead."

I watch a man enter the building, but he's too short and too old to be the Wolf.

"She became a cop because she was tired of being a victim."

I turn to Juanita, my eyebrows rising.

"Kim was mugged twice, once in an evening gown coming from her debutante ball. It scared her and she didn't like the feeling and wanted to do something about it herself."

A cab parks in front of the apartment house and an el-derly lady gets out and enters the building.

"I've never known anyone with a clearer definition be-tween right and wrong," Juanita goes on. "She was a problem solver at scenes, running a guy in for hitting his wife, running a woman in for neglecting her kids, making peace between people more often than not."

I'm not much of a peacemaker.

Juanita readjusts herself, leaning against the door, facing me more as she says, "Why is your middle name Raven?"

"I'm half Lakota."

She's confused, so I explain: "Sioux."

"Oh. Anyone ever call you the Raven?"

"No."

She comes right back with, "I looked up the word in the dictionary this morning. Raven has other meanings, besides the bird. It also means to be predatory, to seek or seize prey and to plunder, and—"

I raise my hand. "I know. But what does that have to do with anything?"

"How many men have you killed?" Her eyes are narrowed, her pouty lips set seriously, and for some reason I can't tell her it's none of her business.

"I quit counting at five."

I figured I'd get a raised eyebrow, but her face remains set.

"The Grand Jury decided all were justifiable homicides. They did cite me, however, for scalping two of them."

"Scalping?" Her eyes go owly.

She's so gullible, I have to play it out, so I reach my left hand around and pull out my black hunting knife from its sheath on my belt. It has a nine-inch blade, a Sioux instrument, sharpened on one side only, a proper knife for a plains warrior.

She folds her arms. "You never scalped them."

Shrugging, I put my knife away. I don't bother telling her I hadn't much choice in shooting the men. Truly. But most cops never shoot anyone and Juanita doesn't have to explain her curiosity. I'm an aberration, either the unluckiest Cajun or a predatory Sioux taking revenge on the white eyes.

"The word *wolf* also means predatory, rapacious, and fierce."

I chuckle finally to ease the pressure and counter, "So what's your point?"

"I want to call you the Raven."

"You can call me Detective Beau, Officer Cruz."

She sits up as if I pinched her and looks out the windshield.

I have to laugh. "I'm just kiddin', Juanita. Beau's fine. I just don't like nicknames."

A minute of silence is broken when she says, "I told you, everyone wants you to be the one to find the Wolf. It's all they're talking about at headquarters."

I don't like where this is going.

"Because you'll kill him."

"You shouldn't hang around headquarters so much." It's my turn to stare out the windshield at the dark night. The apartment building is now bathed in exterior lighting. The night is extra dark because it's moonless and in the darkness I feel a heartache, or rather the memory of heartache.

Her name was Lily and I thought *she* was the one. Soul mate, you know. Only she walked out on me at the lowest point in my life. Lying in that hospital bed after the operation to repair the knee I tore up in the spring game at L.S.U., sophomore season, with my bright future as a quarterback all but gone, Lily told me she didn't love me anymore. I wanted to run after her, convince her it couldn't be over because I still loved her, but I couldn't even get out of bed.

It was for the better, I suppose. And the heartache only returns if I think back. I fidget in my seat thinking how the Wolf reacted to his heartache. Where did he find the fury? I've never felt anger toward Lily and I guess that's the difference. The Wolf let his pain turn into rage. The Raven left his pain where it belongs because life is a series of losses. The Sioux know this and so do the Cajuns, refugees from Canada driven to the swamps of south Louisiana.

"I wish something would happen," Juanita says.

Those chocolate-brown eyes stare into mine for a long

minute and her face looks very relaxed, calm, and lovely in the dim light. I feel my heartbeat now, but the moment is lost as I catch a movement behind Juanita's head and tense a moment, then I see it's a homeless man.

Juanita turns as the man stops and asks if we can spare a buck.

I climb out and he starts to back away until he sees me dig into my pocket. He's middle-aged with a scraggly beard and a well-worn knapsack on his back. I give him a five and he thanks me. I pull out the Wolf's picture and ask him if he's ever seen this man around. He shakes his head and thanks me again and hurries away.

When I climb back in Juanita says, in a shaky voice, "I didn't see him coming up behind me."

"That's what you got me for."

"Partner, right?"

"Almost." She nearly smiles and all the depressing thoughts fade away from my brain. "Saw a bumper sticker yesterday that said, *There are three kinds of people—those who can count and those who can't.*"

It takes her a second and then she laughs.

It hits me as soon as I wake up the following afternoon. The Wolf broke into Kim's apartment and laid in wait for her. I get dressed in a hurry. An ex–Green Beret is no one to mess with but he's the one on the lam, not me. If he's dumb enough to come at me, he'll join the list and I'll cruise through another Grand Jury hearing. I'm thinking maybe I should call Juanita, or at least Jodie, but all I have is this gut feeling and I hate to roust the troops, especially if I'm wrong.

Stepping away from *Sad Lisa*, I see the brown-green water of Lake Pontchartrain is as still as a pond. There's no wind whatsoever, the warm air steamy with humidity and the fishy smell of iodine. The calm is unsettling. To a Lakota warrior, any change in the environment, especially when normally rough waters are suddenly calm, can be a warning from nature. The warning is understood, if that's what it is. It reinforces my gut feeling and I make sure to carry two extra clips of ammo, not that I've ever needed that many bullets to kill someone.

Parking behind Bessie Cleary's apartment house, I walk up to the garage gate and wave to the retired N.O.P.D. man who recognizes me and opens the gate.

"Something wrong?" he asks, pulling out his Glock.

I shake my head. "Just checking."

"She's at work," he calls out behind me, and I wave as I tuck my portable radio into the back pocket of my faded blue jeans. I wear a short-sleeved gray dress shirt over a navy-blue T-shirt. Unbuttoned, the shirt covers my knife and holstered Beretta. My gold star-and-crescent badge is clipped to the front of my belt. I'm breaking in a new pair of black Reebok running shoes.

I go up the back stairs. Bessie lives on the third floor, at the front of the building. I turn into the hall from the back-side and freeze. He's at the far end of the hall dressed in black fatigues and black combat boots. Working on Bessie's door, the Wolf doesn't see me creeping along the hall toward him. I ease out my Beretta and flip off the safety. My heart's already pounding but my hands are steady as I raise my weapon in the standard two-handed police grip.

A door opens between us and a young woman steps into the hall, drawing the Wolf's attention, and he spots me and bolts.

"Police!" I raise the Beretta and the woman falls back against her door. I race past. The Wolf leaps into the front stairwell. My Beretta cupped in both hands, I stop at the opening of the stairwell and hear footsteps descending heavily, thudding on the carpet.

I follow the sound down the stairs, keeping on my toes, pointing my weapon ahead as I take each turn. I can still hear him descending as I reach the landing above the ground floor. A metallic slam echoes up and I stop and ease my way forward until I see the front door slowly closing. He's outside now and I run for the door, catching it before it closes, hitting the metal bar and swinging it outward. I hesitate a second, then scramble through the door.

The Wolf races around the corner, down Howard, not even looking back, moving flat out. I pull my portable radio from my back pocket and charge after him.

I key the mike. "3124—headquarters!"

"Go ahead, 3124," the dispatcher responds.

"I'm in foot pursuit of a signal thirty suspect. River bound on Howard from Constance Street."

I describe what the Wolf's wearing and what I'm wearing, trying my best to keep my voice low and calm. Last thing I want is to sound like a lunatic on the air. Excited voices fill the speaker but I can't hear as I pump my arms, running hard, Beretta in my right hand, radio in my left.

People watch us from the sidewalks and the street, standing with wide eyes, like deer caught in headlights. The Wolf's a half-block ahead of me, running head down, not looking over his shoulder as he cuts between parked cars into the street then back through them, up on the sidewalk in case I'm crazy enough to let off a round or two. He bowls over an elderly couple coming out of a furniture store as he turns another corner.

"Police!" I yell as I jump over the couple, who don't seem

seriously damaged. I try my best to tell headquarters we're on Annunciation now, heading uptown. I'm gaining on him, I think.

When he turns at the next corner, he glances back at me, but doesn't lose stride. I don't know what street this is, but it's even narrower. We're heading toward the river again and there are fewer people here. A man in a hard hat steps from a building in front of the Wolf and then leaps out of the way, crashing against a parked car.

I manage to croak out "Police!" as I pass to keep him out of the way.

The Wolf turns down South Peters and I know this street and try my best to tell headquarters we're heading downtown now. Cars are parked on both sides of this skinny street. A siren echoes in the distance, then another. The cavalry's coming, thank God.

Jesus! This guy's as good a sprinter as me and I run regularly on the levee. My knee's pinching a little now, but I can't fall back. At least my breathing's still coming evenly, although I'm sucking in a lot of air. I feel a surge in my warrior blood and increase my pace. Can't let this fucker get away.

The Wolf crosses the street and I see umbrellas ahead. It's an outdoor café, tables covered in wide Cinzano umbrellas. I get up on the sidewalk as the Wolf skirts the first table and grabs the next one, crashing it and umbrella to the sidewalk. I cut between the parked cars back into the street.

A woman screams and a gunshot echoes. The picture window of the café explodes and I spot the Wolf jumping behind a parked car. The window of the car to my left shatters and I see yellow flashes as he fires at me. I leap behind a van across the street, take to the far sidewalk, and go belly down as more slugs hit the van. I crawl forward and slip behind an

SUV. It's big enough for me to look under, but I can't see the Wolf's position from here.

Six more shots ring out.

Jesus, I hope he's not shooting people in the café! I tell headquarters where we are, steeling myself as I get up and move forward as fast as I can, the parked car shielding me.

When I reach the vehicle directly across from the Wolf's position, a marked police car skids to a stop at the far corner, lights flashing, siren wailing. I take in a deep breath, let half of it out, and peek from between the cars.

The Wolf's on his haunches, looking at the police car. I raise my Beretta as he lifts his weapon, sticks it in his mouth, and shoots himself. He falls face forward, half in the street.

The cops alight from their car. I wave at them as I cross the street.

"He shot himself!" I call out as the patrol officers approach, guns drawn.

"Check the people in the café," I tell them. "Make sure no one's hurt and make sure no one leaves! They're witnesses."

The two move off as another police car screeches up. I put out a code four on my radio, then ask to have the homicide supervisor, the crime lab, the coroner's office, and Jodie Kintyre join us.

As I holster my Beretta, the Wolf's body twitches and I yank out my knife, then laugh at myself, which draws curious looks from the two cops. I feel someone move up behind me and turn to see Juanita Cruz's wide eyes. She's in T-shirt and jeans too, her hair down. Her lips tremble as she stares at me and says, "You *are* the Raven."

I stop myself from snapping at her when I kneel next to the Wolf and check his throat, trying to find a pulse in his carotid artery, not that it'll do him much good with most of his brains on the sidewalk. I find no pulse and calmly slice off a chuck of his hair to slip into my pocket. Juanita's eyes are huge and I see I've nicked the Wolf's forehead with my knife. I feel his warm blood on my fingers.

Slipping my knife back into its sheath, I rub my eyes with my clean hand. When I blink them open, I spot several uniformed men whispering to one another, nodding toward me.

Jodie comes on the air asking me, "Is the subject 10-7?" (Out of service—permanently.)

"10-4. 29-S." I make sure to tell her he killed himself.

"I'm in route." She sounds relieved that I didn't have to shoot anyone.

I call out to the first officer who'd arrived, asking if anyone in the café was hurt. He shakes his head as I turn to the sound of running feet behind me. Lt. Merten lumbers up, sees the body, and looks at me, wheezing as he tries to catch his breath.

I raise both hands and tell him, "I never fired a shot."

He nods and leans both hands against the nearest car.

"You . . . all right?"

"Yeah."

Juanita stands stone-stiff above the Wolf's body, staring down at it. I lean close and ask if she's okay.

"This doesn't make me feel any better," she says.

Boy, do I know that feeling.

She takes in a deep breath and lets it out slowly. I can feel the emotions raging through her tight face. Suddenly, a gust of wind washes over us from the river, a warm summer breeze that rustles Juanita's hair. She peers up at the sun, closing her eyes as it touches her face.

When she opens her eyes, I ask, "How'd you get here so fast?"

' "I remembered how he'd broken into Kim's and decided to check on Bessie's apartment."

"Me too." I reach over and spread the Wolf's blood on Juanita's face in two stripes, painting her like a good plains warrior, the obsidian knife suddenly heavy on my belt. Her eyes grow wide with comprehension. I nod and repeat, "Me too," adding the word she's been looking for, "partner."

JURACÁN

BY R. NARVAEZ

San Juan, Puerto Rico

T here must be more dead dogs on the side of the road in Puerto Rico than anywhere else in the world. The strays must go out of their way to kill themselves there. Or maybe Puerto Ricans just don't like dogs. I was in a cramped rental car, driving my three aunts to my cousin's wedding in Ponce. It was a ten-minute ride, and I'd already seen four dog carcasses. Tongues hanging out. Guts. Blood. It took some of the buzz off.

"Qué pasó con los jodios peros en la highway?" I asked.

"Se dice perrrrros," my Titi Juana said.

"Perrrrrros," I tried.

"Perros," Titi Gloria said.

Then Tía Nidia said, "No sé, mi amor. Toda la gente maneja como loco aquí."

I could see how the roads in PR could drive you crazy. There wasn't always a traffic light where you needed it. A lot of the blacktop hugged the sides of mountains and were crazy-narrow so that your sideview mirror hung over a thousand-foot drop into nothing but jungle. Still everyone on the island seemed to drive fast.

But no one honked. They might not like dogs in PR, but they sure as hell were polite.

"Por favor, mi amor, maneja más rápido," Titi Juana said.

My aunts giggled about something I didn't follow. I wondered if the reception would have an open bar.

The church was dark, big. Polished pews. Bleeding Christ. The ceremony in Spanish. I spent the time shifting my weight from one foot to the other.

At the reception, I went right to the bar. The drinks weren't free, so when the bartender poured, I told him, "Más. Chin más," and he was cool about it. I tipped him a couple of bucks.

At the table, my aunts gossiped, and I tried to listen, nodded a lot, and laughed when I thought I should. I knew everyone at our table except one woman. She had black hair cut straight across the forehead. Copper skin, broad cheeks, thick, dark lips. She sat alone, except for a gift bag in the seat next to her. It was decorated with a coquí wearing a straw hat. I got up and walked around to her side.

"Quieres que yo lo puse ésto con los otros regalos?" I asked, standing over her.

"Qué dices?" she replied, looking up with her eyes.

I gestured to show what I meant. Gift bag. Gift table.

"Grácias, pero es algo diferente," she said and looked down at her manicure.

"No sweat," I said and took a seat next to her. "Me manejó aquí esta noche y vió una cosa . . . rara. Vió, como, cuatro perros en la highway—muertos. It was crazy."

She laughed, covering her teeth like some women do, then shook her head to herself. I hadn't been trying to be funny. She looked completely away from me. I got the hint and so I bounced and went back to the bar.

Some people gave some speeches. I went outside for a smoke. The moon looked like my grandmother's glaucoma eye.

It smelled good out there, green, wet. Palm trees and the sounds of tree frogs all around, like this invisible choir. I'd never seen a coquí before so while I puffed I walked around to see if I could spot one. Then I heard a woman talking in a loud voice. I glanced up and saw a silhouette. A woman talking on a cell phone. I couldn't catch all of it. Something like, How can you do this to me? Then some bad cursing.

I got closer. It was the woman from the table. Framed in the light coming from the reception hall. She had that gift bag with her.

She hung up, saw me standing there. "Estás perdido?" she asked.

"Qué noche bella!" I said.

"Qué noche fea!" she responded and walked past.

"Frío, you mean," I said to her back.

I finished my cigarette and considered calling Julie. I had a vision of her tight, freckled body in a bikini. But it wasn't a good time. So I just went inside.

A band was playing, and my Tía Lidia wanted to know when I would ask her to dance. So I danced with her and then my other aunts and then with every female relative I had. As one salsa finished, another aunt would come up, and so it went. I had a couple more drinks. Then I danced with my cousin Carmen. She was a good egg—a doctor who had just married another doctor.

I asked her who the dark woman was. "Una amiga de colegio. Se llame Itaba," she said. "That's funny, Papo, because she asked me about you."

My cousin was small, thin-hipped, dark-haired, glowing. She was tiny in my arms. At six-four, I towered over her.

"Oh really? What did you tell her?"

"That you were divorced. That you were trying to find your feet. Not too much."

I guess that was the nicest way of saying I'd been unemployed and unemployable for almost a year. "Okay," I said.

"I can't wait to get to Mexico. This humidity is killing me. Is my hair okay?"

"How's mine?" I said, and we laughed. "Leave it to you to get married during hurricane season."

I danced another salsa with Titi Juana. I felt good, energized, buzzed. I figured I'd give that dark lady another shot.

But then I saw my grandmother. She wore a black dress ringed with fluffy edges and sat on the edge of her chair. I could tell she wanted to dance.

"Abuela. Vamos a bailar," I said. She smiled up at me with shiny false teeth. I took her velvet soft hand and led her to the dance floor. She put her white-haired head against my chest.

When the dance ended, she smiled at me again and said, "Coco Duro," the nickname she had for me as a kid. Then she smacked me in the arm because she couldn't reach my head anymore.

When I got back to the table the dark woman was gone.

Maybe she'd left to make a phone call again. I was walking to the door, caught myself in the mirror and put up a hand to fix my hair, when this guy bumped into me. Dark, wraparound shades. I don't like not being able to see a man's eyes. You can't see if you can trust him. He was swarthy. Jet-black hair, combed back. Funny thing was the man's forehead—it was deformed. Flat from his eyebrows to his hairline. And there were thin scars up and down his dark cheeks. The guy caught me looking, his shades turned toward me, but he said nothing, I said nothing, and that was it.

I went back to my hair, making sure the pointed peak I kept on the top was just right. The gel was holding fine.

Outside there was no sign of the woman. Her loss.

The rest of my night I drank enough to feel good, then drove my aunts back to my aunt's house, where I was staying. It rained lightly, making the dark road shiny and slick. I saw four more dead dogs. More guts. More tongues. Or maybe they were the same dogs. The women gossiped in the car—what a nice ceremony, the food could've been better, et cetera.

Back at my aunt's house, in the middle of the night, when everyone else was asleep, I got up and went to the living room, found a bottle of dark rum, and filled a glass with it. I tipped my head back, drained it, burped, and went back to bed.

Outside the drizzle had turned into steady rain.

In the morning, I sat at the kitchen counter in front of a plate filled with eggs, plátanos, half a mango, and buttered bread. Café con leche, orange juice. "Come más," my Tía Lidia said, and before I could answer I got another piece of bread, another fried egg, another mango half. My head was buzzing, my stomach turned, but I kept eating.

"I gotta get ready to go to San Juan," I told them.

My aunt gave me more bread and told me about a tropical storm warning. She was happy my cousin had flown to Mexico that morning for the honeymoon. The warning could turn into a hurricane. She told me I shouldn't travel even though the rain had stopped.

"I'm meeting a friend," I said in English. I was too sour to try Spanish. "And I got to get a little blackjack and poker in while I'm here. Besides, there's not going to be no hurricane."

I went to pack my duffel bag. I wanted to get moving before it started to rain. Through the bars on the window, I saw a taxi park in front of the house. A woman got out. It was my cousin's friend Itaba. Tía Lidia walked out to talk to her.

I was twisting the lid onto my flask when Tía Lidia came in the room. "La amiga de Carmen necesita ir a San Juan." Since I was going to San Juan today, I could give her a ride, no?

"She can't take a cab?"

Cabs are very expensive, my aunt said.

I could see I didn't have a choice.

"Y ella es muy bonita. Parece india."

"Yeah. Well, I got to get ready first."

It's good to make new friends, my aunt said. You need someone to take care of you, she said.

"I have a friend waiting for me in San Juan."

Not that kind of friend, my aunt said.

I took my sweet time with my hair, getting it just the way I like it, and trimmed my beard to make sure it was the same thinness around my jaw. It's hard to get it right sometimes. Then I splashed on some cologne and I was good to go.

When I came out, Itaba was sitting in the patio with a big purse and that gift bag.

"Tantas gracias por hacer ésto," she said, standing up and smiling this big smile at me. I walked past her and went to the car.

When we got into the little vehicle, I noticed that she smelled good, not sweet like perfume, but like trees, like soil, like wood. For some reason it made me hungry.

"Tu huele bien," I said.

At first she looked at me like I'd said something nasty. Then she smiled and thanked me. So I played it off, stayed quiet.

We drove like that for five minutes before she started talking.

"What do you do?" she asked.

"So you speak English?"

"Of course," she said. "Look, I promise not to torture you anymore with my Spanish and you do not have to torture me anymore with yours." She gave me that smile again, full of brilliant white teeth. I wondered if she bleached them.

"Funny lady. Very funny."

"So what do you do?"

"You mean for a living? This and that."

"Is that what you tell everybody?"

I could've told her I had gotten out of prison awhile ago and couldn't find anyone who wanted to hire me. Not that I'm ashamed of that. I just didn't think it was her business. "I do fine. I have money."

"So why are you going to San Juan? To gamble?"

"I like to play cards, you know what I mean? And I'm meeting a friend."

"A lady friend?"

"The best kind."

"I'm sure you'll have a good time."

We were quiet for a little bit, then she said, "Listen, negrito, we first have to make a stop in Utuado."

"What? That's out of my way. It'll take hours to get there."

"It will take all day with the way you drive."

"Fine." I pulled the car sharply to the side of the road. "Take the wheel."

She got behind the driver's seat and slammed on the gas. We burned rubber. I put my seat belt on.

I looked at her dark, caramel fingers on the wheel. No ring.

My cell phone beeped. It was Julie—I had forgotten all about calling her. I looked at Itaba, then took the call.

I tried to whisper. "Nothing's wrong. No one's here," I said, but when she complained that she couldn't hear me I had to speak up. "Yeah. Hey. How are you? What time's your flight get in? . . . That's ridiculous. This is a just a tropical storm . . . Hey, I know you're nervous, but we're going to have a terrific time . . . C'mon, you've always been my good-luck charm . . . Hey, that's not going to happen. He's not going to find out . . . Call me when you know the new arrival time. Yeah. It'll be great. Don't worry."

Itaba kept her eyes on the road and said nothing. I stared out the window. The sky was dark, the clouds looked ready to explode with rain. The palm trees were bowing in the wind. I watched the dark road and—this is funny—I realized I was keeping an eye out for more dead dogs.

Itaba parked the car on the side of the road. We were some-where near Utuado.

"What the hell is this?" I said.

"We're going to the Taino village at Caguana Park."

All I saw were trees. "This doesn't look like anything."

"We're taking the back way."

"Is the front way closed?"

"Do you know anything about the Tainos?"

"The Indians? Oops. Sorry. Native Americans."

She raised her eyebrows. "Tainos were the indigenous people of Boriken, the real name of Puerto Rico. Don't you know anything about your history?"

"I was born and schooled in the Bronx, lady."

"The Tainos were the first people that Columbus met. In a few hundred years most of them were wiped out of existence."

"I heard they all died. Measles and shit. And stuff, I mean. See, I'm not as stupid as I look."

"Smallpox. But no, some survived. And there are many

of us who want to reclaim what is ours. Negrito, I need your help. And for your help I will give you a reward."

I looked at her lips, tried to imagine what she would look like when she was coming. If she was a screamer.

"No me mires así. I can give you money, so you can show your friend more of a good time in San Juan."

"How much?"

"A friend was supposed to drive me but he got delayed. I was going to give him a thousand dollars. I will give you two thousand because I have inconvenienced you."

I pursed my lips. "That's sweet money for a cab ride. But I want to know what this is about."

"Look in the bag," she said.

I took the gift bag from the back. There was something wrapped in plastic and then bubble wrap. I began to unwrap it.

"Be careful!" she snapped, raising her voice.

The stone had three points and was the size of my fist. One point had large eyes and teeth bared like a mad dog.

"You probably don't recognize it. It's a stone carving of Yocahú, a Taino deity."

"Looks like an animal. Check out its fucking teeth."

"Yocahú was the god of good, with no beginning and no end. This was discovered in an excavation at Jacana, near Ponce. I've been working there. I'm an archaeologist. Thank you for asking. The Army Corps of Engineers was clearing land in order to build a dam. They uncovered some of the most important archaeological treasures ever found in Puerto Rico. This one piece is priceless."

"Okay," I said. It was still ugly.

"An American buyer is waiting for me in a hotel in San Juan. But he wants to make sure it comes with a certificate of authenticity. That's why we're here."

"So you stole this?" I waved the stone.

"Please be careful with that."

"It's a rock."

"It's a cemi. It's sacred. The Neo-Taino movement needs money to buy back land. To take back what is ours. This carving is a great sacrifice but it will be worth it."

"And what's a Neo-Taino?"

"According to DNA testing, more than half of Puerto Ricans still have Taino blood in their veins."

"That doesn't make them Indians. They're selling quenepas on the side of the road, not doing rain dances."

She rolled her beautiful hazel eyes. "Listen, the buyer will pay one million dollars for this cemi."

"For this?" I whistled. "So, why not just rent a car? Why did you need me? Or was it just an excuse to get to know me better?"

"Ay, negrito. I didn't want to do this alone. Don't you understand?" she said and got out of the car.

She led me through the trees. The soil was wet and squished under my feet. We came to a wooden fence. With her boots, she began to kick it down.

"Let me do that," I said. With a few kicks, I opened a space big enough for an SUV.

"You didn't have to destroy it."

"I don't know my own strength," I said.

We came out from the trees and into a wide clearing. On one side there were several rectangular spaces of cleared dirt. Around it were stone carvings, one foot to five feet high, with faces and figures in white. Animals, people, and people that looked like animals.

"That is a batey court," she said, "where the warriors

would play in order to settle disputes between different villages. We were wise and peaceful."

"What did they play? Tennis?"

We circled the courts. Light rain began to fall. "There's that tropical storm," I said.

"Have you heard the story of Juracán, who was there at the creation of the world?"

"Nope."

"He was the brother of Yucahú and the son of Atabey, and he was created from elements in the air and therefore without a father."

"Like me."

"Juracán became envious of Yucahú when he saw his brother create the race of humanity, and so he tried to destroy his brother's creations. He became known as the god of strong winds—we get the word hurricane from his name. And the Tainos came to fear and revere him. When the hurricanes blew, they knew they had displeased Juracán."

"Then someone must've pissed him off today."

In the distance we could see a few straw huts. Cone roofs, small doorways. She led me toward what looked like an office building, and we soon passed a hut. She seemed to see something and ran toward it.

The way she gasped—I could tell something was wrong. Then I saw it. A man lay on his back on the ground. His face was stuck in a grin of pain. A line of blood led from a small hole in the man's bright, white guayabera to a black-red pool.

"It's Dr. Arroyo," she said. "He was supposed to give me the certificate."

I was about to bend down to enter the hut when I heard something moving in the grass behind the body. I turned. Somebody hit me.

* * *

I was kissing dirt. I heard talking, but it wasn't English. Some of the words were like Spanish. It was a strange, rhythmic dialect. Like a drumbeat almost.

I tried to move. My hands were tied. I glanced up and saw the flat-headed man from the wedding coming toward me with a big stick. It looked like a giant pilón. In his other hand something was cupped. The man put the hand on my face, covering my nose and mouth. He said something in that strange language. There was a rotten-smelling powder in the man's hand. I tried to shake loose but I couldn't help inhaling the powder. I opened my mouth to breathe and more went in. It hit me like another smack to the back of my head. I began to vomit, all the eggs, plátanos, mango slices, and buttered bread. He came at me with a knife in his hands and cut the rope around my wrists. I tried to move, but my body didn't listen.

I lay there for a thousand years. The sky got brighter and brighter, then dimmed like a flame going out. At the edge of my face tiny insects crawled up and onto my eyes and under my eyelids. I heard the sound of coquís, first low and quiet, then it grew and grew until I thought my eardrums would bleed. I saw a dark beach, black water, black sky. The waves jumped onto the shore like the claws of a giant animal, tearing at the sand, reaching for me. There was a sound like a gunshot, and I tried to shut my eyes, and then I thought I was crying. I looked up and saw a dog licking my face. Small, hairless. It moved its mouth like it was barking but no sound came out. My face felt so wet I thought the dog was drooling all over me, then I realized it was raining.

There was no dog. I was on the ground outside of the hut. My head throbbed.

Soon I heard sirens.

I tried to get up and quickly realized there was a gun in my hand. I saw the body, still lying there. Poor bastard, but there was nothing I could do.

"Fuck," I said.

The dark sky was circling, moving fast. Set up. The gun in my hand—it was a setup.

"Fuck," I said.

I pushed myself up, felt nauseous.

I stood, threw the gun away, then I said, "Stupid. Stupid." I went to pick it up again, fell down, got up again, began running.

I saw the batey courts and tried to remember where we had come in. I fell. I heard the sirens approaching. I got up and ran toward where I thought we had come through the trees.

I pushed back through the trees, saw the big space in the fence, tripped, got up, got to my car. I opened the door, sat down, wiped the powder off my face, checked the back of my head. There was a little blood.

I went to start the car. "Keys," I said. Itaba had the keys. "Fucking fuck fuck fuck."

I grabbed my duffel bag and wobbled away from the car. How far was I from San Juan? Blackjack, I thought. Julie. Blackjack. The cops. I had to get out of there.

I walked five feet, got down on my knees, and felt the hard, wet, cold road, considered laying down, considered throwing up again. Then a vehicle stopped in front of me.

There was a big canoe on the back of the guy's truck. He was an old man, with white, kinky hair, and his skin was as dark as an overripe banana.

"Necesita ayuda?" the man asked.

"I need to go to San Juan," I said. My voice sounded thick, garbled.

"Venga. Entre."

I got in the truck. I thought I looked normal but I was worried that I looked slow, drunk. The man asked if I was okay.

"I need to get to San Juan."

In a thick accent, the man said, "You look bad. You better see a doctor."

"I'll be all right."

There was a big crucifix hanging from the rearview mirror. The radio played old tunes, singers picking at a cuatro. The saddest music ever, the kind of music to slice your wrists to. One song after another.

We drove on, and I concentrated on the blacktop and the highway signs, mile after mile. I saw two more dead dogs, ripped open, lying there like pieces of meat on the road. I had the kind of aching hangover that makes you want to split your own head open and take your brain out to rinse it in cold, clear water. My mouth didn't feel like it belonged to me. My head was numb, throbbed.

All of sudden I said, "You ever heard of the Taino Indians? The Tainos?"

"Sí, los Tainos. A long time ago. In school," the man replied.

"You think you have Taino blood? You think you're a Taino?"

The man laughed, kept his eyes on the road. "My abuela was. At least she said so. Who knows? I respect the history. I respect where I come from. Pero soy lo que soy ahora, en este momento. Puertorriqueño, tu sabes? Boricua."

"Uh huh," I said, although I didn't understand. I felt like sleeping but somehow knew it was important not to.

Mile after mile of blacktop went by. The sky grew darker. Rain started to pelt the windshield.

"My name is Papo," I offered.

"Ángel Luis," the man said and stuck out his hand. We shook and he kept on driving.

When he dropped me off at my hotel on the Condado tourist strip, Ángel Luis warned me about the hurricane. "Storm is coming," he said. "Dios te bendiga."

I waddled with my duffel bag toward the hotel. I was tired all the way to my balls. I was just about to walk in when I saw these two men through the glass doors. Talking to the front desk lady. Plainclothes cops look the same wherever you go. Bad suits, lots of attitude. There was no way they could be after me already. I mean, they could trace me through the rental car, but not that fast.

Still.

I turned around and walked a couple blocks to a cash machine, got out my last five hundred, then headed to a little hotel outside of the Condado.

It was a small room with smelly blankets. One chair, one desk, an AC that rattled. I pulled the blanket off the bed, folded it neatly. Then I sat down, opened my flask, took a shot. It hit my stomach like a bull—I ran to the bathroom to puke. I got some soda, mixed it with another shot. It stayed down, but not for long.

I laid on the bed and stared up at the ceiling. Mosquitoes had arrived from somewhere and were biting me.

Back at the other hotel, there were six dozen roses in vases waiting. A box of candy. Champagne. I had called ahead to prepare everything for my night with Julie. All on credit.

Then I remembered to check my cell phone.

There were two messages, both from Julie. "Papo, where the hell are you? Call!" The second: "I don't know, Papo. The flights are all being delayed. This must be a sign. I don't think I can do this. He's your best friend and it's not right for you to do this either. Goodbye, Papo."

"Fuck," I said.

I turned facedown on the bed and thought of Julie's fine perfect-handful breasts and her pale freckled skin and I woke up twenty hours later.

It was dark outside, and rain hit against the sliding door of the balcony. I took a hot shower, did my hair and beard, put on a jacket, put on cologne. I smoked at the table. The curtains were pulled back and I watched the rain beat at the glass, a million tiny liquid bullets trying to get in.

I had the gun on the table. I knew I should ditch it but it made me feel safer to keep it. I thought about finding Itaba and the man with the flat head. But San Juan was a big town.

Hell, I was here to have fun, to do some gambling. I would cope with whatever hand I was dealt. Why not live it up until the cops found me?

I headed for the casino at the Caribe Hilton—the rain moved in thick, slow strokes across the streets, palm trees were flopping about like they were dancing the salsa—and went inside and warmed up with the slot machines. I ordered a Jack and Coke, but only sipped at it. After $200, I went to the blackjack table. I played without caring, losing deal after deal. This gay couple laughed and joked with the dealer, and I felt like a fourth wheel.

"Lady Luck is not with me tonight," I said to no one but myself.

I turned to order water and that's when I saw her. Straight

back, head held high, firm ass in a tight red dress, Itaba walked past the slot machines. Gift bag in hand.

"Lady Luck." I cashed out and followed her.

Itaba was in a ground-floor suite outside, past the pool. There was tape on all the windows, for the hurricane. When she opened the door, I moved. I pushed her into the room, pulled out my gun, and aimed it at her.

"Bruto," she said.

She was on the floor and her wet skirt was up around her waist. Her thighs were smooth, copper.

"Don't even think about it," she said.

"I wasn't," I replied, and then she kicked me hard in the shin. "Fuck," I said.

"I know men."

I smirked at her. "Sure you do. You led me to that park and left me to hang out for the cops."

"That was not my idea."

"The guy with the weird head?"

"Yes. Kaonabo. It was his idea."

"Ka-nabo?"

"He's my husband."

"No shit," I said and went to close the blinds and the curtains on the windows. I kept my eye and the gun on her the whole time. "So what's up with his forehead anyway?"

"The Tainos believed that a flat forehead was a sign of beauty. Taino mothers carried their babies on their back on a board secured to the baby's forehead to make it that way. His real name is Pedro. He is very serious about the Neo-Taino cause."

"Shit yeah."

"Oye me. I wanted you along, negrito, because I knew he

would do something like this. Like I said, he's very serious."

"You were looking for a bodyguard, then, not a patsy? I don't know about that."

"You have to believe me." She kicked off her shoes, lay back on the couch, her body open. Her wet hair covered part of her face. She looked delicious. "I wanted protection. Your cousin used to talk about you all the time. A big man. She told me you do karate."

"Aikido. I used to." Suddenly I felt like I needed a drink. But there was still a knot in the bottom of my stomach.

"She had your picture in her room. You had a kind face, a vulnerable face. I liked it."

I was standing above her. Water dropped from my hair onto her thighs.

"What was that stuff your husband made me inhale?"

"Cohoba. A hallucinogenic."

"I've had worse. I saw a dog that couldn't bark."

"The Tainos had mute dogs," she said.

"Nice." I didn't want to tell her that the dog saved my life.

I could smell her scent, musky and earthy. Her dark, wet clothes clung to her body like a glistening second skin.

"What happened to your lady friend?"

"Her flight was delayed. Where's your husband?"

"He went to meet the buyer."

I was on my knees, the gun still in my right hand. Then I put my palms on her calves and began to move them up her legs, pulling her dress back and dragging the gun across the copper of her thighs. Goose bumps rose all up and down her skin.

"What are you doing, negrito?"

"Nothing," I said, standing up. I leaned way down, looking

right into her eyes. I kissed her. She let me. But her lips didn't respond. I tried again. She stared at me.

"Are you done?" she said.

"Looks like I am."

"Your cousin also told me you were a mujeriego—a womanizer."

"I know what it means. Wait till I see Carmen again."

I was half hanging off the couch. I should've seen it coming.

Itaba kneed me hard in the balls and yanked the gun easily out of my hand. I curled up and she kicked me off to the side. I smacked the coffee table with my head and hit the floor.

I wasn't hurt. Coco duro. I just looked at the ceiling and sighed. Stupid. Stupid. Stupid.

She sat up on the couch and didn't even bother pointing the gun at me. "Oyeme, negrito. Kaonabo is coming, and he's dangerous."

"Looks like you can take care of yourself fine."

"He doesn't just want to sell the cemi to buy land. He wants to become a drug king."

I got up on my elbows. "What?"

"He thinks we can get more land and more power if we buy and sell drugs."

"He's right. You'd have money coming in all the time. I—"

"It disgusts me," she said, getting up. "I knew he was coming to Ponce to try to get the cemi from me. I knew he would do something stupid. But I didn't know he would kill Dr. Arroyo."

"Why did he?"

"To start his drug business without witnesses."

Outside the wind and rain had picked up and smacked against the windows. The taped glass was throbbing like it wanted to bust.

"I need your help. I want your help." She waved the gun like it was no more than a hairbrush. "It's Pedro."

"So you want to stop him?"

"He is a very violent man. I may have to use this."

"I believe you could," I said.

We listened to the growing storm for what seemed like an hour. It had begun a slow conga rhythm against the windows, against the walls. I was itchy for a drink. I was so used to having a drink in my hand it was strange not to have one. Itaba just sat there and stared at me. She kept the gun near her the whole time.

When the man with the flat forehead opened the door, he was drenched from the storm. He did not look happy to see me. In fact, it looked like he wanted to rip my heart out of my chest and eat it.

"Hola, Pedro," I said. "How's it going?"

He stood there, saying nothing. He had his dark shades on. Behind him was a short white man, late fifties, I'd guess. Bald head, yellow-white beard soaked with rain. He looked even more shocked. Probably didn't expect a party. He had a satchel in one hand.

The conga rhythm of the storm seemed to suddenly pick up in intensity.

"This must be the buyer?" I said.

The flat-headed man said something to Itaba in that strange language. His voice was deep and came out like a growl. She spoke back to him and he seemed to calm down.

Itaba walked up to the white guy and they shook hands. "Mr. Hubbard," she said. "Welcome to Puerto Rico."

"Thank you," Hubbard replied. "I look forward to seeing the amazing cemi you've told me about."

He kept his eyes on me. I glanced at the couch. The gun wasn't there.

"This is an associate of mine," Itaba explained. "Don't worry about him." From where I stood I could see she had the weapon tucked into the back of her belt. She turned and said to me, "Please hand me the cemi, Papo."

I could feel that rhythm, that storm, beating in my own head. I picked up the gift bag from where it sat on the couch. I was tired of being at the sucky end of all this. I handed her the bag and in the same motion I grabbed the gun.

"Get back," I said.

The buyer yelped. Like a puppy. Pedro muttered something in Spanish, fast. I didn't get all of it, but I think he called me a stupid, fat American. Itaba stared at me. Wondering what I was going to do next. I had no idea.

"Give me that satchel," I told the buyer. "You guys can divide up your rock. All I want is the cash."

The buyer stood still, hesitating.

Pedro spoke again before the buyer could move. This time in English, with a heavy accent. It sounded like it hurt him to say each word: "You fool. Destroyer of the Earth. You have no regard."

"At least I try to recycle. I'm reusing this gun, for example."

The storm continued to bang against the windows and in my head with that conga rhythm, hard and fast. And loud.

"The Tainos are a good, noble people!" Kaonabo yelled above the noise. "You are not noble."

"And you call stealing and killing and selling drugs good and noble?" I shouted back. "You're living in the past, my man. I know from experience that gets you nowhere."

"What's this about?" the buyer said.

Kaonabo turned to Itaba. "Puta! Mentirosa!"

"Hey!" I snapped. I scratched my head. "Listen up. If things were different, I could help you. I know about this sort of thing. You could probably use my help."

Kaonabo cursed me more in Spanish.

Itaba came to my side. "Negrito, he won't listen. You have to stop him."

"Wait a second."

She took another step toward me, and I turned to point the gun at her. There was something in the look of her eyes that was hitting me wrong. I never said I was smart, but she seemed a little too excited to get rid of her husband.

The flat-headed man took a step forward. The buyer took a step back.

Then there was a knock on the door.

It was a man from the hotel. Through the door he said, in Spanish, something like, "We would like you to move to the main part of the hotel. For safety. The hurricane is here."

"Itaba, get that," I said. I turned to face her and, in that instant, Kaonabo picked a glass from the table and threw it at me. It smashed against my skull and I dropped the gun. I was reeling.

He grabbed Itaba, pulled the door open, and ran out. The buyer ran too, in the other direction. I got the gun, wobbled on my feet, and moved to the doorway. The confused hotel man looked at me. It was wild outside. The rain came down in black sheets and the wind howled like a baby giant dying for attention. I could barely see more than a few feet in from of me. I ran after Itaba.

I saw a flash of color ahead—Itaba's skirt—headed down the path toward the beach.

I followed through the throbbing storm, onto the sand.

"Stop, you son of a bitch!" I yelled into the wind, then remembered I had the gun. I shot into the air. The pop barely registered in the storm.

But Kaonabo let go of Itaba and turned. "Nuyoriqueño!" he shouted.

Just then the giant got nasty, smacking us down with a huge slap of wind.

Kaonabo was on me, elbowing my head and kneeing the gun out of my hand. I tried to get up, but the wind kept me off balance.

I really should've gone after the guy with the satchel. Stupid.

Kaonabo head-butted me in the stomach and, as I bent over, in the chin.

I fell back on the sand. The wild surf curled in large, foamy waves onto the shore, only a few feet away. The sky over the sea was dark, but there was something black and gigantic on the horizon, moving closer.

I reached for Kaonabo, but he ducked and kicked me twice in the ribs. His sandals were not soft. I went down, spitting up, almost vomiting. We wrestled, moving closer to the waves, getting wet. Kaonabo was about to hit me again, when I moved, then used his momentum to throw him to the ground. He came at me, I turned on my left foot, and dropped him down again. He got right back up, came in low. I smacked my flat palm into his nose, hard, and Kaonabo fell back. I went to stomp him, but he kicked my feet out from under me. I fell on the cold, wet sand—it was like hitting concrete. I felt the ocean spraying on my back.

Kaonabo got my head and neck in a choke hold. "Hijo de la gran puta," he said.

Then there was a shot. In a haze, I turned, looked up, and

saw a small hole in Kaonabo's flat forehead. He fell back onto the dark sand.

Itaba stood there with the gun. The gift bag lay on the wet sand between us, closer to me. She ran toward it, and I leaped like a frog across the beach. Our fingers closed on the bag at the same time. I yanked and she fell on the sand.

She sat up quickly and pointed the gun at me.

"Itaba. Wait," I pleaded, standing, the bag in my hand.

"Lo siento, negrito. But I need this," she said and fired. The bullet whizzed past my face. I fell back; a wave clawed at me and pulled me under.

I don't believe in magic. I pray at night but don't expect any answers. I do it just in case—like making a side bet.

I went deep. I swallowed water. There was darkness and cold and then maybe even small glowing lights. I could've imagined that. But somehow I survived. Clutching the plastic bag with the stone cemi inside. I can't explain it. If I had to give an answer, I'd say it was just dumb luck.

This time there was barking. When I lifted my face from the sand, there was a small, hairy dog yelping at me, stepping forward, moving back, stepping forward. Sand in its fur. I glanced up and saw dull sunshine. All around me—seaweed, dark wood, things tossed out by the ocean, just like me.

I turned my head to one side and saw Kaonabo's body on the drying sand. Moving toward us were police and paramedics. A gurney. Some tourists.

It began to make sense. I think Kaonabo wasn't the one who wanted to start a drug empire. It was Itaba. She'd wanted Kaonabo out of the way, maybe because he didn't approve, maybe to keep the money for herself. He could've killed the doctor for her. But my money was on her—she'd had plenty of time to do it then come back and pick me up to be her patsy.

Now all she had was her gift bag with the little coquí on it. Bienvenidos a La Isla del Encanto.

I thought about what was going to happen to me. I didn't know.

I thought about what was going to happen to the dog. It kept licking me. It was still there. It existed. It looked like a stray. "It's my dog," I told the first policeman who bent down to see if I was alive. "Mi perrrro."

He must've thought I was crazy. I was glad to be alive. But my hair must've been a mess.

PART III

WEST

PART III

JANEJOHNDOE.COM

BY DAVID COLE

Tucson, Arizona

I'm watching Ronald Jumps the Train speed-shop through Safeway. He crams his cart with frozen pizzas and Hungry-Man dinners, corn chips, Cheetos, potato chips, a case of Negra Modelo, two sixes of Classic Coke, and another two sixes of Mountain Dew—all the quick-to-cook, quickly eaten, and sweetish crap that crystal meth tweakers often devour.

"Ma'am? Can I help you, ma'am?"

"No." An eager Safeway employee. Do I look that much like a geezer?

I've been tracking Ronald for five days, ever since dark rumors swirled up from Sonora about a drug cartel takedown war against La Bruja de los Cielos, the rarely seen head of the methamphetamine cartel in northern Sonora. The war brought assassinations by the dozens. La Bruja, herself a vicious stone killer, was believed to have planned last week's assassination of Sonora's state chief of police at a Nogales hotel, AK-47s and grenades pouring down from an upstairs window just as the chief entered the place. Federal pressure got intense. La Bruja's world collapsed, her smuggling routes hijacked, her truckloads of drugs no longer safe because bribed U.S. Customs guards were arrested, and nothing made easier by increased U.S. Border Patrol arrests running parallel to the fence along the P-28 Tucson section. The border was sealed, the border was chaos, the border was dangerous. All of these

things shredded the previous maps and players in organiza-
tional drug trafficking from the border north through Tucson
and Phoenix. Nobody knew anyone they could trust. Including me.

I do intel surveillance of meth dealers on Indian reservations; I'm a private investigator working for the Navajo Tribal
Police. Despite the chaos in Mexico, nothing much had happened for me until I tagged Ronald in the Safeway around 10
in the morning.

I knew the drug cartel world was in turmoil, but I'm just a
small player. I track Navajo meth dealers off the rez, but nobody else. An hour ago, I'm thinking it's mainly another beautiful, quiet Tucson morning. Kids in school, parents working,
geezers shopping. Now, watching Ronald cram his cart full,
I'm realizing that he's stocking up to lay low, to take a forced
vacation from dealing crystal meth up on the Gila River rez
and east toward Casa Grande.

But why?

Ronald's a shrimpy guy, half Apache, half Mexican, an
old-time tweaker born on the Ute reservation in Colorado.
He runs across the front of the store, kinda dancing behind
the cart, he *so* wants to get *outta* there quick. So, *why?* He
can't possibly know I'm tracking him.

I watch from the back aisle of the large Safeway, my hands
on a shopping cart loaded with I-don't-care-off-the-shelf-
whatever, as I pretend to browse while following him. I whip
past the meat cases to see him in the produce section, piling
on boxes of all kinds of berries and even a huge sack of raw
carrots—lots of sugar in carrots, tweakers love sugar—when a
man moves quickly behind Ronald, bellies up to Ronald's back
like a lover, one hand in his Arizona Wildcats lightweight nylon rain jacket. Ronald's shoulders slump, he sags against the

cart but nods resignedly. The two men walk slowly, almost a sex dance, the man urging Ronald out the entrance. I'm dashing with my cart up the produce aisle to follow them, except two *other* guys surround me.

"Don't be a chili pepper."

Behind me to the left, a rough whisper, like a rasp across soft white pine. One hand squeezes the back of my neck, the other extends to pry my fingers off the Safeway cart. Hands in leather golf or driving gloves, wearing a tee, his arms rife with intricate tattoos, not prison ballpoint-pen black but professional, multicolored inks swirling around the name *Dial*. I can see that the tat artist who did the full sleeves on both arms used thicker ink; the word *Dial* covers an ancient tat reading *Diablo*.

I half duck, trying to turn away, but a smaller man on my right wedges his body against me, so I pull the cart toward us, taking tension momentarily off Dial's fingers, and then shove the cart toward the organic apples, peaches, and pears, an elderly couple recoiling as it punches into a free-standing display, the man's face puckering with indignation then quickly dropping a plastic bag of tomatoes, shrinking away from Dial's tats and his cold stare. The tomatoes roll across the floor but nobody pays them any attention.

"She might have a gun," the smaller man says, his voice strangely familiar, "tucked down in her back."

"Forget the gun," Dial responds. "Is this her?"

"Yes."

I'm trying to see their faces, but Dial puts a martial arts grip on my upper left shoulder, pinches a nerve. I recoil, gasp, my left arm flops around, I'm staggering from the pain but they hold me upright and, like a two-person team carrying a bashed-up athlete off the playing field, they frog-march me out the wide Safeway entrance. Dial's hand shifts from my neck to under my arm and across my left breast, almost lifting and carrying me along. Sweat pops everywhere from underneath my headband, running down my face. My body flowers with sweat that fountains between my breasts and underneath the sports bra. I'm sweating from panic but also the rapid transition from Safeway's aircon into the muggy April ninety-degree Tucson midmorning air.

The parking lot is jammed, but nobody really notices us. I decide to shout for help but Dial squeezes my throat. I can barely breath. I can't see an out, so I relax my muscles, trying to flex my fingers, get strength back. The other man's hand slides under my tee and against my bare back, moving down inside my waistband.

"You still tuck that pistola back there," the second man says.

I recognize the voice.

"Rey?" I say. "*Rey?*" Disbelief.

"When you went running, you carried it back there."

He palms my Beretta from the small of my back where I carry it in an unbelted nylon rig. Dial fumbles in my handbag, grabs my keys.

"*Rey Villaneuva?*"

"Yeah," he says quietly.

"Is that really *you?*"

Rey Villaneuva. Once my PI partner. Once my lover. I haven't seen him in, in, I have to think, it's been . . . what . . . five years? Seven? I cut a glance at his worried still-handsome face half hidden by that familiar shock of unruly black hair, which glistens with water as though he'd stuck his head under a faucet and run his fingers through it instead of a comb. He's wearing brown khakis, the kind he once creased daily with his own iron, but now looking like he's worn them for weeks without washing. The direct sunlight catches flecks of gray in his hair and his week-old whiskers.

"What do you want from me?"

"To create a legend," he says.

They hustle me to a silver Escalade with tinted windows, parked next to my Subaru Baja. Ronald Jumps the Train sits behind my steering wheel, the other man in the passenger seat. Dial swings me hard against the Escalade; Rey's shoulders slump, he won't meet my eyes.

"Rey," I say. "What are you doing here?"

"Working, working," he answers finally. "Just working." He still can't look up at me, he cuts his eyes left and right repeatedly. Dial tosses my car keys to the guy in my Subaru's passenger seat. Dial pulls out a Glock fitted with a laser sight. He pops a switch, the red laser dances across his palm, across my face.

"You know what this is?" I nod. "Right now, there's another on your daughter."

"Ex*cuse* me?"

"She's vacationing up in Sedona. With your granddaughter."

I nod again, mute. He gently strokes a thumb down my nose.

"You're a PI?"

"Yes. Yeah, yes. Why?"

"You work for the Navajo Tribal Police? The drug unit?"

"Why are you, why, why are you doing this?"

Dial nods at Rey, like, *Your turn here.*

"Laura," Rey says. "Do you still find people? Create legends? New ID, everything?"

"My daughter? How is she involved in this? My *grand*daughter?"

"What he's really asking," Dial says, "do you still make up really good ID?"

"Yes, but—"

"ID can pass any test? Even if it's fake?"

"Yes, yeah, but listen, listen, just . . . *listen* to me. If you've kidnapped my daughter—"

"Don't fuck with me," Dial says, but quiet, he's really confident of himself. "Don't you fucking *think* you can fuck with me."

"Rey, Rey, Jesus, Rey, what are you guys telling me?"

"You help us, nobody gets hurt."

"Help you do *what*?"

"We need you to create a legend," he says.

"I won't."

"I told you. I said, don't you fuck with me." Dial pulls my Beretta out of Rey's hand. "You want to see what happens, you fuck with me?" Turning toward the two men in my Subaru, the passenger's face in shadows. Ronald Jumps the Train looks at me, he's so terrified I can smell fresh urine. "Tell me again. You're a private investigator?"

"Yes. Yes, yes, *yes*."

"Lady?" Ronald whimpers. "Lady, can you get me out of this?" But I have little sympathy for him. Ronald Jumps the Train got his name at the age of eleven when he rode boxcars pulling into Flagstaff, throwing marijuana bales out the open door. Now he deals crystal meth, the major supplier for Gila River and Casa Grande, so I try not to feel any sympathy at all. But Jesus, a sudden *pop-pop*, a double tap as Dial shoots Ronald dead, then *pop*, one more guarantee shot through his forehead before he turns the Glock at the passenger who is already starting to open his door.

"Me jodí!" the passenger shouts before Dial pops him too.

I'm screwed.

Dial tosses my Beretta onto Ronald's lap. What's really *really* scary about Dial is that he's totally cool about just having murdered two men, and in that moment I believe him about my daughter. He shoves me into the passenger seat of the Escalade, sits behind me.

"Seat belt," he says. "We're going where it's quiet, you either say what we want or you don't. You don't got what we want, we kill you." He checks his watch. "Yes or no?"

"Yes," I say.

Rey drives. Nobody talks. We take Ina to I-10 and head south until Rey exits onto I-19. Soon I see my past rising in front of me. Mission San Xavier del Bac, a gorgeous white mission, the white dove of the desert. Mission San Xavier del Bac, where Rey and I were once responsible for killing and burning a teenager.

Five years ago.

Or seven, I don't want to think about it.

Rey slows at the edge of the mission parking lot, a barren, uneven and unpaved stretch of ground, just a few hundred yards from the Tohono O'odham Tribal Police center. We swing past the W:ak shopping center, the People of the River, the gates open but nobody in sight. The Escalade bumps past some of the concrete block houses, moves briefly along a dirt road with, amazingly, a sign. *Gok Kawulk Wog*. Tohono O'odham words. No sense to me.

Dial's cell rings. He motions Rey to stop next to an ancient saguaro cactus with seven arms and two huge holes up where somebody'd shotgunned it in the main stem. Dial listens, murmurs a word, flips the cell closed, and holds up a hand at Rey.

Engine running, aircon set at meat locker, we sit there for two hours or so, gas gauge near empty. Dial occasionally leans forward between the seats, studying my face. The full tats on his arms are layered three deep, the most faded seem to be 81st Airborne tats from Nam. On the left arm, *Killing Is Our Business*, on the right arm, *Business Is Good*.

A family of Gambel's quail bustles across the road, Dad in front, Mom behind, both sandwiching a dozen new chicks the size of fluffy walnuts, urging them from a creosote bush to shelter under a clump of teddy bear cholla. Dial lasers the chicks one at a time, smacking his lips in a silent *pow*, and then he centers the red dot on my left eye. His cell rings again. He listens, nods at my computer bag.

"Is that enough equipment?" he says to me as Rey checks out the bag.

"The laptop and the satellite phone," I say. "Yes, maybe. I can try. But not until you guarantee my daughter's safety. And my granddaughter. Why are you doing this, Rey?"

"I work for Verónica Luna de los Angeles Talancón," Rey answers quickly; he wants to get her name out there and over with.

"Verónica Talancón? The drug cartel woman?"

Dial slaps the back of my head. "Show some respect. Respect for La Bruja de los Cielos."

"Rey? You work for Sonora's biggest drug cartel?" My jaw slack, mouth open.

"Listen."

"The drug lord? You work for her cartel?"

"Yeah," sighing, shrugging, "*yeah*, okay? Jesus, will you just listen to me?"

"La Bruja de los Cielos? The Witch of the Skies?" Dial slaps my head again; Rey turns away, nodding, his chin so low it bumps his chest. "You're threatening my family because of a vicious woman who runs a drug cartel?"

"Listen," he says. "I mean, just listen to this, okay? I mean, I'm just a go-between. Just a connection, a fixer. Just trying to stay alive here."

"You're wasting time," Dial says. "You're useless. Let's go. Drive."

"Wait, wait a minute. What do you want?" I ask again. "And where are you taking me?"

"What Talancón wants, what she *needs*, Laura," Rey says quietly, but looking me right in the eyes, "what Talancón needs is a brand-new, best-quality, never-fail, platinum-grade U.S. identity. What you call, in your business, you call it creating a legend."

"I don't do that anymore. I'm legitimate. I do computer forensics on corporation databases. I'm completely, totally legal. Rey. Listen to me. This is a bad idea."

"This is *way* past a bad idea," Rey says.

"You're not listening to *me*." Dial flips open his cell, a finger on the keypad. "I've got five minutes left to call Sedona. I don't call, a sicario pops your daughter."

"*Jesus Christ*, Rey. You're just making this up." I talk directly to Rey, I won't acknowledge that Dial is in charge. He doesn't care what I acknowledge or think or whatever, he just dials, listens, puts the cell on speaker-phone. "Five minutes my ass. This is a bluff."

"Eating dinner at L'Auberge de Sedona," a voice says. "Down by the creek. Kid's in a high chair, wearing a pink jumpsuit, Mommy's in a yellow tank top. Nice tits."

"Okay, okay," I say into the cell. It's not a bluff. Panic, trying to sound calm, hoping I project willingness to go along instead of terror at the situation, and in the back of my mind, nothing forming, but back there, trying to figure a plan to get out of this alive. "Okay, I'll do it. Don't—"

Dial flips the cell closed, motions to Rey who just nods and shifts into drive.

"Where are we going?"

"Talancón is hiding in Sahuarita. She got across the border, but no time for plastic surgery, so she's got to fly out of Tucson quick, like, tomorrow. She can't do that without a whole new identity. And you're the expert."

"Just to find the right connections will take days. A week, maybe more."

"Talancón figures she's got eight, maybe ten hours to arrange a safe out."

"Impossible. *Ugh.*" Dial slaps the back of my head. He knows the sweet spots back there, three times he's whacked the same place and it's starting to vibrate with pain.

"I'm nothing here, Laura," Rey says. "Don't you see that? If you do this, Talancón will pay whatever you ask."

"Don't shit me, Rey. You've already threatened my daughter, my granddaughter. If I give this woman, this Talancón, if I give her a new identity, she'll kill me. She'll kill you, she'll kill anybody in her way just like those two back there."

"Yeah. Well. I don't bring you to Talancón right now, Mr. Dial here will pop me and you, no hesitation. That's your choice. Come with us or die." The sunset lights up his face, his color bleaching to white, corners of his mouth sagging. "Yes or no?"

Dial slaps my head again.

"Yes," I say finally. "Yes. I'll do it."

Sahuarita, Arizona. Just south of Indian reservation lands. Bustling with new houses going up, their framed skeletons crowded with carpenters, plumbers, electricians, everybody trying to get rich.

Rey winds along a narrow street, twisting through smaller roads until we stop at the dead end of Calle Zapata at the edge of a pecan orchard. A Ford crew-cab pickup faces out to the street and a woman sits at a battered redwood picnic table behind the gated front wall, a vivid view of the Santa Rita mountains behind her. Dial grips my upper arms, marches me in front of him toward the table.

Verónica Talancón bites carefully into a Sonoran hot dog, sipping occasionally from a bottle of Diet Sprite. A slim, tiny woman, barely taller than five feet. Gorgeous, beautiful, stunning, the Witch of the Skies.

"Miss Winslow," a quiet voice, calm, measured, steady. She wipes bits of chili from her chin. "Thank you for coming."

"You threatened my family. Did you really expect I'd *not* come?"

"Look at this," she says, gesturing at what's left of her food. "The all-American hot dog, made in Mexico, wrapped in bacon, stuffed inside a fresh bun and loaded up with tomato and onion chunks, grilled onions, mustard and mayo and a jalapeño sauce with a guerito pepper. Two nights ago, I had lobster flown in from Maine on my private jet. Tonight," gesturing at the cracked adobe house and yard full of weeds, "this is my whole kingdom."

"You threatened my family," I say again.

"Look. You're alive. Usually, when somebody's threatening me, beating on me with a hammer, I'm not going to duck. I'll grab a machete, whack off his arms and some other parts. So. You know what I want. Fix it for me, your family will live."

"I'm not threatening you in any way. Don't bullshit me about why I'm here."

188 // INDIAN COUNTRY NOIR

"Reymundo," she says, "am I not a woman of honor?"

"You'd have a sicario tell me about honor?" I say.

"Reymundo's a lover, not a shooter."

Rey nods without hesitation.

"He has no honor working for you," I say.

"Then let's get to business. You know what I want."

"No, no," I say. "You know what *I* want."

"You want to live," she laughs. "That's entirely what this is about. We *all* want to live. I control you and your family; you control my future. I will trade one for the other. And money. Do you have enough of the proper equipment to find me a, how do you say it, a legend?"

I just shake my head, work at controlling my panic, searching for an edge. She sips the Diet Sprite, muscles flexing in her temples, a tectonic shift in her calculations as she nods. "You want a drink? Beer? Water? Tequila?"

"No. Just stop threatening my family."

"How about some Ritalin?" she says and I freeze. She reaches under her chair, grabs a plastic folder, sets it on the table without opening it. "I know all about you, Miss Winslow."

"I haven't used Ritalin in years," I say angrily.

"Fascinating." She opens the folder and flips through a few pages. "You didn't use, you abused. I wholesale thousands of pounds of methamphetamines. You once took methamphetamines. So in a way, we're not all that different."

I'm really furious now, the fury conquering my panic. "And your crystal meth has ruined a thousand lives. Ten thousand lives. You can't threaten me. And if you threaten my family, I won't help you in any way."

"Okay," she says. "Let's try something else. Your Hopi name is Kauwanyauma. Butterfly Revealing Wings of Beauty. See? We've both got grand names. I'm La Bruja. The Witch. You're a butterfly, with an arrest record and a drug-user record. Rey's told me everything about you." She finishes the Diet Sprite, opens another bottle, studies me carefully. "Okay." Nods. "You don't really get threatened, do you?" When I say nothing she turns to Dial. "Diablo, call Jesús." Dial flicks open his cell, speed-dials a number, holds the phone aside after hearing a voice. "Tell Jesús to return."

"Whoa, whoa," I say. "Why would I believe you?"

"I offer proof of life," she replies, holding up a small GPS unit. "Tell that man to leave his cell on, and give me his number." Talancón nods at Dial, who flips open the cell to display the last number dialed. She punches it into the GPS, waits until the map screen shows Sedona. "His cell has GPS on it. He's headed toward I-10 and Phoenix."

"Why should I believe you?"

"Don't listen to this puta," Dial says, but Talancón flicks her palm, shakes her head.

Twenty-five minutes later, the GPS shows the cell location—out of red rock country and headed south toward Phoenix.

"Now. I've guaranteed your daughter's life," Talancón says. She shrugs off her wristwatch, presses a button on the side, and lays it on the picnic table in front of me. "A Rolex Cosmograph Daytona. Diamonds, rubies, gold, twelve thousand dollars, I could care less. Right now, it's just a stopwatch. Look at the numbers. Nine hours, fifty-eight minutes. That's how much time you've got. I've arranged an out in Chicago, but I've got to get there first. So in nine hours, we'll be headed for the Tucson airport for the early flight. You've got that long to set up a whole new identity."

"Impossible."

"Driver's license. Social Security card. Let's say four credit cards, whatever else you can provide."

"Impossible," I insist. "Not for a totally clean package." She points at the chronometer dial, the seconds shrinking back toward zero. "We're talking about special paper, special inks. Official seals, photographs, and bottom line, a Social Security number that's absolutely guaranteed to be genuine."

"You've got somebody who stores up these numbers, somebody who verifies they're clean."

"I don't think you really understand," I say. "I haven't arranged an entire identity kit in over a year."

"My personal motto of life," she counters. "If you don't ask for something, nobody says yes. I visit New York, the hottest Broadway show, I can get tickets anywhere in the house. Restaurants booked three months in advance. I can get a table. When they told me my son couldn't get into a prestigious high school, I threatened a lawsuit on the basis of discrimination against Latinos. He got in. Nothing is impossible. So I'm asking you again, can you do this for me?"

"No. Maybe. I don't know."

"Come with me," she says, turning sideways, a slight bow and nod into the house. "Let me show you something, Miss Winslow. Please. No harm, just come inside for a moment."

I walk ahead of her into an entranceway. She gestures down a hall to the door of the main bedroom.

"On the bed. Look."

Two bodies sprawl on pink and purple flowered sheets. A man and woman, bloodied, dead. One hand across my mouth, I freeze. Talancón spins me around, pushes me back outside.

"Okay," she says. "Without hesitation, if you won't do this, just as I killed them, I'll kill your entire family. In front of your eyes."

"You promised, you guaranteed their safety."

"I lie. Usually it works."

And there it is.

I have few bargaining chips. Nine hours, during which I can fake a process, hoping to convince Rey to get me out of this mess, or I can work what few contacts I still have, gambling that if I create a new identity Talancón will let me live.

"Okay," I say. I mean, what else am I going to say?

Except I suddenly realize I have an edge.

"I think I've got you figured," I say. She just waits, face set in stone, no flickers, no tells. "You're on the run. You've been forced out of controlling your cartel. That means you'll probably just go somewhere else, change your identity, use some connections, spend a lot of money, and start up again dealing drugs somewhere else. Thailand. Manila. Wherever."

"Agreed. Okay. Your point?"

"I figure you'll fly to Chicago, then jump around the country, or head outside the country to get plastic surgery. I'll get you a perfect new ID on one condition."

She cocks her head, her expression unchanged.

"Let me tell you a short story."

"Don't beg," she says. "We're well past that."

"Up on the Navajo rez," I say, "my husband's mother is from the Start of the Red Streak People. The Deeshchii'nii clan. His sister married a man from the Jaa'yaalóolii. The Sticking-Up-Ears People. They had two sons."

"Please," Talancón says. "I know where this is going."

"Both sons got totally bored with high school and turned to drugs. Both worked their way up the drug ladder to making crystal meth. They blew themselves up in their lab one day."

"What's the point, okay?"

"If I fly with you to Chicago, I figure there's a good chance you'll just disappear and let me live. I'll take that chance if . . . what I want, what you'll have to do . . . if you'll give me a complete list of all the meth dealers on all Arizona Indian reservations."

She studies me for a long time. A long, long time. And then nods abruptly.

"Okay. You've got everything you need?"

"Just so you understand," I explain. "First, I've got to find an identity, find a legend. That's a name I can use without challenge by law enforcement databases. A name that's got a birth date near enough to yours, a somewhat facial resemblance."

"That's going to be altered here," she says. "Depending on what you tell me I've got to do. I'll dye my hair, cut it, stuff cotton wads into my cheeks and nose, whatever it takes so I look like whatever picture you provide. So find me a golden legend."

"Even after I find the legend, I'll have to locate somebody who'll work up the identity materials. That will take some hours. I might not be able to guarantee delivery."

"Then now is the best time to start." She stabs a finger at the watch. Not needing to say anything, the chronometer dial winding down.

"Even if I can create the legend, I can't get the documents to you down here."

"Not here," she says. "Tucson airport. And the credit cards have to be good enough to get me a ticket on any airline connecting to Chicago. And you'll have to use all your skills to make it look like the tickets were purchased weeks ago. That's it, okay?"

She dismisses me, moves inside the house. Dial sits on a rusted wrought-iron chair, pistol in his lap. Rey slumps in another chair, refusing to look at me. I have to test my chances, have to know if I have an edge. I go to him, kneel and put my hands on his face, turning his eyes to mine.

"Rey," I say. "How did you get into this dirty business?"

"Don't play me, Laura. No way can I help you."

Dial finishes a Sonoran hot dog, smacks his lips. When I look at him, he blows me a kiss. In that moment, I get busy. Open my carryall, take out my gear, boot up my laptop, turn on my ComSat phone, and get online.

"Lovitta," I say. I've dialed her private number. "Lovitta. Wake up."

Lovitta Kovich groans. "Laura?" Lovitta is a sergeant with the Tucson narcotics department, my inside source, my treasured coordinator of drug dealer information.

"Yes."

"Where are, what are you doing?" Groggy. "I've been working twenty hours. What?"

"Hello," I say carefully. "How are you? Have you arrived safely."

"Arrived . . . ah, oh yeah. Laura. Still sending pretty little pics?"

"To everyone I know in my postcard perfect world." The most basic of voice codes, an agreed-on exchange to indicate urgency.

"Where are you?"

"I can't tell you that."

"How can I help?"

"I need a legend."

"How quick?"

"Six hours."

"Impossible."

"Six hours," I repeat.

"What kind of documents?"

"Everything. SSN card. Driver's license. At least three

working credit cards, each with a purchase and payment legend. Medical records, if you can do that. Miscellaneous stuff. Safeway card, whatever."

"Passport?"

"No."

"Well, that saves time. Not impossible. But improbable."

"Who've you got?"

"Larry Marshall. Mary Emich. Alex Emerine. Mary can Photoshop the documents, Larry can coordinate sources for printing, he knows a nonprofit that will let him use a flatbed press and special inks. Alex can set up computer legends for bank accounts, credit, hospitals. She knows just where to hack into records, add a new identity. But. You've got to get a name. A legend is no good without the right name."

"I'll have that in an hour," I say. "You get them set up, wait for my call."

Disconnecting the cell, I sit in front of my laptop. Small, sudden nods of my head as I think through each step. I start typing.

"What are you doing?" Rey asks.

Opening a web browser, I call up a website, begin typing in physical and age characteristics. Rey watches over my shoulder as a series of photo images scrolls down the screen.

"Jane . . . JaneJohnDoe dot com?" he says. "What kind of website is that?"

"People who disappeared."

"What help is that?"

"I don't have time to buy a name. Usually that would take days. Weeks for something really specific. This is a national database of people who've disappeared—men, women, and children who've vanished from their jobs, their homes, their loved ones."

"I don't get it."

"We're looking for women who disappeared five to ten years ago. Once I get those compiled, I'll search the photos for a face that resembles Talancón. When I find that, I'll cross-check the name of the missing person with other databases to get a Social Security number. And then anything is possible."

"How many people are in here?"

"Lots. Probably three to five thousand. And that's just people who've disappeared. There are hundreds more who are dead but unidentified. Rey, stop asking me questions. Leave me alone."

"I just want to help."

"You have nothing to offer me. Not anymore. You," I say to Dial, "get your boss out here. I need to ask her something."

Talancón appears in the doorway, stripped to bra and panties, a bath towel over her shoulder, her hair already cut very short. Dial stands, pulls out his Glock as though there's been a prearranged signal.

"Kill me now," I say, "you get nothing."

"Are you afraid of Diablo?" Her smiling face caught in a sudden, cold light from the sun. I see she wears no makeup, small beads of sweat form on her upper lip, her pupils dilate, and then a flatness comes into her eyes. "Okay, there's nothing left. Diablo, give me your gun."

Dial hands over the Glock. Talancón thumbs back the slide, checking that a live round is chambered. She has an odd way of holding the Glock; her middle finger is on the trigger, and without hesitation she targets Dial.

"Pela las nalgas, puta," he says bitterly as she cranks a double-tap to his chest, striding quickly to stand over his twitching body to put another round directly into his forehead.

"Jesus Christ!" Rey gasps, hands out in front, thinking he's next.

"Not you, loverboy. You're intocable. Untouchable, so far. Anything else?" she says to me. I shake my head, ears ringing from the gunshots. Talancón tosses the weapon to Rey. "Drag him inside." She turns to me with a look and shrugs. "Vámanos, señora! Ahorita!"

Get busy. Now!

And I'm wondering what seed she sprang from, what made this bitter fruit.

Fifty minutes later I have a name, ten minutes after that I get the information I really want when I call Lovitta to get data from NCIC, the national crime database.

"Judith Dunnigan Fletcher," I shout at the house. Talancón comes to the doorway, pressing her hands up against the inside of the door sill and taking three long, deep breaths.

"Okay," she says. "You have a picture?"

I swivel my laptop so she can see the screen. She studies the photograph of a woman with short-cropped graying hair, an open-necked button-down shirt, and tortoise-shell glasses.

"Tell me about her."

"Judith Dunnigan Fletcher. Missing since July 3, 1997. Thirty-six years old then, makes her mid-forties now. Missing from Omaha, Nebraska. At time of disappearance, five-one, 105 pounds. White woman, but she looks a bit Latina. Graying hair, some brown left, brown eyes. No tattoos, no scars, no birthmarks. No nickname, not married at time of disappearance, no children, both parents deceased, no siblings. If seen, notify the Omaha Police Department. She's perfect."

"Let me see," Talancón says, flicking her fingers on the

keyboard, scrolling up and down, reading and rereading the information, finally clicking on the picture to enlarge the image. "There's gray hair dye inside." She suddenly frowns. "Why does it say to contact Omaha PD?"

"She's been missing for years. It's routine with missing people." She nods. "I'll get my people on it. Except . . ."

"Yes?"

"If I deliver this, how do I know I'm safe?"

"Safe?" she says. "You mean, that you'll stay alive?"

"Yes."

"There are suitcases inside the house." Not answering my question. "We'll stuff them with clothes; when we get to Tucson, we'll go to an all-night drugstore, buy bathroom things, whatever else is handy. We'll buy carry-on bags, at the airport we'll get newspapers, everything normal. Then all three of us will buy coach tickets and check the luggage. "

"First things first," I say.

"Now what?"

"I want to call the Sedona sheriff's department. I want officers to protect my family. You won't do this for me, I do nothing for you."

"Call them," she orders Rey, then stands six inches from my face. "Okay. I give you the guarantee. Don't push on me anymore, señora. Now get busy."

Her Rolex chronometer reads just under four hours. I call Lovitta, direct her to the website JaneJohnDoe.com, and give her the name I've chosen.

"You've got three hours plus," I say. "Then all the documents have to be at the Tucson airport. You know me, Lovitta. Serious I seldom get. So now I say to you . . ."

Another of our message codes. My heart pounding while she works it through until she suddenly gasps.

"Ah," she says. "Don't worry. Tag, you're it."

Less than three hours later, Rey slings four suitcases into the backseat of the Ford pickup and starts the engine. I'm sandwiched between him and the remodeled Talancón. Hair shorter and grayer, Talancón wears a yellow sundress, a light cotton shawl across her bare neck and shoulders, an iPod hanging around her neck.

We drive north, few cars on the road, but the Mexican produce trucks already headed up from Nogales. Predawn light on the desert, the sun rising past mountains to the east. Behind my right shoulder, loose gray clouds, the promise of an early monsoon coming up from Mexico. We drive in silence to Valencia Road, turn east, and ten minutes later leave the pickup in the short-term parking lot.

Inside the terminal, Talancón quickly scans the departure boards and heads us to the American Airlines ticket counter. No problems picking up a waiting envelope containing her documents and three round-trip tickets to Chicago, no problems collecting our boarding passes. A quick trip inside the airport store for carry-on bags, mixed nuts, two newspapers, the latest *People* and *Newsweek* magazines, and some beef jerky. At security, we all take off our shoes, drop everything in the X-ray buckets.

"Boarding pass, please," the TSA man says to Talancón.

"Sure," she replies with a smile.

Through the checkpoint, moving toward the departure gate, twenty-seven minutes to boarding time. We buy water, then Talancón points at three seats in the waiting area amidst other passengers, mostly seniors, all sitting as far away as they can from a mother and baby.

"Oh, come on," I complain. "I've got a fierce headache.

This tension, this, all of this, it's just, I feel sick. Let's sit over there, away from that squalling baby."

"Sure," Talancón says. "Why not?"

I move slowly, hands massaging my temples as I drop into a seat facing away from the security checkpoint. Talancón hesitates, then sits beside me and motions Rey to sit across from us. I crack the seal on my water bottle, drink from the nipple, then unscrew it and drink half the bottle.

"The list," I say.

"I'll give it to you in Chicago."

"Now," I say as lightly as I can against my tension. "I just need to see it."

She snaps open her handbag, passes four pages to me, handwritten on legal paper. I make a rough count. Well over a hundred major meth dealers, all across the state, twenty-seven on the Navajo rez alone.

Rey's eyes suddenly open wide at something behind me and I drop my water bottle, liquid spilling across my lap and onto Talancón's shoes. Snorting angrily, she bends over to brush off the water and I leap out of the seat and run sideways. Talancón's quick to react, half rising to chase me before a green-uniformed Border Patrol guard raps a handgun against her head. Talancón staggers before two other BP guards batter her to the floor and handcuff her.

"You've made a bad mistake," Talancón says to me in a hiss.

"I'm *your* biggest mistake," I shoot back.

She doesn't know what I'm talking about.

"You don't know computers," I say. "You knew what to ask for, but you didn't know why I chose that legend." She shakes her head rapidly, trying to clear the fog, her eyes alert, half-narrowed, menacing. "Judith Dunnigan Fletcher. You didn't ask me *why* she disappeared."

Talancón is very, very puzzled, suddenly very, very afraid.

"She murdered her entire family. Embezzled several hundred thousand dollars from her corporation. And just disappeared."

"Where is she now?" Talancón croaks.

"Right here," I say, inches from her face. I rip out her wallet, open it to her brand-new, platinum-grade driver's license with her photo and new name. "And here's your new U.S. passport. Judith Dunnigan Fletcher. Plano, Texas."

"I'm not her," she protests. A strong surge of passengers floods by, exiting an American gate. She bolts to her feet, shrugging off deputies, tries to run and blend with the passengers.

Two suited men block her way, grasp at her arms, fighting to contain her manic energy while holding her subdued.

"Meet Jackson Caller, U.S. Marshal," I say. "Here to take you to Texas where you'll quickly be tried for murder."

"I'm a Mexican national," she announces boldly. Still a tigress. "I can prove that in any court. The documents are fake."

"Meet Jack Bob Deeter, U.S. State Department," I say. "He'll verify that your U.S. passport is absolutely, entirely authentic. These aren't counterfeit IDs. I arranged for real paper."

"You arrogant whore," she hisses. "You've killed me."

"You threatened my daughter," I say. "My *daughter*. She's my life—you threatened my life. No longer. No more. We're done."

"When I'm free," she shouts back over her shoulder, "when I prove who I really am, I'll come for you!"

I figure I've got at least a year before she beats our legal system. By then, I'll be lost myself, adrift on the Navajo rez with a new name and a new life.

LAME ELK

BY LEONARD SCHONBERG

Ashland, Montana

L ame Elk awoke suddenly. He knew he had been dreaming. Now he tried to catch the dream before it disappeared down the dark hole dreams escape to when you're not fast enough to catch them. For a few moments he almost had it. Then it was gone.

His tongue stuck to the roof of his mouth and the bilious taste told him he was going to be sick. He rolled off the cot onto the cement floor. Propped on his hands and knees in the darkness, he retched, the dry heaves tightening his abdomen like a fist. Gasping for breath, he fell onto his side, then pushed himself into a sitting position. Assaulted by the stink of his vomit-encrusted clothes, he forced himself to breathe through his mouth even though it made the dryness worse.

A metal gate screeched and the corridor outside his cell was flooded with light. Lame Elk blinked at the knife thrust of light that penetrated his skull. At least now he could see where he was. Staggering to his feet, he filled the plastic cup on the dirty sink with cold water and drank. He was on his third cupful when he heard footsteps approaching The deputy, Tyler Erickson, was staring at him through the bars of the cell door.

"You are one sorry son of a bitch, Lame Brain," said Erickson, inserting a key in the lock and swinging the door open.

The Indian tried to force a smile but his lips were too bruised and swollen. The deputy, a tall, wiry man, stood with his thumb hooked in his belt, the hand resting next to the butt of his revolver.

"How the hell can you stand your own stink? I told the sheriff we should have left you lying out there in the snow, but you know how good-hearted he is."

"I don't remember anything," Lame Elk said. He had difficulty recognizing his own voice. "What happened to my face?"

Erickson snorted and shook his head in disgust. "Russ says if you try to come into his bar again he'll send you to the happy hunting ground. You owe him for a busted stool and a smashed mirror. Here's the bill. He says you should put the money in this envelope and mail it to him by the first of the month or he's going to press charges."

"Did he do this to my face?"

"You got into a fight with three guys. Not from around here. Russ called us but by the time we got there they were gone. You were lying in the street. Twenty below zero and you were just lying there."

"You should have left me there."

"If it was up to me, I would've. Let's go. I have your jacket and stuff in the office. You can go back to the rez and sleep it off. This jail ain't a motel."

Lame Elk, unsteady on his feet, shambled after the deputy down the brightly lit corridor. His large bulk filled the doorway as he followed Erickson into the office. The deputy picked up a form from the desk and pointed to the items lying next to it. "One wallet containing six dollars. A pocketknife. One sheepskin coat. Sign here."

The Indian leaned over the desk and rested his wrist on the paper to control the trembling of his hand. At that moment the front door of the office opened and a ruddy-faced man entered, his Stetson pushed low on his head. The burst of frigid air that accompanied him into the room blew the paper from the desk as Lame Elk turned to face him.

Ignoring the two men in the room, the man took off his coat and hat and hung them on a rack in the corner. He smoothed back his thinning gray hair and rubbed his hands briskly together.

"Mighty cold," he said, acknowledging the deputy for the first time.

"He's ready to go." Erickson gestured toward the Indian.

"Hello, sheriff," Lame Elk mumbled, unwilling to meet the man's gaze. Instead, he stared at the star pinned on the guy's shirt.

The sheriff squeezed behind his desk and sat down heavily in a swivel chair. The deputy had picked up the signed form off the floor and placed it in front of the sheriff, who ignored it.

Lame Elk took his belongings from the desk and awkwardly put on his jacket. The sheriff regarded him thoughtfully. Whenever he saw Lame Elk, he thought of the Indian's father, Bear Hunter. The same broad shoulders and barrel chest. Long black hair and piercing eyes. The difference was that Bear Hunter had been a chief of the Northern Cheyenne, a man who commanded respect, not a drunken saloon Indian. It was the memory of Bear Hunter, a man he considered a friend until his death, that tempered his disgust when he looked at Lame Elk.

"Wait," he called out as Lame Elk reached the door. The Indian hesitated, turning to face the sheriff. The deputy, busying himself at the file cabinet, also paused and swung his head around.

The sheriff pointed to the chair in front of his desk. Tyler

Erickson, disgusted by the stink of puke and alcohol fumes in the office, grimaced and turned back to his files. Lecturing these Indians was, he knew, a waste of time, but he wasn't about to tell the sheriff that. If Moran hadn't learned that in his twenty-two years as sheriff, he hadn't learned anything.

Lame Elk sat down but refused to meet the man's eyes. The sheriff rummaged through his desk drawer before pulling out a small object from the very back.

"Do you know what this is?" he asked.

The Indian stared at the deer hide pouch. "A medicine bundle?"

"A medicine bundle," Sheriff Moran agreed. "I thought you'd like to have it. It belonged to your father."

Lame Elk looked directly at the sheriff. "How come you have it?"

"Bear Hunter gave it to me before he died. He told me to keep it for you until the time came when you needed it most. I think that time has come."

Erickson, his back to the two men, scowled. What the hell had gotten into Moran?

The sheriff held the pouch out to Lame Elk. For several moments the Indian sat immobile, then reached for it. He was unable to control the trembling of his hand. Staring at the beaded borders of the medicine bundle, he thought not of Bear Hunter, but of his mother, Star Woman. He remembered the winter she had sewn those beads on the pouch. It had been a time of brutal cold and heavy snows. Game was scarce and supplies were not getting through to the reservation. Many people died that winter, including his brother and sister. His mother, too, was sick with consumption. The dark spots on the deer hide of the bundle were, he knew, flecks of blood that had escaped from between her fingers when she covered her mouth while coughing. He scraped at them with his thumbnail, but they were now part of the hide, just as his mother's gaunt face was part of his memory.

"Your father will need this," she had told him. Perhaps she was right. Bear Hunter had survived and become a chief. He, Lame Elk, had survived too, although he often wished he hadn't. Star Woman, the mother he loved, had died before she could see another winter.

"There's a man you should see today before you go back to the reservation," Sheriff Moran said.

Lame Elk blinked. He had forgotten he was still in the sheriff's office.

"His name is Johnson. Hugh Johnson. He's got an office above the hardware store. He wants to meet you."

"Why?"

The sheriff shrugged. "I'll let him tell you. I told him you'd stop by this morning."

Leaving the warmth of the office, Lame Elk shivered as the first blast of icy wind hit him. He thrust his hands into his sheepskin jacket pockets and, leaning into the wind, walked down Ashland's main street. Unconsciously, he fingered the medicine bundle, still held in his right hand.

On this frigid Saturday morning in January, the town seemed deserted. A pickup truck stacked with bales of hay drove slowly down the street, exhaust vapors billowing behind it. The snow crunched beneath Lame Elk's boots as he headed for the café, the lettering of its sign blurred by the wind-induced tears that obscured his vision.

At first, the waitress ignored him. Two white men seated at the counter gave Lame Elk a dirty look when he sat down near them. They picked up their plates and coffees and headed to a booth.

"Can I get some coffee, please?" Lame Elk said to the frizzy-haired woman busying herself to his left, arranging pie slices on a turntable at the counter.

She glanced at him with disgust. "You got money?"

Lame Elk pulled out his wallet and extracted the six dollars it contained. He held the bills up in the air so she could see them. The waitress set a cup in front of him, hard enough so that coffee overflowed the rim and ran onto the counter. Lame Elk sopped it up with a napkin. He stretched his arm out for the sugar container and picked out a handful of packets. Meticulously, he emptied six of them into his cup and stirred the now thick brew. He closed his eyes and sipped the coffee. He nodded contentedly to himself when the bad taste in his mouth finally disappeared.

Lame Elk's nausea had subsided and he was hungry. The waitress ignored him again when he raised his hand to get her attention and he decided not to ask her for anything else. Standing up, he slapped a dollar down on the counter and walked to the door. The two white men in the booth glared at him when he left.

Midmorning and still bitterly cold. Lame Elk looked up and down the street, his breath rising in a cloud above his head. He couldn't bear the thought of returning to his hovel on the rez. The sheriff had mentioned someone named Johnson, a man who wanted to meet him. Lame Elk couldn't imagine why. He didn't know any Hugh Johnson. Yet the hardware store was only a block away. Might as well, Lame Elk thought. Got nothing else to do.

Standing in front of the store, he peered up at the dark second-floor windows. There was no sign indicating what kind of office it was. Lame Elk pushed open the door at the side of the store's display window and trudged up a flight of wooden steps. Black letters were printed on the frosted glass of a closed door. *Office of Economic Opportunity.* The words meant nothing to Lame Elk. He turned the knob and found himself in a room with a metal desk and three straight-backed chairs. A door at the opposite end of the room was closed. Lame Elk stopped in front of the desk, as if whoever usually sat there might reappear. He stared at a painting hanging on the wall behind it. Mounted Indians on a high bluff pointed at white men approaching in the distance.

Lame Elk scratched his head, wondering why the sheriff had sent him here, if no one was around. He was on the verge of leaving when a slender man with a neatly trimmed beard entered the room from the inner door. He was dressed in a flannel shirt and jeans, no different from Lame Elk's attire, but the man's clothes were clean. "I thought I heard someone come in," he said. "Secretary's not here on Saturdays. I'm Hugh Johnson."

"The sheriff said you wanted to see me." Lame Elk became aware once again of the dismal sight he presented with his filthy, foul-smelling clothes.

"You Lame Elk?"

He nodded. He wasn't proud of it.

"What happened to your face?"

"I don't remember."

Johnson frowned. "Come inside to my office. We can talk there."

Lame Elk followed him through the door and into a small office. A bookcase, a desk, a padded chair, and a straight-back chair for visitors comprised its furnishings.

"Have a seat," Johnson said, easing himself into the chair behind the desk.

"Sheriff Moran told me you wanted to talk to me."

"The sheriff tells me you've been having a rough time."

Lame Elk shrugged, not knowing if he was supposed to answer.

"Maybe I should tell you exactly what the sheriff told me. If you disagree with any of it, you can say so. He said he was a friend of your father, who was a great chief. After your mother died, you began having a problem with the bottle. Sheriff Moran said he thought many times of trying to help you, but decided you weren't ready for help. Now, for some reason, he thinks you are. Are you?"

"What kind of help?"

"Help that will bring back your self-respect. Job, clean clothes, a decent place to live."

"That takes money."

"It takes more than money. It takes willpower and sobriety. You know what that is?"

Lame Elk lowered his eyes. "Yeah, I know."

"I can help you if you think you're ready."

"What do I have to do?"

"The department I work for will find you a place to live right here in Ashland. Just a room, nothing fancy, but clean. And you'll be responsible for keeping it that way. We'll see that you get a job and clothes for work. You can pay the store back for the clothes from the money you make working. And after you've worked for a month you can decide if you want to stay put in the room or move to a different place. If you decide to stay in the room we found for you, you'll take over the rent, which isn't much."

"Why would you do this for me?"

"Like I said, the sheriff thinks you're ready for a change. But—" He raised the index finger of his right hand. "There's a catch. You have to stay sober, you have to report to work every day, you have to stay out of trouble, and you have to go to meetings. Staying out of trouble should be easy if you're sober. If you break those rules, it's the end of our agreement. You're out of the room and out of a job."

Lame Elk tucked his hands in his jacket pockets. He grasped the medicine bundle, rolling it around in his palm. "What kind of work?"

"You know the feed store on Main Street? Munson's?"

Lame Elk nodded.

"They need someone to receive orders, stack merchandise, wait on customers, clean up at the end of the day. Interested?"

"Yeah."

Johnson glanced at his watch. "I'll go over to the store with you and you can pick out some clothes. After you meet everyone, I'll take you to the room where you'll be living. It's a few blocks from the store."

"When do I start work?"

"Monday. That okay?"

"Good," Lame Elk said. He knew if he was busy it would keep his mind off drink. It was the time after his work day ended that worried him. Would he be able to resist temptation?

"You said something about going to meetings. What kind of meetings?"

"AA, Alcoholics Anonymous. You heard of it?"

Lame Elk nodded.

"They meet every evening at a church here in town. You'll be going to your first meeting Monday when you get out of work."

Lame Elk's first week was tough. Booze was never far from his thoughts, but he was busy enough to push it from his mind.

Trucks rolled in several days a week, their pallets loaded with feed, fencing supplies, stock tanks, all needing to be unloaded. Stacking materials and ordering were daily chores. Lame Elk found himself enjoying the work, and taking pleasure in using his muscles again. What was most difficult for him was standing up in front of the AA group in the evening after work and admitting he was an alcoholic. By the time he got home after buying his dinner at Burger King, he was almost too tired to eat it.

The second week was easier. Days went by without his wanting a drink. He was able to walk past a bar and ignore the smell of beer and cigarette smoke whenever someone opened the door. The aching in his arms and legs from the heavy lifting at work had subsided. His appetite was better and he was sleeping ten hours a night in a clean room with a clean bed. He'd already paid the feed store half of what he owed for the clothes he'd picked out that first day with Hugh Johnson. And he'd forced himself to write a letter to Russ at the Antlers bar with a twenty-dollar bill inside and a promise to pay the balance for the damage he'd caused. *You'll have it all in another three weeks*, Lame Elk wrote.

Hugh Johnson stopped by the feed store during his third week to ask how things were going.

"Good," Lame Elk said. "Very good."

"Great. Munson says nice things about you. Come visit whenever you feel a need to talk. I'm in the office most days and two evenings till 9, Tuesday and Thursday."

Lame Elk nodded. "Thanks."

He was working outside in the feed store yard stacking fence panels later that week, his gloves doing little to warm his hands in the intense cold of late January. The collar of his Carhartt jacket was turned up around his neck. A stone-gray sky promised more snow by evening. A Chevy pickup truck drove through the yard's open gate and a man climbed out. He examined some panels and gates before walking up behind Lame Elk.

"I'm looking for a sixteen-foot gate," he called out.

Lame Elk turned around to encounter a familiar face. The man grinned. "Well, well, look who's here. You seem a little different than the last time I saw you. You stunk to high heaven then. Almost made me lose my breakfast."

"I have a sixteen-foot gate," Lame Elk said. "I'll get it for you. Want me to load it on your truck?"

"Hey, that's mighty white of you. That what you're doing now? Trying to be a white man with good manners?"

"I don't want no trouble."

"Trouble? Who's making trouble, chief? I'm just making small talk. You know, my friend and I didn't appreciate it that day in the café when you ruined our breakfast. Sitting down next to us, stinking of vomit and piss. My friend, he wanted to go out after you when you left to teach you a lesson. I told him a drunken Indian couldn't learn shit."

"I don't drink anymore."

"That so? Well, good for you, chief."

"You want the gate loaded?"

"I'll think about it. I have some things to get inside. I'm leaving my truck here, okay?"

"Sure. It'll be here when you come out."

The man's steely blue eyes met Lame Elk's and held his gaze.

Five minutes later, the guy reappeared followed by someone else Lame Elk knew, Jesse Harpole, the feed store supervisor. Harpole was a man Lame Elk usually tried to avoid. The manager had taken a dislike to him for some reason.

"What the hell do you think you're doing?" Harpole asked, his cheeks flushed in anger.

Confusion covered Lame Elk's face. "What?"

"Customer says you were rude to him, wouldn't help him find what he was looking for. And when he did find what he wanted, he said you wouldn't help him load it."

Lame Elk shook his head. "That's not true. I told him I'd be happy to load the gate for him, but he said he wanted to do some more shopping."

"Go inside and wait for me at the back register. I'll give you your severance pay when I come in. You're fired."

Lame Elk, unable to comprehend what had just happened, kept turning his head to look at the two men as he walked toward the store's rear entrance.

"Every time I hire a goddamn Indian, I get burned," he heard Harpole telling the man.

Lame Elk waited at the register, as Harpole had instructed him. He reached into his pocket and fingered his father's medicine pouch. He pulled it out, sniffed it, and laid it next to the register. He unzipped the Carhartt jacket he'd picked out with Hugh Johnson and dropped it on the floor. Then he unbuttoned his flannel shirt, pulled it off, and let it fall on top of the coat. He bent down and yanked off the boots he'd bought, and unzipped his new Wranglers and stepped out of them. He stood in the emptiness of the back room, his braid a straight black line thick against his spine.

Lame Elk opened the cash register and counted out his wages for the week and scattered the money like dried leaves on the pile of clothing.

He walked out the door, oblivious to the cold and to the first large snowflakes coming down. He walked past the hardware store and looked up at the second-floor windows of Hugh

Johnson's office. Lame Elk clutched Bear Hunter's medicine bundle in his bare hand and headed home.

ANOTHER ROLE

BY REED FARREL COLEMAN

Los Angeles, California

I t wasn't Harry Garson's fault he didn't speak a word of Navajo or Apache or Ute or Hopi or whatever the fuck kind of Indian he was. He didn't know and he didn't give a shit. Never had and he wasn't about to start caring now. Not that he was barking about his genetics, mind you. His classic Indian looks—the rich bronze skin, dark and distant eyes, high cheekbones, proudly bent nose, granite jaw, downturned mouth—had landed him over a hundred and fifty roles, large and small, in A, B, and C oaters dating back to 1938's *Forked River, Forked Tongue*. As he advanced in years, his classic features, once those of the stereotypical proud brave—"Makeup and Costume, c'mon, get over here and get some fucking war paint and feathers on Harry. He's got a wagon train to ambush. We're losing the light, goddammit!"—had morphed into those of the sage chief. The distant eyes were now achingly sad, the brow above them knitted and furrowed. His cheeks had gone hollow and his angular jaw was now crooked thanks to a bar fight with Lock Martin—*Klaatu barada nickto*. Yes, *that* Lock Martin, all 7'1" of the guy who played Gort in *The Day the Earth Stood Still*—at Musso and Frank's in '53. Word was that Harry was getting the better of it until the normally gentle giant introduced the leg of a bar stool to Harry's chops.

"Harry, you're turning my kishkas inside out," said movie agent Irv Rothenberg when he visited his client in the hospital. "Who picks a fight with a guy bigger than Mount Shasta, for chrissakes? Lock is a sweetheart. What did you say to him to set him off like that?"

"I said Patricia Neal told me he had a small shwantz," Harry replied, waving his right pinky at his agent. "Big man, little pecker." Harry even managed a laugh, though his mouth was wired shut.

"Oy gevalt, you're killing me, Harry!"

Harry was blessed—Irv would say cursed—with the genuine gift of gab, which he could use for good—like talking his way into a part or into a starlet's bed—or for bad, à la Lock Martin. He also had a facility for doing impersonations. When he was on the set with John Ford, Duke Wayne used to pay Harry to call up the second unit director and give him all manner of insane orders in Ford's voice. It got so bad that Ford had to start giving special code words to his staff so that they could recognize him and not the schmuck pretending to be him. The irony for Harry was that he didn't get his first speaking part until 1956's *Red Scout*, and then his only line was, "Blue horse soldier with yellow hair like waves, across running river." Not exactly the stuff of Shakespeare, but the speaking parts came more frequently after that and by the mid-'60s, Harry Garson had landed a regular role as Smells Like Bearstein, Chief of the Sosoomee Tribe, on the short-lived series *Crazy Cavalry*. By the late '60s, as Westerns fell out of favor and parts for aging chief types with a flare for the spoken word grew scarce, Harry settled into an angry semiretirement. The few big roles Harry auditioned for in the late '60s and '70s, he lost to Chief Dan George. That really got him going, especially when reruns of *Little Big Man* and *The Outlaw Josey Wales* played on the movie channels.

"That fucking Canadian prick!" Harry would bark at the screen and imitate Chief Dan George's quiet, monotone delivery. "Every eighteen-year-old in this country ran to goddamn Canada to avoid the draft and this is who we got in exchange? I bet they had to write out his lines in pictographs, the senile old bastard."

He was a charmer, Harry, but he had the bitterness in him too, and it began to overtake him as the years passed and the parts—those in the movies and those on his body—shriveled up. These weren't the only things shriveling up either. He had never been good with money, especially when it was plentiful. Although he denied it until the day he died, Randy "The Crooning Cowpoke" Butterworth of B-movie and early TV fame, was known to have once told Harry he was "the only redskin who acts like a kike, speaks like Olivier, and spends like a nigger." By the summer of '83, Harry Garson was about tapped out. Fourteen years since his last meaningful paying gig, he was living on fast food and five-buck-a-blowjob drug whores in a SRO hotel in downtown L.A. Then the phone rang in the hall outside his room and that all changed.

"Chief, the phone's for y'all!" It was Marissa LaTerre, the black drag queen from two doors down. "Come on, y'ole redskin, you. Man on the phone got me all wet with that sexy voice a his."

"Wet!" Harry said. "What, he make you piss your pants?"

Harry, long used to being called "chief," pulled the door open to behold the slender, 6'4" man with dark coffee skin and features as delicate as a first kiss. Without her makeup, lamé outfits, and wig, Marissa was just plain old Morris Terry, formerly of Camden, New Jersey and myriad points in between.

"He says it's about a part, chief," Morris cooed like a teenage girl, but it simply didn't work without the feminine accoutrements. Frankly, delicate features notwithstanding, his golf ball–sized Adam's apple and towering stature made it a tough sell to begin with. "Y'all think if I do him, there'll be a part in it for Marissa?"

Harry didn't answer, pushing his way past Morris-Marissa and to the pay phone, its receiver dangling in midair.

"Yeah," he barked. "Who is this?"

"Harry Garson, is that you?"

"Last time I checked. Who is this?"

"Dylan Rothenberg, Irv's kid."

"Irv's kid?" Harry was drawing a blank.

"Your old agent, I'm his youngest boy. Remember me? You used to come to my birthday parties when I was little. I've got home movies. You gave me my first cigarette and first sip of scotch."

"Sure. Sure. I remember you. You were the blond-haired kid with the blue eyes. You looked like your shiksa-goddess mother. What was her name . . . Kitt, right? Kitt was her name. Christ, she was hot."

"And you're still the picture of tact and diplomacy, I see."

"Sorry, kid."

"No worries, Harry. She still speaks fondly of you as well."

Harry wisely shifted gears, remembering he'd once nailed Kitt Rothenberg after a movie premier Irv was too sick to attend. "So what's this about a part? You following in your old man's footsteps?"

"God no, I teach physics at Hofstra University on Long Island. Someone tracked me down because of my dad having been your agent. I still have some friends and contacts back home who found you for me."

"So you found me, kid. Now what?"

"You got a pen and a piece of paper?"

He knew he didn't, but Harry unconsciously patted his pockets.

"Here, honey, you looking for these?" It was Morris, who'd been watching the whole time, handing Harry a little yellow note pad and a pencil. "You can thank me later." Morris blew Harry a kiss.

They made quite the couple, strolling down Sunset: Harry, stoop-shouldered in his pink Salvation Army leisure suit and the now 6'7" Marissa in her heels, khaki miniskirt, fishnets, and green chiffon blouse. Harry didn't like acknowledging it, but age and too many Maker's Marks had rendered his once steel-trap memory rusty and full of holes. Lines, no problem. He could remember reams of dialogue like when he played Geronimo in *Mission Apache* or the rebel brave Eyes Like Knife in the cult favorite *Hunting Ground*. He tested himself, running lines with his ersatz escort before they left for the audition.

Harry's trouble was with figures and his sense of direction. His navigation system was shot and he couldn't recall phone numbers for shit, not that he'd been in need of that facility any time recently. What Harry needed was someone's help getting him to the address on Sunset, and it wasn't like he had thousands of eager candidates from which to choose. He supposed he might've gone stag and taken a taxi, but that meant he'd have to pay cab fare in both directions. In turn, that meant he would have to sacrifice a few meals this week. He'd had to do that a lot lately. When he'd weighed the unlikely prospect of getting the part and a paycheck versus lost Big Macs, Whoppers, and Potato World cheese fries—his favorites—Harry decided Marissa's company and help was worth the four bus fares.

"Will you slow up, goddamnit!" he growled at Marrisa. "You take longer strides than a fucking giraffe!"

"I didn't know giraffes took long strides when they were fucking, chief."

"Funny lady."

"Streisand already got that part."

"You're so tall, they could have made a disaster movie about you in the '70s: *Towering Transvestite*."

"Steve McQueen and Paul Neuman can climb all over me whenever they want. Here we are," Marissa said, looking up at the nondescript building wedged between a dry cleaner and an abandoned music store.

The interior of the building was even less impressive than its exterior. Harry had seen furrier putting greens than the threadbare carpet that lined the lobby floor. Come to think of it, he'd seen *cleaner* putting greens, and putting greens were half dirt. It wasn't encouraging and all he could think about as he and Marissa rode the creaking elevator up to the fourth floor were the burgers and cheese fries he'd sacrificed to cover the public transportation. Still, when the elevator jerked to a stop at four, Harry took his traditional deep breaths and mentally flicked up his on switch. Irv Rothenberg had always said that no one auditioned like Harry.

"I got stars in my stable, sure," Irv once told a junior associate, "but Harry Garson is the guy who bought my house and paid for my first son's bar mitzvah. He's automatic, like a given in geometry. He gets the audition, he gets the part." Problem was that after *Crazy Cavalry*, Harry couldn't get many auditions. Charm is less charming on a typecast actor with a bad off-screen rep and too many years on his bones.

Suite 403
The Rights Agency, LLC

"This is the place," Marissa said, reading Harry's chicken scratch off the sheet of yellow paper. "The Rights Agency."

Now this was better, Harry thought. The carpeting in the fourth-floor hallway was clean, and while the pile didn't exactly tickle your shins, it was at least soft under your shoes. And he liked that the company name was painted in gold and black on the door the way people with class did it in the old days. No cheap plastic piece-of-shit sign or gold-plated tin placard. Class. Harry appreciated class.

"You going to wait for me here or downstairs?" he asked.

"No way, chief, nuh uh. I didn't take y'all to the church just to get jilted at the altar."

Harry thought about arguing the point, but he knew better than to use up his limited energy on futile arguments. He knocked, turned the knob, and strode in, his escort looming behind him. The eyes on the two well-dressed men inside the office got big as dinner plates at the sight of Marissa LaTerre. Harry had expected nothing less. Helen Keller, he thought, would've gotten big eyes in the presence of the power-forward drag queen, especially dressed up in that outfit.

"I'm Harry Garson," he said, walking up to the older of the two men. He slid his ancient black-and-white head shot and CV across the top of the fancy etched glass desktop.

"Paul Spiegelman," the man replied, shaking Harry's hand. His eyes were still on Marissa. "This is my partner, Mel Abbott." Spiegelman nodded his head at the man at the adjoining desk. Abbott, who looked about thirty—twenty or so years younger than his partner—stood and shook Harry's hand.

"And this is . . ." Abbott said, gesturing at Marissa.

"My agent, Marissa LaTerre," Harry said, immediately regretting it. He was more nervous than he suspected he would be and the words just came out.

The partners managed not to roll their eyes at that. There was a second round of handshakes.

"Let's get down to business, shall we?" Spiegelman said, gesturing at the two red leather chairs facing the desks.

Spiegelman was a fit fifty. Compact and thin with probing hazel eyes that looked through Elvis Costello glasses, an angular jawline, a sharp nose, and a crooked but ingratiating smile. He was dressed in a gray, light wool pinstripe suit and his accessories were all silk and gold. To Harry, Paul Spiegelman smelled of Yale Law School and twenty years at a New York firm, a big New York firm. He was definitely a lawyer or a money man. In the business, they were sometimes one and the same. Mel Abbott, on the other hand, was a Hollywood hyena, all lean and hungry looks. Harry would have to keep an eye out for him.

"The part," Harry said, unable to contain himself any longer. "What about the part? Where are my lines?"

"Lines?" Abbott asked, seemingly confused.

Spiegelman waved a calming hand at his partner. "I'm afraid you misunderstand, Harry. This isn't that kind of part."

"Christ, I knew it!" He jumped out of his chair. "What is this? Listen I—"

"Harry, Harry, please . . . sit down. Relax. Let me explain." Spiegelman kept his voice even and reassuring. But what Harry found most reassuring were the two bundles of crisp, rubber-banded bills the older partner was pushing across the top of his desk. "That's ten thousand dollars there, Harry."

Now it was Marissa LaTerre's eyes that got big. Harry's weren't exactly squinty either. It was all Harry Garson could do not to reach out and snatch the money. Instead, he sat back down and tried not drooling over the notions of what he could do with that much cash. Visions of cheese fries and hookers, a lot of hookers, danced in his head . . .

Marissa decided to take her role as agent to heart. "So what are you gentlemen speaking about here for my client?"

"It's more theater than film work, though it's a little bit of both, frankly," Abbott said.

"We want Harry to play the part of an Indian," Spiegelman added. "We need him and only him for the part, and this ten grand is only a down payment."

Suddenly, the buzz all came back into Harry's bones and he was rushing harder than a junkie who'd just gotten fixed with the purest skag on Earth. He was barely thinking of the money anymore. It was about the role. He was so juiced by the thought of being in front of the cameras again, he nearly broke into one of those stupid war dances he'd done in fifteen movies and on almost every episode of Crazy Cavalry.

"But I'm still not hearing what the role is exactly for Harry," Marissa persisted.

"Harry, do you think you can stay in character for a long period of time?"

"No problem, Mr. Abbott. I worked for some directors who demanded we stay in character for the whole shoot. It was a pain in the balls, but I did it. I'm a professional."

"See, Mel, I told you Harry was our man," Spiegelman spoke up. He then launched into a long stroking session, naming several movie roles and commenting on just how well Harry Garson had done this or that. "And even in your comedic roles, you always stood out. My favorite was in the 'Bismark Goes West' episode on CC. Your timing was great when you did the line about the Goodyear blimp."

Harry chuckled. "Yeah, the trooper asks Bearstein how his future will be and I say, 'It will be a good year . . .' Then I look up and yell, 'Blimp!' And there's Bismark and his Siamese kitten Cleo flying overhead in a zeppelin."

Now they were all laughing. All except Marissa. "I'll ask this one more time. What's the role?"

"Fair enough," Spiegelman said. "Look, we've been hired to make training films for Native American tribes looking to set up gaming establishments on reservation lands. It's about time the indigenous peoples of this country make some profits off the lands the government ceded to them. It's a difficult and arcane process, as you might imagine, and it just makes sense to the lawyers who do this kind of work to have a tool they can use to train the tribes."

"Okay," Marissa said, "that's better, but—"

Spiegelman held up his palms like traffic cop. "I understand your concerns. Here's the deal. Harry will have to relocate to the Tucson, Arizona area and live as . . ." he looked down at a sheet of paper, "Ben Hart, the long-lost son of an elder of the Tohono O'odham tribe, they're a Pima people. Actually, you'd be part of a subgroup of theirs, but we can discuss all that later. We will have film crews following you and have you miked whenever you leave your house. We will supply you with paperwork, references, etc., and we will walk you through the process of dealing with government agencies and the tribes themselves. But you absolutely must remain in character during this whole period. When you go out to a store or to a diner or go to the bathroom, you go as Ben Hart. Do you understand that, Harry?"

"Who's Harry? I'm Ben Hart, the long-lost son of a tribal elder of the Tohono O'odham," he said, perfectly mimicking Spiegelman's pronunciation. "When do we get going?"

"Well . . ." Mel Abbott hesitated, "first you're gonna have to go through some schooling while you're in L.A. We need you to get very familiar with the role and then we'll send you down to Tucson. It won't be a cakewalk, this will be—"

"Stop being such a worrier, Mel. Harry—I mean, Ben Hart is up to it. Right, chief?"

"No problem."

"Very well then," Paul Spiegelman said, pushing one of the money piles toward Harry and pulling the other one back. "Here's half as an advance. When you complete your education for the role up here, you'll get the second half. I trust you, but our clients need some guarantees, you understand."

"Well, I don't!" Marissa stood up and walked over to Mel Abbott's desk. She sensed he was the more easily intimidated of the two and, at 6'7", she was pretty intimidating. "What about a little thing called a contract?"

Abbott's mouth moved silently as he fumbled for an answer. The hyena was looking mighty scared. Harry was enjoying it all and thought Marissa LaTerre born to the role of agent. An image of Irv Rothenberg in fishnets, a miniskirt, and high heels flashed through his mind and Harry shuddered. One of Kitt followed quickly thereafter and Harry almost got hard. Almost.

"Contract. You want a contract?" Spiegelman asked. "You got one. We'll have it drawn up, but first we had to see if Harry would take the part. It's only reasonable, no?"

Harry said sure, sure. Marissa was still skeptical. Harry took the money and shoved it in his jacket pocket.

"Now, Harry," Mel said, "don't disappear on us with that five grand."

Harry was really starting to dislike Mel. Most people, he guessed, would dislike Mel. "Listen, mister, I'm a professional. I was never late on set in 150-plus movies. I never called in sick or injured, ever. As hard up as I am, I'm not going anywhere."

Spiegelman chided his partner. "Mel, I keep telling you, Harry Garson is a pro. Besides, he knows the five large is *bubkes* compared to what he'll make for the whole shoot."

"And speaking of that," Marissa chimed in, "what are we talking about for the whole gig?"

"Minimum of fifty grand, less the ten up front. Depends how long the shoot goes. Anything over a month, Harry will receive five grand a week. The clock on the shoot starts ticking once he lands at the airport in Tucson. One month from that day, the five grand per kicks in. Once the shoot spills over into the next week, five grand will be prorated. How does that sound to everyone?"

"Wonderful," Harry said. "When can we sign the papers and get started?"

Mel answered: "It'll take a day or two to draw up the contract, then we'll have them messengered over to your hotel and you can have the signed copies sent back here."

Marissa kept at it. "And you have no issue with a lawyer looking the contracts over?"

"None at all," said Spiegelman. "Contracts are meant to protect both parties. For now, Harry, go home and enjoy yourself a little. It's going to be tough work once we get rolling." He stood and offered his hand to Harry and Marissa. "Mel and I have to get things started on our end, so please excuse us. I think this is going to work out very nicely. Very nicely indeed."

In the elevator on the way back down, Harry Garson peeled off five crisp hundred-dollar bills and handed them to his new agent. "You should give up the drag queen routine, kid. You're a natural as an agent."

"Harry, I can't take this."

"Take it. Take it!" he insisted, shoving the money through

the low-buttoned chiffon blouse and into Marissa's thickly foamed bra. "You earned it. Besides, you heard Spiegelman. I'm looking at home-run city here."

"About that, I—"

"Forget it. When the contracts come, we'll worry about it."

"But—"

"No buts. Come on, I'm treating for a cab."

Paul Spiegelman and Mel Abbott stood silently, watching out their office window as Harry Garson and his drag queen agent stood on Sunset trying to flag down a cab. It was almost as if they wouldn't speak until the oddest of odd couples was completely out of sight. Of course they understood that no one, not even people in the hallway outside their door, could hear their conversation. Still, they waited. When a cab finally pulled to the curb out front, gobbled up the two riders, and sped off, Spiegelman and Abbott sighed with relief. The older of the two began whistling "We're in the Money," but all Mel could do was pace.

"Why the fuck did he have to bring that fucking African queen with him? He— She's gonna fuck everything up."

"Mel, will you calm down, for goodness sakes? You're going to give yourself a stroke."

"'Calm down,' he says. How can I calm down? You know what's at stake here?"

"I know, Mel. I know."

"I told you we should have sent a car to pick him up. I told you."

"If we sent a car for him, he would have gotten suspicious. Harry's dumb and hungry, but he's not stupid. He knows the business. He knows that someone who hasn't worked in nearly fifteen years doesn't get picked up in a limo for an audition. That would have queered the deal right there."

"Stooping to puns now, Paul?"

Spiegelman thought about that for a second, snickered quietly, and said, "I didn't realize."

"Never mind. So what are we gonna do about Sheena, Queen of the Jungle?"

"Go round up Joey Potholes for me. Tell him I need to see him here. In the meantime, I've got Harry Garson's contract to write up."

At 4:27 a.m. the next morning, Marissa LaTerre stumbled out of Midnight Cruiser, an after-hours club frequented by freaks, geeks, and beautiful people alike. She'd had a hell of a night, giving head in a back room to a pretty-boy British film star and having the favor returned by the guy's fifteen-year-old date. She'd also managed to spend every dime of her agent's fee and then some.

A tall, elegantly thin man with pocked skin and fish eyes leaned against the front fender of a Lincoln Town Car. He watched Marissa come out of the club and turn in his direction. He'd made sure to shoot out the streetlamp under which he'd parked the stolen Lincoln. When Marissa got close to the back bumper of the car, the thin man pulled open the rear passenger side door.

"For you, Miss LaTerre," he said. "Compliments of Harry Garson."

If she hadn't had so much coke and Dom in her system, Marissa might have listened to the alarm bells her street-smart former self, Morris Terry, was ringing as loudly as he could. But even then, it wouldn't have mattered. It was already half past too late. She couldn't have known that every stitch of clothing, every piece of jewelry, every wig and false eyelash, everything she owned was in the trunk of the stolen car and that she would soon be keeping her possessions company. She couldn't have known that the desk clerk at the hotel had been paid off to check her out and box up all of her worldly goods. It was only when she felt the ring of cold metal press against the back of her skull as she entered the car that Marissa finally heard Morris's alarm bells. With a flash, a snap, and a wisp of smoke, Marissa collapsed in a heap across the backseat.

Harry Garson loved Tucson. He'd shot on location in Arizona about thirty times, but being here on his own and getting to step outside his own persona was a revelation. After the first few days wearing the Nagra recorder taped to his body, he'd learned to forget about it, and since he never knew where the film crew was, it was as if they weren't there at all. Somehow he felt, for the first time in his life, at home. In the past, on movie shoots, he'd always been a part of the crew and his exploration of the area tended to be of the local bars and brothels. Sure, there were a few times he and some of the other actors had taken their horses out into the surrounding mountains and desert when the day's shoot didn't involve Indian or battle sequences, but that too wound up being about someone having a few bottles and getting *shickered*. That's what Irv said the Yiddish word was for getting drunk.

Irv. These days, Harry found himself thinking a lot about his old agent. It was only with Irv that he had ever spoken about his Indian roots and his puzzlement over how he'd come to be raised by the sweet but clueless Garson family in northern Wisconsin. He knew his adoptive parents had been Lutheran missionaries, but they never spoke too much about it. They never spoke much about anything. What he remembered most about his childhood was the silence of it.

"I never felt a part of the life there," he'd confided to Irv.

"Look, we're all members of a tribe."

"Yeah, Irv, but what tribe?"

Irv had just shrugged his shoulders. In Harry's seventy-five-plus years, it had been his one and only conversation on the subject. Now when Irv crossed his mind, Harry's thoughts inevitably turned to Marissa LaTerre. He was still pretty pissed at the fruitcake for abandoning him like she had and without a word. He tried figuring out why she'd done it and turned her back on the 10 percent he would have given her, but it was a waste of time and energy. Who could figure out someone like that? They couldn't even figure themselves out, Harry reasoned. Besides, the contracts had been signed; Harry having paid a C-note to a disbarred lawyer from the hotel to give the documents the once over to make sure they were in order. He'd done his studying up on Tucson and the Pima. For instance, he knew that Ira Hayes, one of the guys who held up the American flag at Iwo Jima, was a Pima Indian. That the name Tucson was taken from a Spanish bastardization of the O'odham name Cuk Son, meaning at the base of the black hill. He'd been an apt pupil and the second five-grand installment had been paid in full in cash.

They'd flown him down to Tucson first class and set him up in a neat little adobe bungalow in the foothills of the Santa Catalina Mountains. When the cab dropped him off, Harry found a 1980 Ford F150 pickup in the driveway with the keys in the ignition. It had been ten years since he'd driven, but with a little practice it all came right back to him. It was wonderful to be behind the wheel again, to feel in control of something other than his bodily functions. Driving, he thought, was like humping: it felt great no matter how rusty you were.

He'd been supplied with property department ID of the best quality in the name of Ben Hart.

Once or twice a week, he'd get documents of one sort or another delivered to the bungalow, and those deliveries were inevitably followed by phone instructions. They were usually about driving over to some federal building or municipal office in this county or that. He'd driven along the Salt, Gila, Yaqui, and Sonora rivers. He'd visited with tribal elders and councils and filed papers of every kind with every kind of bureaucrat—black-skinned, red-skinned, white-skinned, and just about every shade of skin in between. He'd stood in lines longer than the one at the Department of Motor Vehicles. He liked to laugh to himself that they were eventually going to ask for a urine sample, have him read an eye chart, and then give him some goddamn road test. No wonder they needed training films. This shit was confusing and stupifyingly boring. He could only imagine how much more boring it would have been had he actually had to read all the crap he was signing and filing.

Still, it was worth it to Harry. Most days were his to spend as he pleased as long as he stayed in character. That was pretty easy, as he was a virtual stranger in Tucson. Even when his role didn't require him to do so, he'd take long drives in all directions. And that was another amazing thing about coming back to the Tucson area; Harry had somehow recovered his once impeccable sense of direction. Even when it let him down and he got lost, Harry looked at it as an opportunity to explore. Sometimes he'd head out at the dawn of the day and sometimes at dusk. The scenery and the landscapes were breathtaking, almost otherworldy. It was as if his eyes were reborn and could now see what he had missed or ignored during his many acting gigs. Duke Wayne once told him that if you live in the desert long enough, brown becomes just another shade of green. Only now did Harry see the truth of this. More than anything, he'd come to love the rich redness of the rock and soil, a shade not so different from the color of his skin as a young man. There was something comforting about it. From the moment he landed, Harry knew he fit here. He just didn't know how.

There was a knock on the door and Mel Abbott shouted, "Come in!"

"These must be them," Paul Spiegelman said, rubbing his palms together.

The office door pushed back. A stocky Latino in blue spandex bicycle shorts, a wet Los Lobos T-shirt, a backpack, and a helmet stepped into the office and laid a fat envelope on Mel's desk. "Sign here." He pointed at the receipt.

The pen shook in Mel's right hand. It took him so long to put his name down, it was like he was etching rather than signing.

"Some time today would be nice, jefe," the messenger said, staring at his watch.

Spiegelman smiled. Not Mel.

"Here." Abbott shoved the receipt at the messenger. "What's the matter, you afraid you'll be late for your date with your chica?"

The messenger snatched the receipt, balled a copy of it, and threw it in Mel's face. "I don't know about my chica, but your mama don't like me to be late. She dries up quick these days." He took his time leaving the office, not exactly fearing for his life.

"Can you believe that motherfucker?" Mel said. But Spiegelman could barely contain his laughter. "Very funny, Paul.

Very funny. Just shut up and give me the package."

When he opened the envelope, Spiegelman started whistling "We're in the Money."

"What should I do with all these fucking audio tapes we got from Harry?"

"Toss 'em. I can't believe he still thinks he's being followed around by a camera crew. You gotta love actors!" Spiegelman said, then went back to whistling.

Mel was already dialing Joey Pothole's number.

There was a knock at Harry's door. He dreaded answering it. Not only because it was barely daylight, but because it had been five days since he had received a package of documents or a phone call. An actor, even one as old as dirt who hadn't worked for a decade and a half, knew when a shoot was winding down, and this shoot was definitely winding down. He hadn't wanted to think about it, but it couldn't be avoided any longer. The truth was that as much as he felt he belonged in Tucson, Harry wouldn't be able to afford to relocate here. Sure, it was all great now, but in the end it was an illusion, no more real than any of the other movies he'd been a part of. The house, the pickup, his groceries, the utilities, his cable TV bill were all being paid for by the folks who cast him in the role. And as many cheese fries as fifty grand would buy him, it wouldn't go very far if he were responsible for the things the film people were footing at the moment. No, it was back to burgers, L.A., and cheap hotels for Harry. Who knew, he thought, maybe when he got back Marissa LaTerre would be back too and together they could rekindle Harry's career.

But when he reluctantly pulled open the heavy, hand-carved front door, it wasn't a UPS or Federal Express man who greeted him.

"Can I help you?" he said to the impassive young Indian woman who stared at him across the threshold. She was quite pretty, with almond eyes, a broad nose, full lips, and a head of the blackest hair. In tight, faded jeans, a light denim blouse, and cowboy boots, she was dressed just like many of the young women in Tuscon.

"My great-grandmother would like to speak with you. She's in my truck." The woman turned and pointed to a beat-up old Chevy in the dirt driveway next to Harry's Ford.

"What's your name?"

"Rebecca. Please come. She is very old and it is very hot in the truck."

Harry followed Rebecca to the truck and there in the front seat sat a frail, ancient woman with hair as gray as her great-granddaughter's was black. Her deep brown leathery skin was wrinkled and heavily lined. She looked familiar to him. He remembered seeing her, but not where or when. It might have been on his trip to the Gila River compound or maybe it was when he was standing on one of those endless lines in some county or federal office. As he was about to find out, it was less important that he remembered her than she remembered him. When Harry stepped up to the door, the woman held an old black-and-white photo out to him.

"Isaac Hart," she said. "Your father."

Looking at it, Harry nearly fainted. At thirty, Harry had been the spitting image of the man in the photograph.

Mel Abbott and Paul Spiegelman sat across the table from the man who had acted as the buffer between them and the mining company. He was the man who had availed them of Joey Pothole's services and who had supplied them with the expense cash they needed to pull off the scam. He said his name was Walter Hogan. Con men themselves, neither Abbott nor Spiegelman—neither of whom were actually named Abbott or Spiegelman—believed him.

"Do you have the package?" Walter asked.

Mel's lip twitched. "I might ask you the same question."

Walter placed an attaché case on the table, flipped the latches, pulled the lid open, and spun the case around.

"Five hundred large," Walter said. When Mel went to reach for a pile of bills, Walter slammed the attaché closed. "This isn't the time to get sloppy or foolish. What were you going to do, fan a stack by your ear like some moron in a movie, or did you want to show off to the waitress?"

"Sorry."

"And the other half?" Paul piped up.

"When the documents check out. You'll get your percentage when the client starts pulling copper out of the ground. Now, don't make me ask again. The package."

As Paul Spiegelman slid the fat envelope across the table to Walter, the man relaxed his grip on the attaché case and smiled. "You sure everything's here?"

"Everything," Mel said.

"Everything," Paul chimed in. "Everything: a copy of the original birth certificate, the dummy contracts he signed, the original adoption papers, copy of the father's will, the deed on the house in Tucson in Ben Hart's name, a copy of the truck registration and insurance in his name, the tribal papers acknowledging Ben Hart's rightful heritage, the land deed that his father held on the acres your guys are going to mine. And, of course, the coup de grâce: Ben Hart's will, which we wrote and he signed without a second look. In it, as per your instructions, he bequeaths all his assets to Robert T. Ramsland. A friend of yours, I imagine, who will no doubt turn right around and sell it to Francoeur Mineral and Mining."

"A fair assumption," Walter agreed. "How did you get the guy to do all this?"

"Shit, Walter, we even got the idiot to make us cosigners on his bank accounts, so we can draw out his money and give it back to you once he's dead. Actors are the easiest marks in the world! Jesus, they're so fucking narcissistic. Stroke 'em a little and they lay down like a two-buck whore. He probably never even read a single one of the documents. Besides, for him it was just a gig, a role."

"Keep it," Walter said.

"Keep what?"

"The money in bank account, as a tip for a job well done." He actually shook both men's hands. "Good work, boys. Now I'm going to leave. Give me a ten-minute head start and then enjoy the rest of your lives!"

Neither Mel nor Paul could figure out how they'd run out of gas this far short of Phoenix. They had filled up just before meeting with Walter outside of Palm Springs, but it was a moot point now. Help was here in the shape of a Jeep pulling up behind their car. The tall, elegantly thin man with pocked skin shot Paul in the heart as he stepped out of the car. He put a second shot in the dying man's head as insurance. Mel ran. Joey didn't waste time chasing him. He was heading straight for the two holes he had already dug for them in the desert. First thing he did was put the attaché case into the Jeep.

Now Harry Garson finally understood why he fit. He'd been born here and was of the Pima people, but he wouldn't be of them for very much longer if he didn't get a handle on what was going on. It occurred to him that Marissa LaTerre had probably not taken off of her own free will and that she had more than likely come to the end of the road prematurely and violently. Harry spent the rest of the morning and afternoon visiting many of the offices he had visited in the last few weeks, trying to collect copies of the documents he'd signed and blindly filed without taking a second look. And once he had gathered as much of the paperwork as he could, he made two last stops.

While he drove back to the bungalow, a bungalow he was shocked to discover he owned free and clear, in a pickup truck he also owned free and clear, Harry ignored the thick envelope on the seat next to him and kept staring at the photograph of his biological father. Even after more than seventy-five years of life, it was an amazing feeling to fit in and to belong, to know your place in the world. Maybe all those years made it that much sweeter. Rebecca and the ancient woman, Issac Hart's youngest sister and Harry's aunt, explained that his father had fallen deeply in love with a teacher at the Indian school and had gotten her pregnant. He had wanted to marry her, but she refused. She'd had the baby, but disappeared a few weeks later. He had never stopped trying to find her and the child he had named Ben.

"He worked hard to purchase many acres of land off tribal territory, so he could prove his worth to the teacher when she returned or he found her," Rebecca explained. "He never found her and she never returned, but in your father's will he left the land to you and your children. Until you returned, it was to be kept by the family. We were not allowed to sell it or use it. I have been told this story since I was a child. The fact that your father bought white land when he did has been a source of great pride for us, but I always thought it was only a story." It was no story and the proof was there on the seat next to Harry.

It was dusk when he got back up to the little abobe house in the foothills, a place he had come to love. He also loved how the light of the vanishing sun lit up the sky with streaks of orange and purple, gold and blue. And although his eyesight wasn't great in the falling darkness without his glasses, he caught sight of the Jeep parked across the road from his house. If he hadn't been looking for a strange vehicle, he probably wouldn't have spotted it, but after what he'd learned today, he expected it to be there. He rolled to the side of the road, reached into the envelope, and pulled out one particular document. He took his deep breaths, flicked up his famous on switch, put the truck back in gear, and pulled onto the dirt driveway. When he got out of the Ford, Harry held the document out in front of him like a shield. He had it all planned, the words he was going to say to save himself. Yet, now out of the truck, he decided not to speak. Harry Garson was an old man, too old to be fully transformed into Ben Hart at this late date. Belonging, being Ben Hart, son of Isaac Hart, even for only a few hours, had answered all the important questions that he'd kept locked up inside all these years. What he really hoped for was that the end wouldn't hurt too much when it came.

The elegantly thin man with the pockmarked skin and cold fish eyes stood in the trashed living room and dialed the untraceable number Walter had given him. He had been thorough, making sure it looked like his target had walked in on a robbery, surprised the thief, and was shot to death in the process. Joey had even used a .45 on the old man, not the kind of weapon a professional killer would generally use.

"You're fucked," Joey said when Walter finally picked up.

"How's that?"

Joey explained about the document the old Indian held when he got out of the truck.

"He was holding a piece of paper in his hand, so what?"

"It's a last will and testament," the assassin said, "a brand-new one, dated today."

"Shit!"

"Shit is right. He left the land to the tribe and some woman named Rebecca to do with as they please. I don't know how he managed it, but the will was witnessed by the mayor of Tucson and a tribal elder. He's got a Polaroid of the signing stapled to the will. You're fucked."

"You said that already."

"My money?"

"You did your job. It'll be in your account in the morning."

There was a click on the other end of the line.

As Joey left, he took one last look at his victim to make sure everything was just so. And as he did, he thought he recognized the old Indian from a TV show he had watched as a kid.

"Bearstein!" he whispered to himself. "Sorry, chief."

PART IV

NORTH

GETTING LUCKY

BY LAWRENCE BLOCK

Upper Peninsula, Michigan

H e was wearing a Western-style shirt, scarlet and black with a lot of gold piping, and one of those bolo string ties, and he should have topped things off with a broad-brimmed Stetson, but that would have hidden his hair. And it was the hair that had drawn her in the first place. It was a rich chestnut with red highlights, and so perfect she'd thought it was a wig. Up close, though, you could see that it was homegrown and not store bought, and it looked the way it did because he'd had one of those $400 haircuts that cost John Edwards the 2008 Iowa primary. This barber had worked hard to produce a haircut that appeared natural and effortless, so much so that it wound up looking like a wig.

He was waiting his turn at the craps table, betting against the shooter and winning steadily as the dice stayed cold, with one shooter after another rolling craps a few times, then finally getting a point and promptly sevening out.

She didn't know dice, didn't care about gambling. Something about this man had drawn her, something about the wig that was not a wig, and she stood beside him and breathed in his aftershave—an inviting lemon-and-leather scent, a little too insistent but nice all the same. The string tie, she saw, had a Navajo slide, a thunderbird accented in turquoise.

Here in Michigan, the slide and its owner were a long way from home.

"Seven," the stickman announced. "New shooter coming out."

And the dice passed to the man with the great haircut.

He cradled them in his palm, held them in front of her face. Without looking at her he said, "Warm these up, sweet thing."

He'd given no indication that he was even aware of her presence, but she wasn't surprised. Men generally noticed her.

She took hold of his wrist, leaned forward, blew warm breath on the dice.

"Now that's just what was needed," he said, and dropped a black chip on the table, then gave the dice a shake and rolled an eleven. A natural, a winner, and that doubled his stake and he let it ride and rolled two sevens before he caught a point, an eight.

Now it became hard for her to follow, because she didn't know the game, and he was pushing his luck, betting numbers, scattering chips here and there, and rolling one combination after another that managed to be neither an eight nor a seven. He made the point, finally, and the one after that, and by the time he finally sevened out he'd won thousands of dollars.

"And that's that." He stepped away from the table, turning to take his first good long look at her. He wasn't shy about letting his eyes travel the length of her body, then return to her face. "When you get lucky," he said, "you got to ride it and push your luck. That's half of it, and the other half is knowing when to stop."

"And you're stopping?"

"For now. You stay at the table long enough, you're sure to give it all back. Luck goes one way and then it goes the other, like a pendulum swinging, and the house always has more money than you do and it can afford to wait you out. Any casino'll break you in the long run, even a pissant low-rent Injun casino way the hell up in the Upper Peninsula." He grinned. "But in the long run, we're all dead—so the hell with the long run. In the short run, a person can get lucky and do himself some good, and it might never have happened if you didn't come along and blow on my dice. You're my lucky charm, sweet thing."

"It was exciting," she said. "I don't really know anything about dice—"

"You sure know how to blow on 'em, darlin'."

"—but once you started rolling everything happened so fast, and everybody got excited about it—"

"Because the ones who followed my play got to win along with me."

"—and I got excited too."

He looked at her. "Excited, huh?"

She nodded.

"And now," he said, "I suppose it's passed, and you're not excited anymore."

"Not in the same way."

"Oh?"

She allowed herself a smile.

"C'mon," he said. "Why don't we sit down and have ourselves some firewater."

They took a table in a darkened corner of the lounge, and a dark-skinned girl with braids brought their drinks. He'd ordered a Dirty Martini, and she'd followed his lead.

"Olive juice," he explained. "Gives a little salty taste to the vodka. But I have to say, what I like most about it is just saying the name of it. 'A Dirty Martini, please. Straight up.' Don't you like the sound of it?"

"And the taste."

"Did you ever tell me your name? Because I can't remember it."

"It's Lucky."

"You're kidding, right?"

"It says Lucky on my driver's license. On my birth certificate it says Lucretia, but my parents didn't realize they'd opened the door for a lifetime of Lucretia Borgia jokes."

"I can imagine."

"You can't, because you don't know the whole story. Lucretia is bad enough, but when you attach it to Eagle Feather it becomes really awful, and—"

"That's your last name? Eagle Feather?"

"Used to be. I chopped the Lucretia and dropped the Feather and went in front of a judge to make it legal. Lucky Eagle's what I wound up with, and it's still pretty dopey."

"You're Indian."

God, he was quick on the uptake, wasn't he? You just couldn't keep anything from this dude.

"My father's half-Chippewa," she improvised, "and my mother's part Apache and part Blackfoot, and some Swedish and Irish and I don't know what else. I worked it all out one time, and I'm one-third Indian."

"A third, huh?"

"Uh-huh."

"Lucky Eagle Feather," he said. She liked that he was willing to skip the Lucretia part, but still wanted to hold onto that Feather. Made her a little bit more exotic, that's how she figured it. A little more Indian. And hadn't he just finished screwing a bunch of Indians out of a few thousand dollars? So why not screw a genuine Indian for dessert?

His name, she learned, was Hank Walker. Short for Henry,

but he'd been Hank since childhood. Seemed to suit him better, he told her, but it still said Henry on his driver's license. And he'd been born in New Jersey, the southern part of the state, near Philadelphia, but he'd moved west as soon as he could, because that seemed to suit him better too. He indicated the Western shirt, the string tie. "Sort of a uniform," he said, and grinned.

"It suits you," she agreed.

He lived in Nevada these days, outside of Carson City. And right now he was driving across the country, seeking out casinos wherever he went.

"I guess you like to play."

"When I'm on a roll," he said. "But these out-of-the-way places, I come here for the chips as much as the action."

"The chips?"

"Casino chips. People collect them."

"You sure collected a batch at the crap table."

What people collected, he explained, just as other collected coins and stamps, were the small-denomination chips the casinos issued, especially the one-dollar chips. At each casino he visited, he'd buy twenty or thirty or fifty of the dollar chips, and they'd be added to his stock when he got back home. He had a collection of his own, of course, but he also had a business, selling chips to collectors at chip shows—who knew there were chip shows?—and on his website.

"Ever since the government decided the tribes have the right to run casinos," he told her, "they've been popping up like mushrooms. And they come and they go, because not all of the tribes know a whole lot about running a gaming operation. You belong to the tribe that's operating this place?"

She didn't.

"Well, nothing against them, and I hope they make a go

of it, but there are a few things they're doing wrong." She half-listened while he took the casino's inventory; she had another sip of her Dirty Martini (which, all things considered, sounded better than it tasted) and breathed in his aftershave and an undertone of perspiration.

He finished his casino critique and reached across the table to put his hand on hers. "Now it seems to me we've got a decision to make. Do we have another round of drinks before we go to my room?"

For an answer she picked up his hand, lowered her head, and blew her warm breath into his palm. "For luck," she said without looking up, and then her tongue darted out and she licked his palm. His sweat, she noticed, tasted not all that different from the Dirty Martini.

He had a nice body. Barrel-chested, with a little more of a gut than she might have preferred, and a lot of chest hair. No hair on his back, though, and she supposed he got it waxed at the same salon that provided his million-dollar haircuts.

Muscular arms, muscular shoulders, and that meant regular gym workouts, because he couldn't have gotten those muscles simply by throwing his own weight around. An all-over tan, too, that probably came from a tanning bed. You could shake your head at the artifice, or you could go with the result—a fit, good-looking man in his late forties, who, it had to be said, was as impressive in the sack as he'd been at the craps table. And if he owed some of that to Viagra, well, so what? He got her hot and he got her off, and what more could a poor girl desire?

And the best was yet to be.

Optima futura—that was the Latin for it, and she knew it because it had been her high school's motto. It was, she'd always thought, singularly apt, because anything the future held had to be better than high school.

Somewhere along the way, after high school years were just a blur, she'd come across some lines from Robert Browning, and perhaps it was the high school motto that made her commit them to memory, but it had worked, because she remembered them still:

> Grow old along with me!
> The best is yet to be
> The last of life, for which the first was made . . .

"Part Indian, huh? I bet I know which part is Indian."

And he reached out a hand and touched the part he had in mind. She put her hand on top of his, rubbed his fingers against her.

"A third Indian," she reminded him.

"So you said. You know, I was wondering—"

She put her hand on him, curled her fingers around him. She worked him artfully, and he sighed.

"Lucky," he said. "Man, I'd say I got Lucky, didn't I? But I think I'm tapped out for this evening."

"You think so?"

"You drained me to the dregs, babe. About all I can do right now is sleep."

"I bet you're wrong."

"Oh?"

"What we did so far," she said, "was just a warm-up."

"Yeah, right."

"Can I ask you something?"

He raised his eyebrows.

"Have you ever been tied up?"

"Jesus."

"Just imagine," she said, her hands still busy. "You're tied up, you can't move, and the entire focus is giving you pleasure. I'll do things to you nobody's ever done to you before, Hank. You think this has been your lucky night? You just wait."

"Uh—"

"I've got all the gear in my bag," she said. "Everything we could possibly need. You're gonna love this."

Handcuffs, silk scarves, nylon cords. She had everything she needed, and she knew just how to employ them.

The last time she'd done this she'd given her partner a couple of roofies first, and let the pills knock him out before she trussed him up. That had worked fine, but she'd been stuck with a two-hour wait for the son of a bitch to wake up, and who needed that?

This was much simpler. And he cooperated, putting his hands where she told him, spread-eagling himself on the bed. And making little jokes while she did what she had to do.

By the time she was done, he was already semi-erect. She wrapped the base with an elastic band. "Sort of a roach motel," she said. "The blood gets in and it can't get out, so you stay firm."

"Is it safe?"

"Absolutely," she said. "It's an old Indian trick. Now you can do something for me, and after that everything will be entirely 100 percent for you." And she sat on his face and he did what he was supposed to do, and he was pretty good at it too. He didn't have to be, she was so excited right now that great technique on his part was by no means required, but this made it even better.

"Now that was just wonderful," she said. She went to her

bag, got out the duct tape, and cut off an eight-inch length. "I wanted to do that first," she went on, "because it's our last chance for that particular activity."

And she slapped the tape over his mouth.

Oh, the look in his eyes! Worth the price of admission right there. He wasn't quite sure whether this was going to make it even more exciting for him, or whether it was maybe something he ought to worry about.

But why worry? What good would it do? What good would anything do?

"See, isn't this neat? You're harder than ever. And you're going to stay that way." She mounted him, felt him swelling impossibly larger inside her. "Mmmm, nice," she said. "Oh, yes. Very nice."

She rode him for a long time. Her climaxes came one after the other, and all they did was pitch her excitement higher. At last she fell forward, her breasts crushed against his chest. A smooth chest would have been nice, but a hairy chest was nice too. Everything was nice when you could do whatever you wanted, and when you knew just how it was going to end.

She got up because she wanted to be able to see his eyes now. "I told you some lies," she said. "My name's not Lucky. Or Lucretia, or any of that. My last name's not Eagle, or Eagle Feather, and don't ask me how I came up with all of that on the spur of the moment. As far as I know, I haven't got a drop of Indian blood in me. A third Indian! How could anybody be a third anything? I mean, you've got two parents, four grandparents, eight great-grandparents—I mean, do the math. You're the one who knows all the odds on the craps table, so you would have to know that you can only be half or a fourth or an eighth or three-sixteenths or whatever you are of anything."

She wagged a finger at him.

"You weren't paying attention, Hank. Little Henry there was doing your thinking for you. And that's another lie I told you, incidentally. That it's safe to wrap you up like that. If you don't loosen it in time, you can do permanent damage."

She left the bed, reached into her purse, found the knife. She let him see the blade. She let the tip of the blade graze his cheek as she mounted him one more time.

"God, it's bigger than ever," she told him. "You're in pain now, aren't you? Oh dear, I'm afraid it's going to get worse. Well, more intense, anyway. *Optima futura*, you know. That's Latin. It means the best is yet to be. For me, that is. For you, well, maybe not."

She left with close to five thousand dollars in cash and chips, and stopped downstairs at the cashier's cage to turn the chips into currency. Then she got in her car and started driving.

She'd left his one-dollar chips in the room. She'd left his credit cards too, and a gold signet ring that had to be worth a few hundred dollars. She took the slide from his string tie, just because she liked it, and she took her cuffs and cords and scarves, because it would be a nuisance to replace them. But she left the elastic band in place.

And she took the scalp, tucked away in a plastic bag. It was just such good theater to scalp him, what with having been drawn to his hair in the first place, and then the whole Indian motif of their encounter. Before she was halfway done with the process she regretted having begun it in the first place, because even minor scalp cuts bleed like crazy, and when you scalp a person altogether—well, the Indians probably waited to scalp people until they were safely dead, and disinclined to bleed, but she went ahead and finished what she'd started, and it was almost worth it when she shook the scalp in front of him and let him gape at it.

She'd cleaned up her fingerprints, but she knew she'd left plenty of DNA evidence, and people at the casino could furnish a description of her. But she'd been working variations on this theme for a good long while now, and she always got away with it, so she figured all she could do was play out the string. And she'd ditch his scalp where it wouldn't be found, and the scalping would guarantee a lot of press, along with a manhunt for some unforgiving Indian seeking vengeance for Wounded Knee.

Yes, she'd just go ahead and play out the string. Because it kept getting better, didn't it? *Optima futura.* That pretty much said it all.

PROWLING WOLVES

BY LIZ MARTÍNEZ

Chicago, Illinois

The Pima Indian huddles on the ground in the fox-hole, his M1 rifle propped upright between his legs. He is awake and watchful while his fellow marine, Bill Faulkner, curls up nearby, getting some shut-eye. The darkness is pervasive, and he sees what he thinks might be shadows. Or maybe they aren't. He keeps his ears open, straining to make sense of the rustling noise. Other marines? The enemy? There isn't any way to tell.

The most important thing is not to fall asleep. He's responsible for keeping himself and Faulkner safe. He has to stay awake. It's not a problem for him, though. If he gets sleepy, he just concentrates on the smell. In the two days they've been on Bougainville, the marines of Easy Company have been pinned down in their foxholes in a monsoon, then trapped under the scorching sun. They all stink.

He turns his head, trying to match shapes to the rustles he hears. He can see better in the darkness out of the corner of his eye than by looking at objects straight on. The change of position causes the stench to hit him again. Not just his own rank body odor, but the smell of blood. And guts. And decaying bodies. Already, there are bodies ready to be shipped home. Young men who knew they'd be the lucky ones to make it back to America—but they'd figured on doing so alive.

He glances over at Faulkner. He's glad his buddy is able

to get some sleep, but he can't figure out how the guy can do it. The adrenaline courses through his own body, keeping him from ever really sleeping. This isn't new. Even back home on the reservation, he could hardly rack up any sack time. Instead of adrenaline, feelings of guilt, remorse, and shame would torture him in the nighttime. Not over anything specific. Or rather, over everything. A white man's purposeful slight. A buddy who made a thoughtless remark. Anything, really. During the day, he could find ways to cope. But at night—that was different.

He turns his head again to try to see what's going on in the darkness around them. He doesn't hear or see anything, but he strains to listen and penetrate the darkness anyway.

He feels an abrupt thud that reverberates down his arms, and he hears screaming right next to him. The adrenaline courses through his body at full speed. He doesn't know what just happened, but his rifle seems to have a mind of its own, jerking and pulling out of his hands. He grabs it back by reflex.

All of a sudden, he realizes what's going on. An enemy soldier tried to sneak up on him, and when he moved to attack, impaled himself on the Indian's bayonet at the end of the rifle.

He yanks the rifle back, pulling the bayonet out of the Jap's stomach. He's running on animal instinct now. He picks up the rifle in both hands and punctures the enemy soldier's body over and over. He's stabbing the man with his bayonet, but the man keeps moving. He knows he must kill him or be killed. So he keeps thrusting. Again and again, he heaves the rifle downward, pulls it back, hurls it into the man's body.

He is so consumed with his own personal combat that he's in another world. "Chief, stop! He's dead. You killed him. Knock it off!"

He can hardly hear the other marine over the roar in his ears. He's barely aware of the guy's hand gripping his shoulder, shaking him. "Ira. Ira!"

His lids popped open. Sergeant Beech's fingers squeezed his shoulder at the nerve point, sending the pain radiating down his arm. The Indian twitched to shake the sergeant's hand off. Beech gripped him by the upper arm to lift him to his feet. The roar of the audience's applause subsided as Rene Gagnon sat down next to Ira on the dais again. Gagnon shot him a disgusted look and turned back to his dessert.

The Indian stood up, stretched, and opened his mouth in a huge yawn. The audience responded in kind. They looked like a sea of goldfish swimming toward the surface for food. Beech grinned. This gave him a kick every time it happened.

He shoved Ira toward the microphone. "Tell 'em . . ."

But the Indian knew what to do. He stood before the microphone and confronted the audience of Chicagoans who had turned out to see the heroes. His mouth always got dry at this point. He was never a man to use many words, and his vocabulary seemed to abandon him in front of a crowd.

"I hope you buy lots of war bonds," he said.

He sat down again.

The crowd in the hotel ballroom erupted in applause and cheering. Ira wasn't really aware of them. He was busy looking around. Beech knew what he wanted and leaned down to whisper in his ear. "Later, chief." He patted the Indian's shoulder reassuringly.

Ira didn't want to wait until *later*. He needed some booze now. He was thinking about how to attract the waiter's attention without attracting the attention of the audience. He barely heard Bradley, now at the microphone, denying they were anything special.

"We're not heroes." Bradley gestured to himself, Gagnon, and Ira Hayes. "We just put up a flag. The real heroes are the ones who died fighting on Iwo Jima. Please buy war bonds to honor their memory."

The crowd went wild. The band started up again, and the room exploded in a cacophony of chatter, laughter, and music.

Beech slapped Ira on the shoulder. "Come on, buddy. Let's go."

Ira got up eagerly. Keyes Beech was always ready to bend an elbow.

Gagnon sneered. "What's the matter, chief? Can't wait to start drinking again? Fuckin' drunken Indian." He muttered the last part.

Ira went cold, then hot. His fists curled.

Then Bradley poked Gagnon. "Hey, come on. Ira's working as hard as we are. Lay off."

Beech steered Ira away from the dais, and it was over. "Don't listen to him. This bond tour is getting to all of us. He's just blowing off a little steam. Hey, a buddy of mine tipped me about this great bar in the Loop. Let's go check it out."

Ira didn't say a word. He just followed Beech out of the hotel, listening to the sergeant's nonstop chatter. He had no need to talk. Beech said enough words for both of them.

Ira didn't feel at home anywhere, but he felt the least uncomfortable in a bar. Just walking inside, inhaling the familiar bar smells—old beer overlayed with cigarette smoke—made the churning in his stomach stop. The act of sitting on a bar stool gave him that relaxed feeling. Then he gripped the glass in his hand, and even before the first swallow, he felt at peace.

The whiskey had just begun spreading its comforting warmth in his stomach when it started.

"Hey, aren't you that guy from the picture?"

"You're a hero, man. Lemme buy you a drink!"

"Look who's here—he's one of the ones who put the flag up! Bartender, this marine's money's no good tonight!"

Beech loved it. His job was to chaperone the three flag-raisers as they toured the country on the 7th War Loan Bond Drive, raising money for the boys overseas. But Bradley was a pretty straight arrow, and Gagnon, with his movie-star good looks, had no trouble fending for himself. Ira was the one he had to babysit. The Indian was likely to wander off somewhere and get into a fight, then not remember how to get back to the latest hotel in the latest city. Or even remember which city he was in.

Not that Beech minded hanging out with Ira. Hell no. The guy attracted attention wherever he went. And he was so modest he hardly said two words in a whole night. So people began talking to Beech instead. Beech was a tech sergeant and war correspondent. He told the war stories that people wanted to hear from Ira, but that Ira would never talk about. After a few drinks, it didn't matter who was talking. Everyone was a hero by that time. And the booze flowed, so Beech was happy. And Ira was happy.

Except Beech didn't think Ira was so happy. Oh well. Nothing he could do about it. The only one Ira would talk to was "Doc" Bradley, and Bradley wasn't really a drinker.

So that left the two of them. Two little Injuns, he thought, and giggled. Snippets of the song ran through his head. *Four little Injuns up on a spree / One got fuddled and then there were three / Three little Injuns out on a canoe / One* something, something, *and then there were two.* He couldn't remember the rest.

"Hey, Ira." He reached across a man who was in the middle of telling a story and grabbed the Pima by the shirt sleeve. "What happened to the three little Injuns?"

Ira glared at him. Oh boy. He must be drunker than he'd thought.

"Never mind," he said, trying to pat Ira's sleeve, placate him. He turned to the storyteller he'd interrupted. "Do *you* know what happened to the three little Injuns?"

The guy shook him off. "Buddy, I think you've had enough."

"I'm fine, I'm fine," he slurred. Then, "Oh shit." He got up and tried to get to the restroom before he tossed his cookies all over the bar floor. He didn't make it.

Then Ira was pulling him out of the bar.

Beech bent over in the street, heaving his guts out. "Must have been something I ate," he croaked.

Ira didn't say anything.

After a minute, Beech stood up and wiped his mouth. "You know, I actually feel better." He could feel a little spring coming back into his step. "Hey! Look over there." He pointed to the warm glow of another barroom.

But Ira had already seen it and was heading toward the inviting lights.

"Geez, wait up, buddy," Beech said.

They elbowed their way up to the bar, and the same drama from the other bar—from all the other bars on this tour—started all over again: "Aren't you the guy from Iwo Jima? I wanna buy you a drink!"

Ira was entering that maudlin stage of his drinking. He couldn't tolerate company, but he did want the free drinks. He made himself as small as possible at the back corner of the bar. He watched the bartender's brogans as the man walked back and forth, hustling drinks. He wished he could just curl up on the floor behind the bar, alone with all the liquor bottles. Just sit on the floor. The rats could keep him company. There must be rats, because there was a box of rat poison, the skull and crossbones warning anyone who came near.

That's not what a real skull looks like, he thought, hunching lower. A real skull has blood on it. And hair. And pieces of brain leaking out.

And there are men screaming all around. And huge explosions as mortar shells rock the island.

The Pima Indian hears a fellow member of Easy Company calling out the password. "Studebaker! Studebaker!" But that's yesterday's password. "Chevrolet! Goddammit, I can't remember! It's me! It's me, Early."

The Indian doesn't know whether the forgetful marine gets to live or dies because the next thing that happens is three of the "prowling wolves" attack him and two of his buddies. General Tadamichi Kuribayashi, the commander of the Japanese forces on Iwo Jima, has given this name to his teams of stalking, crawling night-murderers—the dancing shadows feared by every American fighting man on the island.

The Japs are ruthless. They think it's a big honor to die in combat. Ira just knows it's him or them, and it ain't gonna be him. He shoots the one who's attacking him in the head. The round smashes the Jap's face and leaves his teeth lying on the ground.

The Pima marine wants to be sick, but he's distracted by something even worse than the dead jack-o'-lantern in front of him. A marine is wrestling with an enemy soldier, but he's losing because they're not really wrestling. The Japanese soldier is stabbing him.

"Mom, he's killing me!" the marine cries. "Mom!"

The Indian's eyes flickered. "I'm coming to help you!" he called. He reached out and grabbed the guy's arm.

"Easy, easy," the man told him. "I just got this here tattoo. It's a beaut, ain't it? *Mom* in a heart, that's what I wanted. And that's just what I got." His jacket was off, his shirt sleeve rolled up to display his newest artwork.

Ira squinted. There were two hearts, its seemed, and two *Mom*s. His heart rate slowed down. "Nice," he said. Or tried to say. He couldn't be sure he got the word out. The guy was talking to somebody else now, anyway. It didn't matter.

He was tired of this bar. In fact, he was sick of this two-bit joint and everybody in it. He pushed up from his bar stool and staggered to the door. Somebody came up behind him, and he whirled, ready to throw a haymaker, let this guy's teeth wind up on the floor, like the Jap's.

The man looked frightened. "You forgot your jacket there, buddy." He held it out to Ira at arm's length.

The Indian grabbed it out of the man's hand. Who did he think he was, anyway, following him around? His mom?

He let out a howl, like a wolf in pain. It sounded so good he did it again. It was a mistake, though, because he was attracting attention.

"What are you looking at?" he yelled at the crowd beginning to form outside the bar. "Go back inside."

He turned on his heel and strode away.

Keyes Beech caught up with him. "Ira, Ira, take it easy, man."

Ira shrugged him off and kept going.

"Where you heading? It's cold. Come on, let's go in here. This looks like a quiet neighborhood joint. Nobody'll bother us here. See? I'm going in. Come with me," Beech coaxed. He opened the door and motioned Ira in.

The Indian was going to keep walking, but then he thought, What the hell, and went in.

It was a workingman's bar. Sawdust on the floor. Men in caps and thick jackets. Men who looked like Mike.

Mike Strank is the best platoon leader a guy can have. He understands his marines, and he takes care of them. The Indian respects him. Reveres him. All Mike's men do. And even though the Pima doesn't speak much to anyone, he's practically a chatterbox with Mike. He can tell Mike anything. Mike doesn't judge. He just loves his men back by being the best leader he can be and doing everything he can to keep them safe. That's why they'll do anything for him.

Mike was born in Czechoslovakia but passed through Ellis Island when he was three. He has the strong bone structure common to Eastern Europeans that keep them looking young, even in their old age. Mike's most prominent feature is a pugnacious chin.

The Indian walked up to a man standing at the bar, his hands wrapped around a beer glass. The man wore a cap and had a defiant chin. The Indian peered at him. "Mike?" he said in a small voice.

"Look, I don't know you," the man said, keeping his eyes on his beer. He had an accent.

Ira's head snapped back. "Sorry," he said.

Beech pulled him to the other end of the bar. "What are you doing, huh? You want to get us thrown out of here?" he hissed.

Ira looked down but didn't speak.

"Here, sit at the table. I'll get you something." Beech shoved the Indian into a chair.

The sergeant returned to the table with two beers and drank half of his in one swallow, as though it were his first of the evening, instead of his seventeenth. "We'll just sit here for a little while, huh, Ira? It's a good place just to have a few beers."

It was a quiet place. Every man in there had his own story, and they were all keeping mum. They were just minding their own business after putting in a day's manual labor at the docks or the slaughterhouses.

Then something happened to fracture the silence. The two marines didn't know what set it off. Not being regulars, they didn't know the politics of the place. But somebody obviously stepped out of line because a man crashed into their table, landing with his head practically in the Indian's lap. As the guy attempted to stagger to his feet, the back of his head slammed into the Pima marine's chin. The Indian punched his enemy in the stomach.

The guy cries out, bent double. Mike is trying to lead the Indian and several other marines across a dangerous strip of ground. But Boatwright takes a bullet in the stomach. The impact slams him into a shell hole. The others scramble for cover. The sniper fire is unceasing.

Mike bends down on one knee, surrounded by his beloved troops. He's drawing a plan in the sand to show the marines how to get out of there safely.

But he doesn't get a chance to speak. A shell explodes, ripping his heart out.

He was lying facedown.

The Indian crouched over him, sobbing. "Oh, Mike! Mike!"

Rough hands pulled him up, shoved him away. "Don't you think you've caused enough trouble, buddy?"

"Just go before you get what's coming to you."

Then—"Jesus, Hayes, you can't even have a beer without

all this drama. Let's get the fuck out of here before we have to take on the whole bar."

Good old Beech, bailing his ass out again.

It was cold, but the Indian wasn't aware of the weather. Or much of anything else. He could hardly see straight, and what he did see came in pairs. He felt pretty good, though.

Then he spotted it. It loomed ahead, mocking him. This was the cause of all his troubles. He ran toward it. He was going to pull it out of the ground and get rid of it, once and for all.

The Pima grasps the piece of drainage pipe he and Franklin Sousley found at the top of the mountain. It weighs over a hundred pounds, and they have to drag it over so the flag Gagnon is carrying can be tied to it. Then they all have to hoist up this pole and plant the fucking flag in the ground. Some dumb officer wants to keep the Stars and Stripes that's *already* flying for his own personal souvenir of the invasion of Iwo Jima. So now he and some other guys from Easy Company have to drag ass up the hill and take down a perfectly good flag, just to put up a new one.

They're already on a mission to run telephone wire and batteries up the mountain, so why not have them replace the flag while they're at it? The brass are always sending marines on stupid errands.

The pole is heavy, but he and Sousley are battle-toughened marines. They can do what needs to be done.

He grabbed the pole and tugged with all his might. This time, he wouldn't plant the flag. There would be no photograph of him and his buddies sticking the goddamn thing into the top of Mount Suribachi. He yelled as though the pole could hear him, his voice filled with grief. "You son of a bitch! I hate you! I hate you!" Tears streamed down his face.

The copper was walking his beat when he heard a cry. He quickened his step. At fifty-two, John Flanagan was beginning to feel a little creaky. But he couldn't leave the job. Who would replace him? All the young, able-bodied fellows were off fighting in the European theater or the Pacific or some damn place. The Chicago Police Department needed him. Besides, what would he do with himself? Police work was all he knew.

This hour of night, this part of town, he figured the yelling was coming from some guy who had too much to drink. There was a festive air in town these last couple days, what with the war bond tour and all the Hollywood entertainers who were participating so they could get their names in the papers. Flanagan smoothed his small mustache and pulled himself up to his full five foot six inches.

Sure enough, there was some idiot hanging off a streetlamp, screaming his head off. Flanagan reached down instinctively to check his weapon. He swiped his left sleeve down over his star. He didn't even notice he was doing it, he'd had the habit so long. Wearing a gleaming star on his chest had been a point of pride since he'd joined the force, and he had developed the unconscious routine of shining it up before any potential confrontation.

"All right, what's the problem here?" he bellowed. He didn't know why, but drunks seemed to lose their hearing during the course of a night's imbibing. He'd learned early on that if you don't shout at a drunk, you won't get through to him.

The idiot didn't respond. Just kept banging his fist against the streetlamp and cursing it out.

As he got closer, Flanagan could see that the guy wore a uniform. Great. Another drunken marine. He let out a small sigh.

Then he realized it was even better than he'd thought.

The drunk idiot had a friend with him. Another marine. This one looked three sheets to the wind too, but at least he was quiet. He was crouched on the ground.

Now Flanagan could see what the guy was doing. Why did he always have to get the drunks who puked? He hoped he wouldn't get any vomit on his uniform this time. His wife would have a fit.

"What's going on here?" he called out in his best basso profundo. "What did that streetlamp do to you?"

The idiot didn't pay any attention to him. He sighed again. Louder. Stood with his legs apart and his hands on his hips.

"All right, listen up! Step away from that lamp and you won't get hurt. You hear me?"

It wasn't working. The idiot was still lost in his own world.

Flanagan crossed his arms, then almost jumped out of his skin as he realized that the idiot's buddy was standing right behind him. The guy had sneaked up on him like a thief in the night. He whirled around and dropped his hand to his holster. Then he realized there was no threat.

The sergeant was obviously standing so close to the other guy because he could no longer gauge distance, he was so drunk. He just stood there with a sweet smile on his face, his eyes at half mast, swaying in the breeze. Lovely.

Well, as long as he was upright . . . "Do you think you can get your buddy to leave the poor streetlamp alone?" Flanagan jerked his thumb behind him. "After all, it doesn't look like the light attacked him first. Why does he have to try to punch its lights out?" Flanagan played to an audience of one. Himself. He chuckled slightly.

The marine sergeant just stood there with that big stupid grin on his face. Useless.

Flanagan stopped laughing. He tried again. "Listen, pal, if your friend there doesn't stop his screaming, I'm going to have to lock him up. Let's try to be civilized about this, okay?"

Something must have penetrated because the guy came to life. Well, he moved a little.

"We're—marines," he slurred. "Don't—lock up. Hafta be back for—grblsh."

Flanagan could barely understand him. "I can see you're marines. You want to help your buddy back to camp or wherever you belong, or do you want to spend what's left of the night in jail?"

The sergeant visibly tried to straighten himself up. "It'sh—okay. Fine. I'll take him—"

He thought the guy was going to puke again, so he made a rookie mistake. He backed up, forgetting that the other drunk was behind him.

The Pima marine grabbed him by the coat and whirled him around. "You son of a bitch!" He punched Flanagan in the stomach. "You goddamn son of a bitch! It's all your fault!" Another punch. "I hate you, Rosenthal! Hate you, hate you, hate you!" He underscored every "hate you" with another punch.

Beech revived enough to try pulling him off the policeman. "Ira, enough! Leave him alone!"

Flanagan rolled himself into a ball to make a smaller target. If he could just get to his gun . . . He managed to unsnap his holster. He touched the grip of his pistol. Almost there . . . Then, fireworks. Then, darkness.

The adrenaline coursing through Beech's body rendered him instantly sober. He wrestled with the Pima for possession of the cop's gun.

The Indian is in the foxhole with Franczik when a flare

explodes, lighting up the night. Two enemy soldiers are slashing the guys in the next hole with bayonets. They run over there to aid their fellow marines.

One of the Japs hurls a grenade at them. It's a dud, but it strikes Franczik in the head, and he goes down. The Indian reaches inside Franczik's shirt to pull out the .45 he knows his friend keeps hidden there, but the Jap is right on top of him.

He punches at the enemy soldier and wrestles with him for possession of the handgun. Blood covers the gun, and it's slippery in his hand. He may not be able to hold onto it, but he won't give up. They go back and forth over the .45.

A tug of war for the gun.

"Ira, stop it! Let go!"

Beech grabbed for the policeman's gun again. The Indian was still engaged in mortal combat. He wouldn't loosen his grip. But Beech had sobered up, and Ira's body hadn't yet processed all the alcohol he'd consumed that day.

With a final tug, Beech managed to pull the weapon away from the Pima marine. The gun went off.

"Shit!" Beech cried. "Why isn't the fucking safety on on this piece of shit? You okay, Ira?"

Ira didn't say anything.

Beech scrambled to his feet and jerked Ira up. "Yeah, you're okay. Thank fucking Christ."

Ira looked down at the spreading pool of blood.

"Oh my God," Beech said. "Oh fuck."

The blood pools all over the ground. It sinks in, staining the dirt. There are so many dead and wounded that there's nothing else to smell besides the coppery scent of blood and the stench of decaying bodies.

The Pima Indian crouches down, trying to duck rounds that he can't begin to guess the origins of. The enemy is hidden, and bullets seem to originate from nowhere and everywhere.

He sees blood pouring out of the man in front of him. He presses the man's jacket against his chest wound. "You'll be okay," he reassures him. But he knows he's lying.

Out of the corner of his eye, he spots one of the prowling wolves coming toward him. "Over there!" he shouts. He grabs a gun out of another marine's hands. He hears rounds exploding everywhere. It's impossible to tell whether what he's hearing is his own gunfire or not.

"Oh my god, oh my god, ohmygod ohmygod."

Beech came around behind the Pima and yanked his jacket down to immobilize his arms. "Ira, we have to go. *Now*."

He shoved him toward the street, but not before the Indian spotted the two men lying on the ground. "What happened?" he asked, craning his neck to look.

Beech gritted his teeth. "You were here. You know what happened."

The Indian became desperate. "No! I don't know. Tell me. Please, please, tell me."

"The cop got shot," Beech said shortly. "The other guy saw what happened. Now let's *go*." He shoved the Pima away and frog-marched him down the street.

Beech looked up and saw dawn beginning to peek out of the sky. He had to get this guy back to the hotel and cleaned up for the dog-and-pony show this morning.

As they passed a sewer grate, he shoved the Indian ahead of him and dropped the gun down the hole.

Five blocks later, the Indian asked, "What happened to the other guy?"

Beech didn't answer.

"Beech?"

"What?"

"What happened to the other guy?"

"What other guy?" He was stalling.

"There were two guys on the ground back there, and I'm pretty sure they were both dead. Who was that other guy, and how did he get that way?"

"Ira, you were there. I was there. There's nothing else to say." He stopped walking and jerked the Indian around to face him. "I mean it. You are never to mention this again. Do you understand?"

"No. Why won't you tell me?"

Beech stared at him. "You kidding me? I don't know anything that you don't know. Now, you're to keep your mouth shut about tonight or we're gonna have some real problems." He grabbed the Indian below the collar of his shirt and shook him. "Understand me?"

The Pima just looked at him for a long moment. Then he nodded and said, "Yeah."

Beech let him go. "Good."

Outside the hotel, they passed a poster for the 7th War Loan Bond Drive. It was fastened to a light pole and it danced in the breeze. The Indian looked at the photograph of himself and five others raising the flag on Mount Suribachi. He, Gagnon, and Bradley were the only survivors. The other three were killed in the battle that raged on after they planted the flag. Every time he saw the photo, another little part of his heart withered and died. He missed his buddies from Easy Company, most of whom were gone now.

"I wish Joe Rosenthal had never taken that picture," he said. "Then I wouldn't have to be on this crummy tour."

"Yeah, well, he did and you are," Beech said sourly. "Now you have to get in there and clean yourself up in time to go raise the flag again at Soldier Field."

"I already raised the flag on Iwo. Why do I have to do it again?"

"Because they built a replica of Suribachi, and you *heroes* have to reenact the flag-raising so people will buy more war bonds, so the marines who are still fighting have a half a chance of surviving. Get it?"

They entered the hotel in silence. Beech said, a little friendlier now, "I'll take you up to your room, help you get cleaned up."

"That's okay. You don't have to."

"I *said* I'll take you up."

The Indian didn't respond.

Beech checked his watch. "Never mind. We don't have time anyway. Come on."

He led the Indian down to the staging area. Gagnon and Bradley both shook their heads when they saw the shape he was in. Bradley looked at Beech, exasperated. Wasn't Beech supposed to keep an eye on Ira?

Gagnon stepped over to the catering area and came back with a bucket of ice water. He poured it over Ira's head. "Maybe this'll sober you up, you fuckin' drunk."

"Jesus, Rene. You didn't have to do that," Bradley said.

"Yes, I did. Look at him."

"Enough," Beech snapped. "The Cadillac that's going to drive you around Soldier Field is here. Make sure Hayes sits in the middle so he can't fall out. And Hayes—you drag your ass up that papier-mâché mountain and you plant that flag. And *don't* fall down. Do you understand?"

The Pima marine shook the water off himself like a dog and said nothing.

Beech had watched the whole dog-and-pony show, and unless

you knew what a mess Hayes was, you couldn't tell he was out of it. He always tended to be a little on the sloppy side anyway.

And Beech would be the first one to catch any flak if the brass was upset with the performance of any of the heroes. No news was good news.

But that didn't prevent him from almost having a nervous breakdown. He kept running down to the street to see if there were any extra editions of the Chicago papers highlighting the murder of a policeman and a civilian.

The copper was one thing. Hayes had grabbed for his gun, and Beech had had no choice but to get involved. Too bad the guy bought it, but Beech had to protect Hayes. And himself.

But that other fucking guy had seemed to come out of nowhere. All of a sudden he was standing there, watching the whole thing. It would definitely not be a good thing if the guy shot off his mouth later about seeing two marines and a dead policeman.

And that fucking Hayes, asking him what happened. Hayes wasn't stupid. He was trying to play it coy, maybe setting the stage to shift all the blame to Beech if the shit ever hit the fan.

Beech developed a splitting headache.

After a few days in Detroit and Indianapolis, the tour returned to Chicago. Beech wanted to rip his fingernails out with his teeth. He hadn't had a drink since their last night in Chicago. He took Hayes out to bars every night but kept himself in check so he could watch the Indian. He managed to make sure the captain or the colonel saw Hayes in all his glory, returning to the hotels after his nights on the town.

At the Palmer Hotel in Chicago, Colonel Fordney told

Beech to bring Hayes into his office. The colonel shoved a United Airlines ticket to Hawai'i into Beech's hands. "He's going back to Easy Company. The Fifth Division is training to invade Japan. Hayes is going with them. Make sure he gets on the plane without disgracing the Corps. Dismissed."

Later, as Beech was getting the Indian seated on the plane, he said, "I'm real sorry it turned out this way, Ira. You're a good man. Keep your chin up." He clapped him on the shoulder.

The Pima marine looked at Beech. "What did you do with the gun?"

Beech cupped his hand behind his ear. "Can't hear you."

The Indian raised his voice. "The gun. What did you do with it?"

Beech shrugged and waved his hand, indicating there was too much noise for him to make out what his friend was saying. "Have a safe trip," he called.

The Indian didn't say anything.

Beech jogged back inside the terminal where he could watch the plane, with Hayes inside, take off.

The war bond tour was raising money, that was true, but it was also a fact that the United States government was broke. That meant a lack of weapons, ammunition, tanks, food—a shortage of everything. With diminishing supplies, there was a hell of a good chance Hayes wouldn't make it back from combat alive.

He scanned the morning editions of the Chicago papers. There were follow-up stories on the dead policeman and civilian, but all they amounted to were that there were no witnesses and no leads. The only item of note was that the policeman's gun was missing, but there were no clues and no theories yet.

Beech rubbed his hands together. Now he could relax,

have a drink, and get ready to move on to St. Louis and Tulsa with the bond tour.

QUILT LIKE A NIGHT SKY

BY KIMBERLY ROPPOLO

Alberta, Canada

Going home was the last thing he wanted to do.

In the darkness, Boon Lone Rider walked past Farm Four, a mix of gravel and crusty snow crunching beneath his heavily worn runners. He wished it were summer. He remembered shoes from the past, smaller pairs of canvass ones with rubber soles, dust coating them thinly as it rose in tiny clouds, his child feet dragging patterns like snakes in the road. He thought about stopping at a cousin's place in Little Chicago, but it had been a long time since he had been back here, and not only was Boon unsure of circumstances—the things that had transpired since his last visit, the details of life, always changing, who was cool with what and with whom, who had been caught with whose woman in the backseat of a pow wow van, what shotguns and odd handguns had drifted across the border into whose hands, whether his cousin was even alive—he also knew he needed to do this.

He thought about visiting his mom and his grandma, but he'd have to go by the cemetery soon enough, he figured. He thought about visiting his dad, but that would necessitate finding him, and Boon wasn't sure he was willing to spend the last thing he had, his time. And he wasn't sure if he even had the effort in him to do it. Boon thought about his grandpa and what a good man he had been. He thought about Regina. He guessed she was a woman now, but the girl was the one he held in his mind. He didn't want to wonder how many kids she had now, who was brushing her skin softly as she slept, caught up in the velvety wonder of it all, who was gently lifting her dark hair away from her face and neck to kiss her tenderly . . .

With a twitch like he'd seen in horses, Boon shoved his scarred hands deeper into his jeans pockets. He needed more than a hoodie out here in this cold, but at least tonight, the spirits were dancing. He hadn't seen that in a long time. Boon looked up, his breath rising white into the blackness of night. He scanned the sky for the Lost Boys. This evening, their names suited them a bit too well.

Boon looked up the road. A few houses still had lights blooming softly into the blackness outside the windows. A few more miles west and he would be there.

Boon had been fighting as long as he could remember. The first time he hit someone back, it had been his father. Four years old, Boon's smooth fists pummeled out, surprising even himself, mad tears streaming down his face. The old man should have never come back around, Boon thought. Boon and his mother had been just fine at Grandma's. Grandpa had come in later that morning from an all-night smoke, found Boon curled up in the old quilt in his chair in the corner, taken him into his arms, gently reminded him of the pipe in the house, told him that fighting back would do nothing to take away the black eye from his mother's face, smudged him off, prayed for him. That's when Boon began walking, walking these very roads when the hurt or the anger got too much, when it had to come out of him somehow. Grandpa was right. Even if the pipe hadn't been there, the world of men and the wars they fought belonged outside of women's houses.

Faces he had hit flashed through his mind. Boon didn't always start the fights, and he didn't always finish them. There had been plenty of times he had been left lying somewhere, alone and beaten. Some fights he regretted. The guy who had said one thing too much about his sister when Boon was sixteen and drunk. Fair warning, Boon thought, but at sixteen, he hadn't realized one punch could break someone's face. Sometimes he clenched back the fistfuls of rage and pain, clenched them back, hugged them to himself, plunged them through his own chest, and hit the person he was really aiming at, but usually it wasn't too hard to find another Indian as mad at the world and himself as he was. Boon ran his tongue over his top front teeth, tasting the scars they had left there. The guy had been right about Boon's sister after all, though Boon still missed her terribly.

He saw the outline in the dark. A click or so back from the gravel road, snow drifted in deep piles at the base, further rounding the silhouette softened by time and wind. A frozen tear fell down from the Morning Star, plunged into the snow, blending with the rest of the grinding whiteness, but Boon didn't notice. Fine as sand, snow sifted into his runners as he walked up where the old path ran beneath it. There was still wood in the woodpile, but Boon ignored it, hopped up on the porch, turned the knob, and worked the door, stuck in its frame, until he could just squeeze in. His eyes adjusted as he made out the old chair, still there, with the blue, tatted quilt, purple yarn dotting it like stars, holding the whole thing together. He pulled the gun from the small of his back. Boon walked over, gently lifting it, folding down the edge, letting it fall around his shoulders, sinking at last into the chair, laying the gun in his lap.

Going home was the last thing he wanted to do.

He'd started smoking that shit while he was still with Regina.

As much as Boon tried not to cry, a tear ran down his cheek as he lay curled in the quilt in the empty house. Regina had loved him so much, more than any other woman ever had, but there was something in him, some huge empty wound that made him fuck up everything he touched. He'd done all right for a while, holding down a construction job out on the rez, living with Regina at her mom's in Laverne. Regina had been so proud of him. Boon felt a sharp pain in his chest, worse than the one far below it. His head was light. He could barely keep his eyes open now. How could he have fucked up so much? Regina had been everything he had ever needed or wanted. She was beautiful, and despite how much he had screwed up as a kid, she loved him anyway, loved him with her whole heart. He remembered her long dark hair, how it swayed down and brushed her breasts when they made love, how she looked at him. That's what killed him the most, when she stared at him with that total adoration, him knowing he didn't deserve it.

When Grandpa died, Boon had been fifteen, and he'd just lost it, running the roads, drinking, smoking weed. He and his friends started busting in joints, jacking folks, doing whatever they had to do to get money to get fucked up. But Regina loved him anyway, thought he deserved a second chance in life. Boon was crying harder now, the pain in his chest getting worse and worse. From the waist down, he was already numb. Damn, I should have never left that girl. He wondered now if she would still take him in—a crazy thought, but he wondered anyway. Would she still love him now, even after he'd done this? Boon's lip quivered. The chinook was howling away outside, eating away the snow, singing through the boards of the old house. Boon shifted in the chair, the wet, sticky quilt clinging to his groin and leg as he moved. The blood was starting to freeze. Even if Regina loved him after all this time, she wouldn't after she heard the news, he thought. That was the worst part of all.

He ended up homeless with that other one in Saskatchewan because of the crack, because of the meth. Jennifer had been a common whore, not even attractive, but she was good at being on the streets, and she could get some shit from truckers when all else had failed the two of them—shoplifting and pawning crap, stealing from old ladies, whatever. He hadn't even enjoyed sex with her—all he could think about when he was with her was Regina, and there was no way Jennifer compared to her. Stupid lot lizard, he thought, scurrying from truck to truck giving blowjobs for meth.

If only he'd never left Regina, chasing that glass pipe. It had all started when he was working construction up in Edmonton one winter, building a Mormon church, making pretty good money. At first, Regina had been so proud when he came home for the weekends; even her mother was proud of him. But then that whore Jennifer had taken a room down from his and Trevor's in the motel their boss had put them up in. She'd been in the bar one night when he was drunk, hitting on him pretty hard. But even drunk, he knew she was a whore and an ugly one at that. At twenty-one, she'd looked forty, easy. He must have left the door cracked when he stumbled back to his room that night, though. In his inebriated slumber, he thought he was dreaming of Regina when Jennifer went down on him. When he awoke, exploding in her mouth, it was too late. He knew Regina would hate him for cheating on her, even if he never meant to do it. He hated himself enough, that was for sure. It wasn't long before he was picking fights with Regina on the phone, avoiding coming home, trying to make her hate him. Anything was better than admitting to her what he'd done, drinking again behind her back when he'd cleaned himself up for so long. Soon, he was out of a job, living in Jennifer's room, hitting that pipe with her, walking Edmonton's cold streets while she was screwing her tricks. When the dealer two doors over from her got busted, he hitched with her back to Saskatchewan, the name of the city they landed in only reminding him more of his pain.

Over the years, he hated her more and more, hated her for making him lose Regina, hated her for making him lose himself, hated her for the whore and the thief she was, hated her even for being ugly, the one thing she couldn't help, the one thing that had made him feel sorry for her at first. He thought about his old friend Nolan Little Bear. Nolan had tried to save him when he started smoking that crap on the job site up in Edmonton. He wondered if Nolan would come to his funeral now. Nolan was like that, always a good friend no matter what. Boon remembered Jennifer's body lying in the snow. Maybe not, he thought. Maybe not after this.

The gunshot wound had almost stopped bleeding now. The whore had won in the end, Boon thought. That's what she'd always wanted—to win. That's what she had told him years ago, in that Edmonton bar, playing poker. "I'll win," she leered, holding her cards where everyone could see them. "I'll win." But after he'd done what he did, after his hatred toward her had finally blown up, after they'd come back here, back to his home, where all he could think of was Regina and the loss, he knew it was the only noble thing to do, shooting himself, blasting away the cause of all of his agony. He wasn't a man anymore anyway, not really, and he didn't deserve to die as one.

Boon pulled the quilt closer, thought of his grandma, his mom, of Regina, of all the women he loved who loved him, of

Grandpa. He pulled the quilt closer, and he floated high into the dark blue sky, reaching for those stars that had eluded him, knowing his real home was up there with them.

ABOUT THE CONTRIBUTORS

MISTINA BATES is a transplanted Texan and freelance writer living outside New York City. She is the great-great-granddaughter of a full-blooded member of the Cherokee Nation who served as a Texas Ranger.

JEAN RAE BAXTER'S award-winning short stories have appeared in various anthologies and literary journals. Her debut collection of stories, *A Twist of Malice*, was published in 2005, and her young adult historical novel, *The Way Lies North*, was published in 2007. In 2008, Seraphim Editions released her literary murder mystery, *Looking for Cardenio*. Her ancestry is German, French, English, and Pottawatami.

Athena Gassoumis

LAWRENCE BLOCK has won most of the major mystery awards, and has been called the quintessential New York writer, although he insists the city's far too big to have a quintessential writer. His series characters—Matthew Scudder, Bernie Rhodenbatt, Evan Tanner, Chip Harrison, and Keller—all live in Manhattan; like their creator, they wouldn't really be happy anywhere else.

Martin Benjamin

JOSEPH BRUCHAC, an author of Abenaki, Slovak, and English descent, has edited a number of highly praised anthologies of poetry and fiction. His poems, articles, and stories have appeared in over 500 publications, and his honors include the Cherokee Nation Prose Award, a Rockefeller Humanities Fellowship, and a National Endowment for the Arts Writing Fellowship for Poetry. In 1999, he received the Lifetime Achievement Award from the Native Writers Circle of the Americas.

DAVID COLE has published seven mystery novels set in southern Arizona, dealing largely with problems facing Native Americans and illegal immigrants. His next fiction project, set in Tucson, involves Mexican drug cartels and home invasions. He is also collecting real-life personal stories from women in all phases of law enforcement for a nonfiction book.

REED FARREL COLEMAN is the former executive vice-president of Mystery Writers of America and has published ten novels—two under his pen name Tony Spinosa—in three series. His eleventh novel, *Tower*, cowritten with award-winning Irish author Ken Bruen, was released in 2009. Reed has been nominated for two Edgar Awards and has been the recipient of three Shamus Awards. He is also an adjunct professor in creative writing at Hofstra University.

SARAH CORTEZ is the author of the acclaimed poetry collection *How to Undress a Cop*. Winner of the 1999 PEN Texas Literary Award in poetry, she has edited *Urban-Speak: Poetry of the City* and *Windows into My World: Latino Youth Write Their Lives*, which won the 2008 Skipping Stones Honor Award. She also coedited, with Liz Martínez, *Hit List: The Best of Latino Mystery*. Cortez has been a police officer since 1993. Her blood is Spanish, Mexican, French, and Comanche.

O'NEIL DE NOUX was born in New Orleans. He writes in multiple genres and has published five novels and six short story collections. His story "The Heart Has Reasons" won a Shamus Award in 2007, and his story "Too Wise" won a Derringer Award in 2009. He received the Artist Services Career Advancement Award for 2009–10 from the Louisiana Division of the Arts for work on his forthcoming historical novel set during the Battle of New Orleans.

A.A. HEDGECOKE holds the Paul W. Reynolds and Clarice Kingston Reynolds Endowed Chair of Poetry and Writing at the University of Nebraska, Kearney. Her books include *Dog Road Woman*—winner of the American Book Award—*Off-Season City Pipe*, *Rock, Ghost, Willow, Deer*, and *Blood Run*. HedgeCoke is from Huron and Cherokee heritage.

GERARD HOUARNER lives in the Bronx and works at a psychiatric institution. He has published hundreds of short stories, several novels and story collections, and has edited two anthologies. His most recent books include the story collections *The Oz Suite* and *A Blood of Killers* and the novel *Road from Hell*.

LIZ MARTÍNEZ is of Guachichil (Mexican Indian) heritage. She is a recognized medicine woman and ordained clergy in a Native American church. She combines her spiritual mediumship abilities with her experience as a New York State investigator to assist individuals and police as a forensic psychic. With Sarah Cortez, she has edited the mystery anthology *Hit List: The Best of Latino Mystery*, and is the author of numerous short stories.

R. NARVAEZ was born and raised in Williamsburg, Brooklyn, of Puerto Rican parents with Taino ancestry. His work has been published in *Mississippi Review, Murdaland, Thrilling Detective*, and in the anthology *Hit List: The Best of Latino Mystery*. He is coeditor of *The Lineup* crime poetry chapbook series.

KIMBERLY ROPPOLO, of Cherokee, Choctaw, and Creek descent, is a visiting assistant professor of Native Studies at the University of Oklahoma and the national director of the Wordcraft Circle of Native Writers and Storytellers. She won the Native Writers Circle of the Americas First Book Award for Prose 2004 for *Back to the Blanket: Reading, Writing, and Resistance for American Indian Literary Critics*.

LEONARD SCHONBERG, who died of lung cancer in 2008, has had five novels published by Sunstone Press: *Deadly Indian Summer, Fish Heads, Legacy, Morgen's War*, and *Blackfeet Eyes*. Schonberg has also had articles published in *Boston Magazine, Yankee Magazine*, and *Medical Economics*.

MELISSA YI works as an emergency room physician in Cornwall, Ontario. Her award-winning short stories have appeared in fine venues such as *Nature, Weird Tales*, and *Open Space: A Canadian Anthology of Fantastic Fiction* under the name Melissa Yuan-Innes. She also writes for the *Medical Post*.

Also available from the Akashic Noir Series

BOSTON NOIR
edited by Dennis Lehane
240 pages, trade paperback original, $15.95

Brand-new stories by: Dennis Lehane, Stewart O'Nan, Patricia Powell, John Dufresne, Lynne Heitman, Don Lee, Russ Aborn, J. Itabari Njeri, Jim Fusilli, Brendan DuBois, and Dana Cameron.

"In the best of the eleven stories in this outstanding entry in Akashic's noir series, characters, plot, and setting feed off each other like flames and an arsonist's accelerant . . . [T]his anthology shows that noir can thrive where Raymond Chandler has never set foot."
—*Publishers Weekly* (starred review)

DELHI NOIR
edited by Hirsh Sawhney
300 pages, trade paperback original, $15.95

Brand-new stories by: Meera Nair, Irwin Allan Sealy, Uday Prakash, Radhika Jha, Tabish Khair, Ruchir Joshi, Omair Ahmad, and others.

"[V]icious and poignant . . . *Delhi Noir* is an invigorating and often moving collection."
—*Rain Taxi Review of Books*

"All fourteen stories are briskly paced, beautifully written, and populated by vivid, original characters . . ."
—*Publishers Weekly* (starred review)

BROOKLYN NOIR
edited by Tim McLoughlin
350 pages, trade paperback original, $15.95
*Winner of Shamus Award, Anthony Award, Robert L. Fish Memorial Award; finalist for Edgar Award, Pushcart Prize.

Brand-new stories by: Pete Hamill, Arthur Nersesian, Ellen Miller, Nelson George, Nicole Blackman, Sidney Offit, Ken Bruen, and others.

"*Brooklyn Noir* is such a stunningly perfect combination that you can't believe you haven't read an anthology like this before. But trust me—you haven't . . . The writing is flat-out superb, filled with lines that will sing in your head for a long time to come."
—Laura Lippman, winner of the Edgar, Agatha, and Shamus awards